BLADE

of the
Sun

J.L. CRES

Daelarias

Aruvian Sea

Nixian Sea

Laurealis Sea

Legend	
•	Town
⊙	Capital
⊚	City
⚒	Mine
🌲	Tree

CONTENTS

To my bestie, Kate and her husband, thanks for reading and not judging.

Trigger Warning

GODS OF DAELARIAS

- Valirr: Father of all Gods
- Fallia: Goddess of family and fertility
- Damiv: God of pain and sadness
- Avilt: God of wisdom and knowledge
- Faktirnor: God of War and strength
- Yasmil: Goddess of beauty and cunning
- Patrov: God of patience and self-reflection

GLOSSARY

- Solveig (SOHL-vay)
- Vidarr (VEE-dar)
- Tyr (TEAR)
- Cadoc (CAH-doc)
- Kaeden (KAY-den)
- Batair (BUH-tair)
- Malphas (MAL-fuss)
- Aren (AIR-en)
- Thaemon (THAY-mon)
- Sigurd (SIG-yurd)
- Eirik (AIR-ik)
- Lochlann (LOCK-lan)
- Sindari (SIN-dar-ee)

CHAPTER
One

SOLVEIG

"Get out of my infirmary, Lieutenant!" Healer Thaemon, the highest ranked healer in the castle, shouts loudly. For an older man in his sixties, how far he can project his voice always surprises me. Honestly, he's the best healer in the Kingdom of Laevaris—which I can attest to, as he's taken care of me at least weekly since I turned thirteen.

I watch Lieutenant Victor stomp away out of the infirmary with a smug grin. Thaemon looks down at me from behind the large glasses falling down his nose. His long, white hair, pulled back with a leather strap, matches the mustache I would tease him about as a child. Stroking that silly mustache, he looks over my body and the drying blood-tinged liquid on the cot, analyzing where I'm injured most. Unlike Victor, he views my body in a professional way, trying to piece out what he needs to do.

"What have you gotten yourself into this time, child?" he sighs then yells, "Liv!"

"Coming!" says a voice from around a corner in the castle infirmary. Liv Evellard is one of my best friends in the castle. She only came to the castle to apprentice about a year ago under the tutelage of Thaemon, and although she is common born, she caused quite a stir in the castle on her arrival! Standing only a mere five foot two inches with petite, delicate facial features, she is quite the beauty. Many of the men in the castle longingly gazing after her. Of course, she never notices since she's always so engrossed in studying anatomy and the healing arts. Oh—and the fact that she tends to prefer the female variety.

Walking up to me with a developing frown on her pretty features, she asks Thaemon, "Sir, what can I do to assist you?" She pulls out her small notebook from her apron ready to take notes. She's always *so* organized! Winking subtly at me, she then turns her soft grey eyes to the elderly healer.

"Please examine the patient and report," Thaemon says clinically.

"Yes sir," she says, looking me over with squinted eyes and a calculating look. Liv doesn't look surprised to see me in such an injured state. No, far from it. In fact, she's looking angry now based on the thinning of her lips and the narrowing of her eyes. She's been my caretaker in the castle since she started here and is well aware of my imperfect past.

"The patient is slightly malnourished with possible dehydration …" She swallows roughly from discomfort in the knowledge that I was tortured *again* and looks over to Thaemon. She tucks a piece of curly blonde hair behind an ear, then runs her hands over me examining every inch like the healer she's training to be.

"Given the flushed appearance to her face and upper chest as well as the noticeable sweat coating her skin and rapid heart rate, she appears to have a fever, possibly from infection. Her back, specifically the large lacerations from a whip, are likely the source. She also appears to have deep bruising around her left lateral chest wall from broken ribs, a mostly healed laceration to the right inner thigh, a healed laceration around the right breast and several deformed fingers from incorrectly set finger fractures. The periorbital region around her right eye has faint bruising and minimal swelling but the pupillary response to light appears normal and eye motion appears intact."

"Very good, Liv. Don't forget when assessing the patient to include old or prior injuries as they may play a role in recovery for the patient. We know Princess Solveig well enough through her frequent visits to the infirmary that she does heal rather fast, so the question for you is: why has she not fully healed already? What would your recommended treatment plan be for this patient? And given her special healing capability, how can we assist in her in self recovery?"

I almost feel bad that Liv must do this *every* time I come in here. At least the punishments from my father, King Batair, and Counselor Malphas are good for something! She definitely is the best healer's apprentice in the castle since she has an established patient to practice on every week at least! Some of the other apprentices have tried to take over my care in the past but shortly after arriving each time in the infirmary, Liv will get all crazy eyed like "I'm going to punch you if you don't move out of my way" and they scatter like leaves in different directions. Liv can be scary when necessary, which I love about her. *Too bad I still prefer men … or that is, if I was allowed to have a relationship, I would.*

I've never had anyone be protective of me like Liv is. Well, no one else other than Jorah. Not since my mother died. So, it's … nice. Jorah is my other best friend in the castle, and we grew up together from a young age unlike Liv who is a more recent addition to my inner circle of friends. He's always telling me to stop making hasty decisions or put myself in harms way while Liv tends to think on how she can fix me up after I *do* put myself in dangerous situations. But I will say, they both have my best interests at heart and will defend me in their own ways.

Liv and I developed a common bond shortly after she came here a year ago. Late one night in the infirmary when everyone else was asleep, I came with a broken bloody nose and head injury. She was on shift that night and instead of asking what happened, she gave me my first hug since I was thirteen years old. It's almost as if she knew then that someone was abusing me, not just physically but emotionally.

I promise I will take care of you, she had said, affectionately squeezing my right hand and looking me directly in the eyes. She grabbed bandages and a splint to help set my nose, but I stopped her with a hand on her raised wrist.

There's no need to worry about me, don't trouble yourself. I heal faster than everyone and I have reset my nose more times than I have fingers. Looking into her shocked eyes I grabbed my nose with my hands and quickly reset it.

That night a year ago, we sat together and she told me her mother died when she was a child just like mine had. She says her mother had a blood-related disorder that caused her to waste away. Her mother met with every healer in the Kingdom of Laevaris but none could save her. During that time, Liv learned a lot about the healing arts and vowed to become better than every healer in the Kingdom. Her father who is a blacksmith (one of the best in Falal, our capital city) was understanding of her career choice and allowed her to apprentice here at the castle when it was time. We formed a bond of friendship and understanding regarding the loss of our mothers that was special to me in a castle where affection was desolate.

"Sir, it would be beneficial for the patient to be relocated to a cot nearest the window and light. Per prior visits, her accelerated healing ability is best assisted with sun light and a more outdoor environment. We should then thoroughly clean the wounds and express any pockets of infection. I can give her willow bark tea every two to four hours to reduce fever and pain. Apply a honey-based herbal paste to the wounds on her back and wrap them in clean gauze. A comfrey poultice can be made and applied to the bruising on her abdomen and ribs. We may need to reduce and possibly re-break the healed but deformed fingers to make sure they are set properly for full use of her hands in the future."

"Very good, Liv. A most thorough treatment plan!" Thaemon states pushing his glasses further up his nose and giving Liv a proud smile. I swear Liv practically beams upon hearing his praise. "Anything to share or add to the assessment, princess?"

Rolling my eyes, I knew this was going to be unpleasant, but I could handle it. "No, sir," I respectfully add.

As my mother would always tell me: *grin and bear it but don't share it.*

CHAPTER

Two

VIDARR

I swear if I have to wait one more second for her I'm leaving her behind. *Fuck! Where is she? Petrov, give me fortitude for dealing with late princesses!* Praying to the God of Patience, Petrov, likely won't help me in dealing with her since she has never been known for her punctuality and *obviously* isn't starting now. Swallowing my irritation, I silently move through the ancient trees while scouting the area around our meeting place in case someone decides to spy on us tonight. I'm currently waiting on Solveig in one of our most common rendezvous near the edge of the Broken Forest. We usually meet at least once a week since I met her a couple years ago.

It's just creeping past midnight based on the shining moon above me. We have things to do and people to see …

Hearing a small noise to my right, I start to turn and scan my gaze in the area despite the darkness. My eyes have adjusted to the night at this point, sneaking around in the forest and city at all hours of the night. For a larger man well over six feet and muscular, I am rather agile and stealthy if I say so myself. The only thing that stands out when I'm sneaking around in the dark is my dirty blonde hair but it's nothing I can't alter with a little dye or mud depending on the job that needs done.

Suddenly feeling a small pinch on my left buttcheek, I whirl around hearing a soft chuckling coming from the forest but only seeing glowing blue sapphire eyes within the branches of the nearest tree.

"How do you always sneak up on me, Sol?" Rubbing my sore derriere and giving a fake glare in her direction, I say, "You're late, *again!* We better not miss this upcoming shipment because you sat around primping your pretty-pretty princess hair."

Slowly Solveig, or Sol as I liked to call her, jumps down from the tree branch and walks out of the deeper shadows towards me.

Blessed Yasmil, Goddess of beauty, why do you torture me so? I think to myself while running my hungry gaze over her perfection.

Blinking past the desire I'm sure she can see in my eyes, I become aware of a few subtle changes in her appearance. Her long dark brown hair looks the same, currently in a loose braid to avoid hindering her when fighting. One thing I know about Sol is that she is quite vain when it comes to her hair. She always says it's her favorite and only appealing feature. I swear (which I do a lot) for an insanely intelligent woman she can sometimes be totally brainless when it comes to herself. She is likely the most attractive, desirable female in the whole Kingdom of Laevaris. Unfortunately, for a low-class rebellion leader like me, this puts her far beyond my reach.

She seems to be slightly hunching forward when walking towards me instead of her usual proud, upright posture. This is my first clue that something happened to her. I run my gaze over the rest of her and see some dirty bandages around both hands. Is that a resolving bruise around her right eye?

"I knew you missed me, Vi!" she says making a silly kissing face at me with her lips but instead of making me laugh it makes my pants get tighter. *Damn, the things I could do with those pouty lips of hers.* I think then focus on what she's saying. "Sorry if my hygiene and caring for my appearance offends your … delicate sensibilities. Some of us actually try to smell better than a pig stye. Oh—and by the way, I don't *primp!*" Smirking, she starts to lean against a nearby tree and cross her ankles.

"I don't smell and you know it! I just took a bath two weeks ago!" I sarcastically say, throwing a hand across my chest as though I'm offended, causing her to chuckle.

Folding my arms over my chest to resist grabbing her and examining her injuries myself, instead I say, "What happened to you?"

Instantly she tenses up and puts on an emotionless cold mask, or as I like to say her "princess mask".

"What do you mean?" she says while quickly averting her eyes to the forest then back to me. I keep staring at her unblinkingly to try to get answers out of her stubborn mouth.

Sighing, she says, "Okay, okay! I did... injure my hands yesterday. But Liv and Healer Thaemon fixed me right up. I'm much better now—see?" Holding her hands up for my inspection, she unwraps one showing me slightly bruised fingers that otherwise look normal in the minimal light of the moon.

"Sol, I may joke around more times than not but I'm not an idiot. You know I can read people well based on their body language and posture." Raising one eyebrow, I pointedly run my eyes up and down her torso. "You're hunching your back and you winced when you leaned against the tree. Your posture is stiff when walking unlike your usual graceful gait. You also haven't thrown a dagger—which requires use of your hands—at my head like you usually do when greeting me as your violent self. This tells me something *more* happened and those hands still look pretty bruised up."

She looks at the ground for a moment and when she glances back at me, I see something in her eyes that I never noticed before. Shame. Anguish. Sadness. Then her gaze shutters and she smiles using her "princess" mask and shrugs. "It's nothing to worry about, Vi. I can handle it. And—I'd rather not discuss it right now. Aren't we late anyways?"

Grinding out my response between clenched teeth, I say, "Fine. I'll leave it for now. But I know you're hiding something. Just let me know if you need me. I will always come if you need me, Sol. I hope you know that especially after everything we've been through. You aren't alone in whatever you're dealing with."

I mean, we've been through a lot together over the past two years completing vital jobs for the Rebellion, finding release for our frustrations in the city's underground street fights and meeting up at least once a week for updates and sparring.

But recently, we've been meeting sometimes just to talk about life and the occasional dream for the future.

She nods her head in response and steps forward, wrapping those graceful arms around my waist and surprising me by placing a soft kiss to my right cheek. I swear I saw a glimpse of her eyes being teary.

Covering up my pleased and surprised expression from that small dose of affection from her, I clear my throat and then start whining like a child, "So … Did you get it? Please can I see? Can I see?" I flutter my eyelashes at her and put my hands together like I'm begging.

Chuckling at my antics she steps back and says, "All in good time, Vi." Reaching into the back pocket of her tight black leather pants, she pulls out a map with a flourish and a bow. Wincing as she straightens up her back, that she hides quickly, she hands over the map to me.

"Wow! I can't believe you finally got this! I know you're not close with your father so how in the kingdom did you get this? He must semi-trust you at least to allow you near his office, poor judgement on his part obviously!" Then I spat out, "Narcissistic, useless asshole."

Crouching down and unrolling the map on the ground, I miss her expression as I run my fingers over the trade routes. Over the past two years I've known her, she has made one thing abundantly clear to me... she *hates*, and I mean *hates*, her father King Batair with a passion. She's never really come out and told me what caused her to feel that way, but I assume it's more than the lack of care he shows his people.

This map she stole could change the course of the Rebellion in our kingdom. Being their leader at the age of twenty-four, I feel like I need to prove myself. I knew there had to be a map that King Batair used laying out every trade route and location of his armies. There's even outposts and some written notes regarding timing of silver shipments. Food supplies, location of water, everything is on this map! Feeling some sense of accomplishment, I can't help but smile up at Solveig. But when I look up, her expression isn't what I expected. She seems to be scowling down at the map as if it's caused her problems.

For the past ten days, I've known there was an upcoming shipment of food and possibly valuables crossing into Laevaris. Supposedly, its coming from the neighboring Kingdom of Jaarn which is rich in iron ore, steel, barley, and some goat cheeses, interestingly enough. One of my many spies in Falal reported to me he overheard a gambling merchant complaining that the royal advisor Counselor Malphas denied him trade with the neighboring kingdom. He indulged too much wine that night at a local tavern grumbling that the Counselor has a secret trade route through his own land near the border of Laevaris and is getting this shipment in ten days' time. This is why me and Sol were meeting tonight to hopefully lay out a plan and look over the map if she could obtain it.

Discussing new information at a meeting of the Rebellion a few weeks ago, we decided to start overtaking food shipments and anything we can get our hands on. Our people are starving! And yet the cruel king keeps taxing and taking from the people of his kingdom. I went to Sol and she came up with the idea of seeing if her father had a map. Her argument was that there were at least six different trade routes near that border and we need more information before traveling there. I agreed—but was hesitant. She seemed to not say something regarding her father the King.

I can tell she holds no affection for him and I've witnessed first-hand the compassion she has for her people in this kingdom. The people of Laevaris love her too which infuriates King Batair even more. I always worry if he takes some of his resentment out on Solveig. He would kill her if he knew about her involvement with the Rebellion which is why I'm always hesitant to involve her. But I'm starting to get desperate.

Just last week twenty people died in Falal from starvation and that's not including all the deaths from the surrounding towns. The King's taxes and tithes regarding some of the town's crops mean people have no reserves on their food. Many go hungry and still the King takes. Also, another ten people in the city this week went missing bringing up an additional problem I've been trying to solve. *Where are these people disappearing to?*

The bad thing about our current plan is the timing. Based on the map, the shipment we were tracking is due to be traveling through the border of Laevaris *tonight!* It looks like this shipment is reoccurring every month and tonight is the night.

Looking up from the map and standing, I see her big almond-shaped eyes staring at me and her pointed ears subtly poking through her hair even though I know she tries to hide them. I've never seen their like in this kingdom but I find them exotic and beautiful.

"We need to leave now if we hope to overtake this shipment." Then taking a deep breath and grimacing, I say, "Do you think … you can keep up with your injuries? We could use the extra hand …" Looking at the bandages around her hands and her stiff posture, I'm suddenly doubting her abilities tonight.

"Ugh, Vidarr Rikare! I can still fight just as well as you even *with* my injuries. I can handle pain. It's nothing." Rolling her eyes at me then looking off into the forest, "Besides, you can't navigate the Broken Forest at dark without me and you know it!"

"What do you mean you can *handle* pain?" Confused, I look at her since she seems to be inferring something more serious. She looks back at me with a flat look and no answer. "Fine! You stubborn, stubborn woman!" I say throwing my hands in the air. "But you let me know if you're struggling with something … sunshine." I say smiling and liking my new nickname for her.

"Oh no! You are *not* starting that nickname for me!" She says glaring at me.

"What?! Get it … *sunshine* … meaning Sol?" Smirking in her direction, I start walking to meet up with the three other men from the Rebellion that will be assisting us.

Unexpectedly, my mind shifts to the first time I met Sol.

I'm currently "walking", more likely stumbling, down a back alley from the Green Tavern. My sister Kindra kicked my ass at the poker game we were playing with several other friends from the Rebellion. I swear she robbed me clean! Now, I don't have a cent to my name tonight.

Maybe I should have walked her home since we all overindulged on the famous Gorvian wine tonight. However, she whispered to me before the night was over that Jarron was taking her to his place. They started dating about three months ago and seem to be hitting it off. Its irritating to me since she's only twenty years old, but I know Jarron is a good man and can defend my sister if needed. He joined the Rebellion around the same time that me and my sister did after our parents died.

Paying more attention to my surroundings, I suddenly hear a soft grunt of pain and a light shuffling of feet on the stone alley up ahead. I stop and listen while looking around but it's very late and very dark out.

There! I can see three men standing over a smaller crouched form on the ground against the alley wall. Trying to stay hidden behind some trash, which smelled disgusting by the way, I squint through the darkness and can see the uniformed insignia of the King's guard on the cluster of men. Like a cold splash of water, my inebriated brain is alert once again.

Fuck the King's guard! I don't know what trouble they are causing but either way I will help whatever poor lad has garnered their attention tonight. I send a small prayer up to Valirr, the father of all Gods: I hope my sister will be okay! If the King's guard are out tonight, then there could be a purge going on. Looking past the alley opening I see several other guards running past our alley. She has to be okay! She has Jarron with her and is going straight back to his place. Besides, the last time King Batair did a massive purge on the city it was when our parents died ten years ago. Supposedly, the last purge was to "help" our people by cutting down on the mouths to feed in the city and open up more jobs in the city. I mean what the fuck, who does that?

A small cry of pain echoing down the alley pulls me from my thoughts and causes me to focus on the current situation. The three guardsmen are kicking the poor lad repeatedly. They haven't noticed me yet, so I slowly get closer. The pudgier guardsman grabs the boy by the hair and lifts him. The boy kicks out and manages to nail the guardsman in his kneecap causing the guard to grunt in pain. Nice one! The boy has spunk! He would be a good addition to the Rebellion with some training.

The guardsman with the now bruised kneecap drops the kid and another bulkier and more muscular guardsman picks the lad up by his throat pushing him against the wall. He starts to crowd the boy and thrust his hips into the lad. What the hell is going on?

"Stop fooling around! Let's have some fun with this one and then gut her like the rest of the ones we found. She's actually rather pretty under all that blood and dirt." I can just make out what the guardsman said and am surprised to notice it isn't a lad but a girl that he's holding up by the throat.

"She looks fresh. Young. And I bet … has never been touched," the pudgy guardsman says with a sneer. "I want to pay her back for that cheap shot to my knee."

"We were ordered to just kill any street rats and anyone suspected of associating with the Rebellion scum. The King wants another purge, so let's just get this over with," the third older guardsman says while looking bored.

"Shut up, Gavin! She looks like a street rat to me … doesn't she, Cal? Therefore she meets criteria," the pudgy one says while ripping her shirt open and fondling her small chest.

"Mmm, sure does! Looks better underneath all those clothes. I got a dagger with your name on it after we're done with you, street rat!" the guardsman named Cal says while leering at her chest.

Meanwhile, she doesn't make much of a sound and has a glazed look in her eyes probably indicating she is close to losing consciousness. There's some blood running down her left temple from a head injury and she's covered in bruises. Screw this! Pulling out my father's Jaarnian steel tri-dagger, I stealthily sneak up on the guardsman while they're focused on their victim.

Thrusting up into the first guardsman's right flank for a deep kidney shot, I then twist around and throw an arm around the second guardsman's throat and stab the dagger down into the soft spot above his right collar bone. They both go down instantly and don't get up. Losing the element of surprise, I keep my eyes on the last guardsman who they named Cal and clean my dagger off on his friend. Putting the dagger back in the sheath at my hip, I smile and hold my hands up like I'm innocent. I then shift my weight to be prepared to fight. I want to feel this guy's pain in my hands, while I kill him for what he did to the girl and probably countless others in Laevaris. Sometimes, you want to feel the blood on your hands instead of seeing it on your dagger. It's why I frequent the underground street fights in the city so often.

"Who the fuck are you?" he shouts while spittle flies from his mouth. The girl is quickly thrown to the ground in a heap at his feet while he pulls a short sword out readying to fight. Shuffling her feet on the ground until her back hits the alley wall, she sits up pulling her shirt together with one hand then looks directly at me.

Piercing deep sapphire eyes look at me from under a tangle of dark brown hair. Granted, she looks a mess after all she's been through, but the breath I have in my lungs is suddenly blown away by her beauty. I swear I feel like the world stops in that one moment of eye contact. There is this deep realization that something just intrinsically changed in my life. Quickly looking at the rest of her, she has to be young as she is so small and thin. But it's her eyes that tell another story.

Shaking my head to clear my thoughts, I shift my gaze back to my opponent and focus on the situation. I have to keep his attention away from the girl.

"I'm the Rebellion scum you guys were hunting. I think you've been looking in the wrong direction. Pity your friends got distracted and paid for it," I say looking down at my dirty fingernails out of boredom.

"You Rebellion trash all think you're so smart and will never get caught … well tonight is different. We had a spy amongst you," the guardsman says chuckling and then smiles with a fake expression. My breath catches in my throat. "And—unfortunately for you, they gave us several names and locations which we are currently dealing with. All of your little friends and all of your family are likely already dead."

Thinking of my sister going back to Jarron's place, I suddenly feel sick to my stomach. He is a higher-ranking Rebellion member. Could his name or house be on their list?

I don't have further time to worry about Kindra anymore as the guardsman swiftly rushes at me with his short sword cutting down. I twist to the side but don't avoid all injury as a small gash appears on my left forearm bleeding rather quickly. Pay attention Vidarr!

Shifting my weight to my left leg and crouching slightly, I lunge my right foot forward and sweep around making contact with his feet just below his ankles. He falls backwards, and I wrestle with him slamming his right hand on the stone alley till he releases his sword. Meanwhile, he's throwing decent punches to my right flank which is rather annoying. I straddle him while knocking away the sword from his reach and he reaches up in an attempt to choke me.

Punching his depraved face feels so good that I slowly become aware he isn't fighting me anymore. Oops! His face looks like pulverized meat and his nose is almost nonexistent now that it's been broken in so many places. There's blood everywhere and my hands are covered. I must look a sight!

I become aware of the situation again, when I hear her small gasp. I nearly forgot she is there! I tend to get into this calm distant state of mind when fighting. It is a slowly learned skill that I developed on the streets and in some of the fights occurring in the city.

It's quiet in the alley otherwise now that the guardsmen are all dead but I can hear some distant footsteps and shouting in the city. We need to get a move on so the other guardsmen don't find us!

I walk over to the girl again noticing her distinctive beauty. I've never seen anyone like her. With a shaky hand, she reaches up to push a piece of hair in her face behind her ear and I notice her ear is slightly pointed at the tip. Strange … but beautiful in an exotic type of way.

"Who are you?" Whispering softly, she looks me directly in the eye. I instantly like her. She must have a spine of steel to be able to look at me and not shrink away while I'm covered in splattered blood.

Crouching down to her level, I hold a hand out. "I'm Vidarr. Just another poor city dweller that the King's guards think they can control, kill or starve to death."

"*Thank you,*" *she says grabbing my hand and trying to smile but it turns into a wince. Blood starts to trickle down her temple. I reach to rub the blood away and run my hand through her soft hair feeling for the location of the injury in her scalp. She makes a small gasp and looks up at me with wide eyes.*

"*You have to come with me since this place is teeming with the King's guards. I think they are doing a purge tonight and it's not safe for you out here. Can you walk?*"

"*I'll be fine in a few hours. Don't worry about me,*" *she says looking down at her disheveled state. I look at her, too confused by what she means. "You're right, it's not safe. It was stupid of me to come into the city so late and on such a night. I heard my father talking about that spy the guardsman mentioned and I had to do something. I just couldn't let innocent people die if I could warn them! But—obviously I failed." She starts to sniffle indicating she's about to cry but instead surprises me when she takes a deep breath and calms herself.*

"*Okay, I'm not sure how you or your father would know about that. We can talk later. I need to move fast to check on my sister. Can I carry you?" I ask knowing there's no way she can walk with her injuries and a definite concussion. She hesitates for a second but then nods. I reach my arms behind her back and under her knees, picking her up slowly. She groans in pain and puts her face into my shoulder trying to conceal any sounds.*

"*Easy there. You're going to be ok. We'll just go check on my sister, then I know a safe place we can patch you up and lay low. Okay?" I look down at her since she doesn't respond right away and realize she's already lost consciousness.*

Taking this as my chance, I run through the streets as stealthily as I can while holding an unconscious girl. Horse shit! I never even got her name! Looking around the corner of another alley while I run and try to avoid guardsman, I see Jarron's place up ahead. It's eerily quiet as I walk up to it.

There's no light coming through the window and the curtains are pulled shut. I knock softly on the door but when no one answers, I open the door and shuffle inside. Feeling blindly with my feet for the couch to the left of the living room, I place the girl on the couch gently. I know the small kitchen to the right of the living room has some candles so I walk over there and hear a squishing sound under my boots. Got it! Grabbing a candle and lighting it, I suddenly understand the strange sound on the floor. It's covered in blood! My breath catches and panic starts to make my heart race. It then that I notice the body near the doorway to the kitchen.

Jarron's body is laying in a dark pool of blood around him and his axe is laying embedded in his neck. Suddenly feeling as if I'm not connected to my body, I step over him and walk a few steps down the hall to his bedroom. It's there I notice Kendra's naked body laying on his bed covered in blood with vacant eyes staring at the ceiling.

I walk out of that house of death in a haze and continue on even though it's one of the hardest things I've had to do in life. Kindra was my life, my family, my best friend. And now she's dead. I'm alone.

I think the only thing that keeps me going is "the girl". After I take care of my sister and Jarron's bodies as best I can, I grab the girl off the couch and run as fast as I can to the outskirts of the city.

My parents before their death were close friends with a woman named Sandan, known to our family as Sandy. Therefore, I've known her for nearly my whole life. She always treats me and Kindra as her adopted grandchildren. I usually make a trip at least once a month to visit her and bring her any supplies from the city that she needs. She tends to stay away from most people and lives a quiet life near the edge of the city and the Broken Forest. Her house is the only place I can think of to take the girl that's safe given the purge going on in the city.

Just when dawn is cresting, I make it to Sandy's steps dropping to my knees in exhaustion. I hold onto the girl in my arms though. She seemed to be having nightmares and would reach for me during the long trek but right now looks rather peaceful in sleep. I don't want to disturb her but I'm exhausted.

The door to the farmhouse cracks open and Sandan peeks out looking around. Without looking directly at me she asks, "Were you followed?"

"No, I don't believe so. I'm sorry, Sandy, to bring you into this but I don't know where to go. There's another purge going on in the city."

Looking into my eyes and her face losing all color, "What? Get inside now! Where's Kindra then?"

"Gone." Tearing up, I go to stand with the girl in my arms and avoid eye contact with Sandy. Abruptly there are hands cupping either side of my face gently. I look up into Sandy's sad eyes and notice tears running down her face.

"No. Not again!" Closing her eyes she whispers, "I'm so sorry, Vidarr." I start to step away to walk into her house, but she places one hand on my arm stopping me.

"He has to be stopped! This is madness!" she says.

"I know. But Sandy, now is not the time. I need to grieve and honestly … I'm just tired. I've been running all night and this girl needs looked over."

"You're right. I'm sorry. Come in and put her in the guest bedroom then we will talk. Who is she?"

"I don't know yet."

CHAPTER
Three

SOLVEIG

"Princess, well met," Finn says with a respectful nod and bowing at the waist. He's one of the newer rebellion members that we just met up with to overtake the shipment going into Laevaris tonight. The idea is to use only a small group with a specific set of skills.

"Don't call her that, idiot!" Darritt says smacking the back of Finn's head making Vidarr chuckle softly. "You call her Sol when out in public to avoid drawing anyone's attention" He turns his eyes to me then. "Hey Sol! Sorry about the new one." He walks to me and clasps my right forearm in greeting with his.

I've known Darritt since shortly after joining the Rebellion movement. He's stern and doesn't show much affection to others in our group but he always has a softer spot for me. It's always amazing how quietly he moves for how big he is. I mean one of the man's arms are the size of both my legs for goodness sake! Might be because he's a blacksmith during the day. He's one of the few who can come close to matching me when sparring but tends to use his strength whereas I use more agility. If Vi goes on any assignments for the Rebellion, he tends to take Darritt with him acting in a sense as his right hand man.

"Greetings, Darritt. I missed seeing you last time." It's been a while since I saw him since he wasn't at the last rebellion gathering. Supposedly, he was the one gathering intel on Counselor Malphas at the time. "When are you going to let me grind your face into the dirt again?" Smirking at him, I cross my arms.

"Anytime, sweetheart. You know where to find me." Cracking his knuckles, he smiles at me.

Vidarr interrupts any further banter between us. "Alright, children. Now that everyone is here, let's get this show on the road." Unrolling the map on the ground, everyone bends over to look.

Darritt makes a sharp whistle threw his teeth, "Well, I'll be … I can't believe what I'm seeing. You guys managed to get it."

"Yup! And we need to move fast since the shipment you heard about from that merchant is moving tonight based on these notes." He runs his finger over some notes near the border of Laevaris. "We have to cut through the Broken Forest to make it there in time. Sol?" Everyone's eyes turn to me then.

"Since Finn and Darritt haven't been in the forest yet with me, we'll need to go over some ground rules …" I look directly into their eyes and try to impart this is serious that they understand.

"My night vision is better than most people and likely better than yours. So, you need to trust me when I tell you to do something." At this, Darritt shrugs his shoulders in acceptance. Finn looks nervous but focused on what I'm saying.

"Do not run anywhere that I don't lead. The Broken Forest can change to confuse you. If you step away from me … then you are lost. Also, no talking, only hand signals until I say it's okay. There are creatures in the forest that you don't want noticing you, especially at dark. Okay?"

"Got it. Don't talk, don't breathe, run as fast as you can and do whatever you tell us. Right?" says Darritt with a smirk.

"Right. Let's go. Move fast. Oh, and Vi? Don't touch Tyr. He's not a pet."

"No problem, sunshine. I wouldn't want to almost lose a finger again like last time," he says to me with a wide-eyed expression and a fake shudder. Hopefully, Tyr makes an appearance during our journey. Unpredictable but friendly, he's a male goshawk that I've grown close with since childhood and has superb vision for spotting threats in the forest.

Vidarr turns away, checks his weapons, and starts to roll up the map preparing to head out. Looking over Vi, I give myself a second to appreciate what a fine male specimen he is. Taller than most, he stands over the other men with me today and is covered in tattoos that span over his muscular arms and chest. Biting my bottom lip, I think about the last time we went swimming in Silver Lake and how far down those tattoos on his chest go. *Damn! Bad Sol! Totally not the time to think about the sexy rebel in front of me.* I swear he only thinks of me as his little sister since he rescued me two years ago. *Shame.*

He looks back at me suddenly, almost as if he feels my heated gaze on his body. I look up into his light blue-grey eyes that seem to fill with heat, but I must be imagining it. He shakes his head causing this dirty blonde hair to fall over one eye. He tends to keep his hair shaved on the sides and long on the top similar to a lot of the city dwellers. His face is handsome and defined except for the slightly hooked nose from too many street fights. But to me, I feel like it just gives him more character.

Overall, Vi gives off a safe feeling which is foreign to me given my history with my father. I've never felt safe even when my mother was alive. It's baffling Vi projects safety and comfort since he's probably one of the most dangerous men in the city. I mean … he is the leader of the Rebellion for a reason. Even though at the end of this life everyone ends up alone, he makes me feel like it might be different. Like, maybe he'll always be there for me. Steady and safe.

I turn and start to walk ahead of the three rebel leaders towards the edge of the Broken Forest. The moon is shining overhead as we enter the forest but once beneath its branches most of the light is gone. This forest is old and has a resounding aura of knowledge. Like it knows what you are planning, or what your darkest secrets are (which is probably why most people avoid it).

My thoughts travel to a fond memory and one of my many secrets. It's from when Vi took me to Silver Lake the first time. At the time I was struggling, dealing with issues I found difficult to discuss. We went for a swim there, enjoying the crisp forest air and cool waters. When Vidarr went off to gather firewood just before dusk, I came across a young woman. She looked similar in age to me but her eyes gave off a look of maturity far beyond my years. She approached me, telling me she was from far away living in northern Jaarn, said she traveled here to clear her head for the day. It was strange … I remember thinking at the time, why did she travel so far just to "clear her head"? We talked for over an hour and I told her things I never told another.

"You look like you could use a day to clear your head. Just like me" the woman says glancing over at me. "Tell me something…a secret. Let me unload some of that weight on your shoulders. You're too young to look so troubled and I've honed the perfection of listening over the years."

"If I'm young, then so are you. You look nearly the same age as me!" I defensively reply with a confused look. "And I don't know you well enough to tell you any of my secrets. Not that you don't seem nice and all but…I just… it's hard to trust anyone."

She nods her head somberly before laying back on the ground with her arms crossed behind her head. The perfect picture of poise and calmness. "I'm older than I look. Trust me. It's smart to be cautious and it is your choice to trust others or not. However, proving you right is my choice."

We sit in silence for a few minutes before she turns onto her side facing me. "I'm lonely. There I said it…take it for what you will. It's one of my secrets. Also, the fact that my family is gone. My people, dead. I don't have many close friends and sometimes it gets to be too much. I have such a long life ahead of me and I hate the idea of spending it alone" she somberly says looking off into the forest behind me deep in thought.

I take a deep breath before saying, "I feel alone too in a similar sense. I do have a few good friends though, but I still feel alone sometimes. I lost my mother when I was younger, so I know how it feels. What do you mean your people are dead? You mean the ones in Jaarn?"

Her intense gaze soaks up every word I say before her concentration is pulled back towards the forest. "Your attractive male friend is almost back. I need to go. Maybe… maybe we can be companions to each other's loneliness? Or at least strangers who share some of their memories? I know some people enter our life giving us temporary happiness, but I hope we can be more, Solveig. I feel like I'll see you again one day."

I could hear Vidarr frantically yelling for me, and by the time I turned back around she had disappeared. In her place was a small hand-sized notebook. Just inside the cover it said *I'll hold your friendship in my heart, while you hold mine in your hand. Write to me* … And it was signed Jicquara. I didn't figure out what it meant until nearly a year later when I wrote in the notebook and got a response immediately on the paper.

Closing my eyes, I tilt my head up and take a deep breath of the forest air to ground myself in the present. Immediately, I feel at peace. Sometimes, I would even say the Broken Forest feels like my home. It just feels *right* here. It resonates with me. Smiling about the fond memory of Jicquara, I start forward and glance back to see the others cautiously following me since they cannot see clearly in the dark.

Traveling at a jog without making a sound, we move through the trees for just over an hour. I can hear the newbie, Finn, making louder breaths in the back of our group. I slow down to a stop and signal the others to me.

"What is it?" whispers Vi.

"Finn, you need to catch your breath. You're going to attract the Catchki," I softly say to him.

The Catchki are a larger cat predator species that love to hunt at dark. They use their advanced hearing to hunt since their vision is rather poor. The problem most people encounter is you usually cannot see them until it's too late. They have a beautiful coat with fur that camouflages perfectly with the surrounding forest. They also tend to rest in the tree branches rather than on the ground. They've never been hostile to me, however I am very, *very*, quiet and agile. The only reason Finn was picked for this trip was because another Rebellion member (who is a damn good fighter) broke his leg after falling off a spooked horse.

"Sorry, Prin—Sol!" Looking sheepish he works on calming his breathing but ends of puffing out more air loudly.

"Slow deep breaths. Like this …" I grab his right hand with mine and place it on the center of my chest. "Follow my breathing. Put your tongue on the roof of your mouth, take a gentle breath through your nose and gently release your breath through your lips while relaxing your tongue. There you go." Even in the darkness of the night, I can see Finn's blush. He replicates a few breaths following mine before the forest is silent again.

"Ready?" I look over at Darritt and then Vi. Vi has this scowling look on his face and is focused on where Finn's hand was just on my chest. He looks up and relaxes his expression then nods to me.

We make good time and have no encounters with any creatures or Catchki. *Thank Valirr!*

Hearing the distant sound of a wagon and clopping of hooves up ahead, I quickly signal the others to wait. Crouching down, I then crawl through the undergrowth over a small rise that overlooks a hidden ravine within the forest where a dirt road is running. That's where I see the convoy. I take a second to scout their numbers and count how many men and wagons before I crawl back towards my group.

I see them all crouching around the unrolled map spread out on the forest floor. Vi looks up as I get closer. I wave them back a bit farther from the ridge to speak.

Motioning to lean in closely, I softly say, "Over that ridge is our convoy. The trade road is at the bottom of the ravine but should be rather easy to navigate down if you scurry from tree to tree. The problem is that any loose soil or rock could echo down and alert the guards to us before we make it to the bottom. I counted three wagons which appear to be heavy and moving slow. There are four armed guards to each wagon and one driver per wagon."

"Perfect, Sol. That's about what we thought based on our info right Darritt?" Vi looks over at Darritt.

"Yes, that should leave one of us for each group of four guards while Finn here takes out the lead wagon driver. Once the leading wagon is stopped, Finn you need to subdue the other two drivers and take cover." Darritt states while scratching his jawline.

"Got it! I won't let you guys down!" Finn nods pulling out his longbow and rearranging the quiver of arrows on his back.

"We need a distraction so they don't notice us coming down the ravine otherwise they will hear us. I think the bushes and trees will be able to provide some cover but if anything rolls down, it will be noticeable," Vidarr says while rolling up the map and looking around.

Cak-cak-cak! The noise echoes through the area and then a soft rustling of wings disturbing the air is all the warning I get before a large male goshawk lands abruptly on my right shoulder throwing me forward a bit from his weight. Luckily, this morning I donned a tight black shirt with leather shoulder pads overtop that connect to my weapon harness and prevent his sharp talons from pinching too far into my skin.

Surprised looks encompass the group except for myself. "Hey baby." I say with a large smile reaching up to pet Tyr. He snaps his beak at my fingers causing me to chuckle. "Sorry! Just teasing you—good evening, Sir Tyr." I greet him again while turning my head and nuzzling the soft pale feathers of his belly. He preens a bit and looks contemptuously at Vi.

"I swear to Valirr that hawk is giving me a *don't mess with me* look right now." He mutters looking into Tyr's sapphire blue eyes which are so similar to mine.

"Well, I suppose we have our distraction right here." I proudly say as Tyr stretches his wings out and puffs his chest.

"Guess we do! Let go then before the convoy gets any further down the road." Darritt tilts his head toward the ravine.

CHAPTER
Four

SOLVEIG

Crouching down in position on the top of the ridge overlooking the trade road, I look to the right and signal to Finn. He nods in acknowledgement then aims his arrow at the lead wagon driver.

I begin to quickly and stealthily run down the ravine grabbing on to the ancient trees that are protruding from the earth. In my peripheral vision, I can see Vi and Darritt doing the same. Vi is supposed to take the first wagon, me the second and Darritt the last.

Just as we advance halfway down the ravine, I can hear a shrill *kee-eeee-arr* from Tyr. I glance up and see him dive towards the first wagon. The guards all look that way and one even tries to throw a dagger at Tyr! *Halfwit! You're going to pay for that*! If he harms Tyr, I'll make sure he dies a slow painful death!

Twang! The soft sound from Finn's longbow can be barely heard over the thundering of my heart even with exceptional hearing. I race towards the guards nearest the middle wagon. The following thump of a body hitting the road is much more noticeable in addition to the echoing yells of the guards who are realizing they're under attack. *Thump.* Just as the second wagon driver's body falls to the road, I've already simultaneously withdrawn my two katanas from my back harness.

Leaping up and pushing a foot against the wagon to propel me up higher, I quickly behead one of the guardsmen with flawless execution before he even turns his head fully around. As his body tumbles to the ground and his horse races off, I spin to confront the second guard. He attempts throwing a dagger at me just as I look up and I quickly bend backwards turning my face to the side.

Schnick. The dagger swipes by the side of my right cheek making a tiny cut.

Ahh. So this is the man that threw that dagger at Tyr! Halfwit with a death sentence! Standing up quickly and thanking Faktirnor, God of war, for my speed and agility, I swiftly run at the guardsman just as he is swiping his longsword down for a killing blow. Twisting myself to the side to avoid his sword, I then stab up under his rib cage towards his heart showering myself with his blood since I'm standing nearly a foot shorter than him on the ground.

Two down. Two to go. I think while I see the last two guardsman for my wagon riding their horses towards me at the same time. *Going to have to be fast for this one.* Taking off at a sprint with my katanas out aiming for between the two horses, I wedge my left katana into the ground just as the horses' approach. Then in a maneuver that defies logic, I throw my weight onto it trusting the craftsmanship of the steel blade before I swing my whole body up into the air. My right foot kicks into the guard unseating him and knocking him directly into the path of the second guards' downward sword that was meant for me.

Smiling in a blood-thirsty way, I look up into the surprised but angry face of the final guard on his horse. And without looking away from his stare I quickly flick my katana across the throat of the unconscious bleeding guard on the ground. *Just to make sure he's dead. For completion's sake.*

With an angry shout, the last guard charges at me using his horse as an advantage to throw me off balance as he attempts to stab me with his sword. *As if I could be thrown off balance by this brute.* Rolling my eyes, I then duck and roll under his sword popping up behind him and his horse. During this I irritatingly dropped one of my katanas in the blood-soaked dirt. *I hate getting my katanas muddy.* Ready for the fight to be over now, I unsheathe one of my jaarnian steel daggers and throw it directly into the jugular vein of his neck as he turns the horse back around.

Thump. He dies quickly bleeding out on the ground while I grab his horse and mount it all in a single graceful move. I put my katanas swiftly back in their harness in a well-practiced maneuver in order to grab the reins.

Pulling the horse around, I scan the area and notice Vidarr has two guards that he's still fighting simultaneously. Finn has the lead wagon's horses under control which is blocking the other wagons from going anywhere. Darritt is in a battle with a large brute of a man using an axe but seems to have the upper hand.

I start to head towards Vi since it's two against one. *Not worrisome.* I think shrugging my shoulders. I've seen him take on five men before by himself, however these are trained fighters.

As I'm cantering my horse over to him, I'm startled to see one of the men get under his guard and wound him in the left shoulder. Vi doesn't shout out but I can see him grimace through the pain and he manages to pull up his short sword in time to deflect a blow from the other guard.

Unsheathing my katanas again in a single move, I flip my body to the left off the horse. I land softly on my feet in the dirt behind the *asswipe* that stabbed Vi. Then I thrust both katanas up and into his torso below the rib cage crossing them before pulling them out. *Smooth as butter.* I watch his body fall limp to the ground with a sick sense of satisfaction. *No one hurts Vi.* I then clean off my katanas while I watch Vidarr finish off the last guard.

Darritt walks up with a new bloody axe in his hand, right as I say, "Vi, you okay? Seems like you're losing your touch."

"I was handling it fine," he states while panting slightly and then grimacing while blood leaks from his shoulder wound. "But *you* distracted me— riding up on your horse covered head to toe in blood. And—for your information— my *touch* is fine … better than fine if you want me to prove it to you later." He tries to smirk in a teasing manner while I can't help the embarrassed blush that spreads across my cheeks at his innuendo. *Did he mean …?*

"What happened?" Darritt asks looking back and forth between us.

"Sunshine here distracted me just because she always finishes her fights fast. I got a teensy tiny cut in my shoulder."

"Let me look. It seems to be bleeding quite a lot for a *teensy tiny* cut," I say with a doubtful look.

Walking up to him after I put my katanas in my harness again, I grab his shirt at the collar and rip it open over his left shoulder to expose the "cut" as he calls it. Seeing the shocked look on Vi's face makes it so worth it.

As I put my hands on his chest around the wound, I hear a subtle gasp. I look up into his eyes concerned I caused him pain and realize his half-lidded eyes are full of desire. And heat. *For me? Am I imaging this? Damiv!* I curse the God of pain, thinking maybe Vidarr's a masochist since he's turned on while I'm inspecting a shoulder wound in the middle of a battlefield.

"I didn't know you could rip open a shirt like that, sunshine … I always thought you would be feisty in the bedroom but now I know," he whispers into my ear causing me to shiver and heat to grow between my legs.

He then places his hands on my hips, while I inspect his wound. "I like your hands on me, Sol. Damiv!" he curses out and flinches when my finger prods into the wound.

"Sit down. I'm going to have to stitch it. It's bleeding far too much for us to make it back before you pass out. Finn, do you have the medical kit?" I yell looking over at the fourth person in our group. He's crouching in the front of the lead wagon still keeping the horses controlled.

"Yeah, one second!" Rustling around in his bag that he had slung over his back, he pulls out a smaller leather pouch and tosses it to me.

"Darritt. You and Finn should look over the cargo in the wagons and see if we can consolidate it into one or two wagons. Tie any loose horses to the last wagon. We can sell some of them for more supplies to help feed some Laevarians in need."

"Good thinking, Sol! Also nice work. I saw some of those fancy moves you were pulling out against those guardsmen," he says with an amused smile and an arched brow before turning to complete the tasks I set him.

"Yeah! I've never seen moves like that before! You were faster than I could follow with my eyes! It's almost like you slowed down time with that move taking down two men!" Finn rambles while gesturing his hands in the air and a slight blush on his face. "All I know is that I am never, and I mean *never*, sparring with you!"

Chuckling and looking intently at me. Vidarr softly says, "I think you have an admirer. Several in fact …"

I roll my eyes and start cleaning the wound with a cloth that I see in the pouch. "He's new … probably doesn't have much weapon training. So everything is impressive. Now, hold still!" I demand while pushing a needle and catgut thread through his wound repeatedly until it's closed. "There. All done!" I sing while smiling and then pat his head like a puppy which earns me a chuckle from him. He's lucky that sword missed anything vital and didn't push all the way through. I then place an ointment with honey over the wound and bandage it. *Thank you, Liv, for teaching me some of your healing skills!*

"You're good at this. Thank you, Sol," he says while taking a hand and running the back of his knuckles along my cheek. "What happened here?" he asks looking at my cheek where I forgot I had a small cut.

"Nothing, just a *teensy tiny cut.*" I smirk at him. "One of those halfwits threw a dagger at me and nicked my face. It'll be healed soon." Standing up and starting to pack up the supplies, Vi grasps my hand to stop me. Confused, I look at him. But he just reaches for the honey ointment. Looking intensely into my eyes, he— *oh so slowly*— rubs a small amount on the cut gently before he puts it back into the pouch. I swear, I've never been more turned on than with that intimate little touch. *Get it together, Sol! Now's not the time to be thinking dirty!* But unfortunately, my mind considers other possibilities. *What would it be like to have him rubbing his hands over other parts of my body? Mmm …*

"You still here with me, sunshine?" he asks, snapping my eyes back open that I didn't realize had closed. "You need to take care of yourself. I can't—*literally can't*—tolerate seeing you hurt or broken in anyway."

"It's just a scratch, Vi," I state looking at him and blowing a piece of hair out of my face that must have fallen out of my braid.

"I'm not talking about the scratch, Sol. I'm talking about the other injuries you keep showing up with since I've known you. I don't want to see you broken like the first time I met you two years ago. You never talk to me about it and I'm worried about you. I … care for you," he says seriously and then clears his throat almost like he's embarrassed. Which looks strange on a muscular, tattooed man that just killed several men.

"Everything's made to be broken, Vi," I softly say while looking away from his intense stare.

"Maybe. Not you. Never you, Solveig. You're too strong- much stronger than you realize." He leans into my view trying to catch my gaze again and pushing that pesky strand of my hair behind my ear.

"You don't always have to be the one to pick up the pieces and put them back together. You can ask for help, you know. Let someone see those broken parts. We all have them ... some cracks are just more visible than others," he says with a pained expression. I can tell he's starting to think about his sister, so I try to change the subject and ... deflect his concern away from me. If there's one thing I *hate*, it's being vulnerable and talking about *feelings*.

"Come on, I guess we should help the others and see why these wagons needed all those guards!" I say with a bit too much enthusiasm before tugging him back towards the wagons.

"Finally! Hey guys, look at this!" shouts Darritt, while he throws back the canvas of the second wagon. Underneath stacked tightly are a few bars of silver alongside several crates of iron ore and steel.

Shocked and optimistic we look into the other two wagons finding more large crates of iron ore. "No wonder those wagons were traveling so slow! They must be extremely heavy with all that metal and ore," says an excited Finn.

"Oh, the things I can do with all this iron!" Darritt smiles while rubbing his hands together in a greedy way. Given that he is the best blacksmith and a renowned swordsmith in the Kingdom, I would say he *should* be excited.

"What's this?" I ask seeing a red velvet bag hidden in the back of the first wagon. Opening up the drawstring I pour some of the contents into my hand and see small rough shaped diamonds.

"This could fund weeks of food for the city!" I enthusiastically show the others.

"It could also buy the Rebellion more weapons and mercenaries," Vidarr states with a calculating gleam in his eyes. With his bulging arms crossed over his wide chest and that vicious look on his face, I'm reminded why so many fear Vidarr and why he's considered the underground "King" of the streets. He's the leader of the Rebellion for a reason, no one messes with him. It's just hard to think that when he's constantly joking around with me or lately, looking at me with a different type of gaze.

"Alright, so obviously we can't combine the wagons. Each of you will have to drive a wagon back. I'll take one of the guardsman's horses and lead us back through the forest but we will have to use an old trail I know of since the wagons are so wide." Tossing the velvet bag with the diamonds at Vi which he swiftly catches and pockets, I then ask, "Now, the issue is what do we do with all the metal? It will look too suspicious to bring all this back to the city."

"I think I know where to hide it," Darritt states while rubbing his chin. "My mother lives in a cottage not far from here in Tillian. She has this old stone cellar under her cottage which you can access through a door in the back. It would be perfect for hiding this until we can use it or sell it."

Tillian is a tiny town outside of Falal, the capital of Laevaris, which is where we all currently live and need to get back to before morning.

"Alright then. Shouldn't be too far, probably only a half hour by horse if I'm correct based on our location, but given these wagons move so slow, it could take an hour or two," I say while whistling loudly and looking up towards the branches.

A fluttering of wings precedes Tyr as he swoops down and lands on my right shoulder. Nuzzling my face, I notice that the cut from earlier is already healed now. I jog back and untie the horse I used earlier. Quickly, I undo the saddle that was in place and take off the bridle from his head. I then drop them to the ground and place a hand on the beautiful gelding's neck. I didn't realize what a stunning horse he was when I was in the midst of battle.

He turns his neck, arching it up and looks back at me with a look saying, *Are you just going to stare at me all day or are we going to go now?*

Smirking and silently chuckling in my head. I look over his sleek black body for any injuries and find none. He has to be at least eighteen hands tall from the ground to his withers. *Big boy,* I think to myself. I also observe he has a small streak of white hair in his mane and forelock giving him a distinctive look. Focusing my thoughts, I project: *Well friend, what do I call you? Will you help me lead this journey?*

Stomping his large hoof and shaking his mane out, I get the subconscious word, *Sindari,* pushed into my head. Also the thought, *hurry up already.*

I run my hand down his neck and then his flank, smiling. Since I was a child, I always had an affinity for animals and nature. The animals around the castle would always watch me, observe me. As if they were waiting to see what I would do. I could almost feel their thoughts (if that makes any sense). The hunting hounds would lay down, wagging their tails when I approached. Horses were easily tamed by me. Sheep could be herded with a thought visualizing the pen. It caused my father, King Batair, to be concerned with a speculating look on his face. It's not that I could necessarily "talk" to animals out loud. It's more that I can project thoughts, sometimes words, and feelings to an animal just as they can project to me. Not all animals can do this ... usually the more intelligent ones are able to figure it out, such as Sindari so it seems. It took me a while to master this new skill given that I was a child when it started. But as I got older, it became easier.

The first time it happened I was terrified. I remember I went out to the stables and felt all the horses' attention shift to me before I was flooded with thoughts and questions. I could *feel* they were hungry! I ran straight out of the barn to my mother and like any eight-year-old child, I tattled to her that the horses told me they were hungry and yelled at me. After getting over her shock, she softly smoothed my hair out of my face and behind my pointed ears. She told me everything would be okay. She calmly explained that it's a special skill I likely inherited from her mother, my grandmother. She said that I can practice to quiet the thoughts and hone the skill so it's not so overwhelming. *It's a blessing not a curse.* She imparted to me.

Looking directly into her almond shaped eyes so similar to mine, she told me to *never* tell my father.

But why mother? I asked in my child-like voice.

He doesn't understand and when your father doesn't understand something it scares him. He wouldn't take well to knowing you have something more powerful than he does, she said to me all those many years ago.

My mother and I shared only two distinctive characteristics that I could remember well. Our blue eyes and our ... unruliness, as my father puts it. Strangely, I can't see many similarities to my father but then again it's hard to see yourself in someone you hate.

I once heard the castle's cook talking about my mother while I hid in the pantry looking for a treat to give to a new puppy. *The Princess is too much like her mother. The King will break her spirit just like he did the Queen. We should find a way to help her, Ger. I worry for her. She's wild just like her mother was and now that counselor has risen in the king's favor. The way he looks at the girl ... I could see* the cook shutter and run a shaky hand over her flour dusted hair from my hiding spot. *It's no good, Ger. I'm telling you.*

I focus back on the present and my inspection of such a beautiful animal knowing we need to get moving.

"Sindari? I think based on how prickly you are…" Sindari throws his head up shaking his mane, "and how vain, we should call you Sin for short." I say smiling and then leaping up onto his bare back. I grip his mane just as he turns his head around and yinnies at me in acceptance. I always ride my horses bareback. It makes it easier to communicate with horses having that constant skin to skin contact for some reason. And who needs a bridle to control a horse when you can just ask them where to go?

"Anytime you and 'Sin' will be ready?" Vidarr asks sardonically with an eyebrow raised. "Don't let us interrupt you."

Rolling my eyes, I project the thought of snapping teeth at Vidarr then of trotting away down the trail. Sindari quickly takes to the idea chomping his teeth at Vidarr who practically falls backwards off the wagon in his attempt to avoid Sindari's teeth.

Chuckling I look behind me as we trot away and see Vidarr shake his fist at me. He mutters under his breath as though I can't hear him, "Damn animals. I swear she tells them to eat me. First the bird …"

Ouch! I get a slight pinching sensation in my right ear and realize Tyr is trying to get my attention. *Well, someone is jealous!* I project to him while reaching up to rub his belly.

Goshawks do not *get jealous. But feel free to keep rubbing, hmm—that spot.* He sends back feelings of contentment to me.

Alright, off you go, you lazy bird. I need someone to scout ahead. Perhaps you aren't getting enough exercise based on this fluffy belly you're carrying around. He offensively squawks before taking off into the trees.

S ilently (or as silent three wagons can be), our opportunistic group approaches the edge of the small town of Tillian.

Ugh, it's nearly dawn! I don't know how I'm going to make it back to the castle before someone notices. I've been gone all night. Biting my lower lip in concern and nervousness, I think about all the possible punishments my father or Counselor Malphas will enact. Without warning, I'm thrown into a flashback from about six months ago.

Sneaking through the halls of the castle just after everyone went to bed, I was on my way to the city, specifically, to meet up with Vi for one of his underground fights and maybe to get a drink after.

Hopefully, he'll notice my tight fighting leather outfit that I've made. Liv's newest lover's a tailor in the city who's exceptional at creating a perfect fit for all my curves. Liv did tell me her lover knows her way around a woman's body. Guess she was right. Although, the shirt is a bit low-cut in the front showing off a generous amount of my cleavage. Luckily, the cape I'm wearing provides some extra coverage so I'm not accosted in the street for them misinterpreting my outfit. Maybe … Vidarr will look at me other than as a little sister he needs to protect? A girl can hope!

I usually meet up with Vidarr every other week at a local tavern where I let my more viscous nature run free. The underground street fights provide an outlet for my pent up anger and murderous, revengeful thoughts as well as being a somewhat "safe" place to practice my fighting skills. Vi introduced the idea thinking it would help me physically and more importantly mentally. He was right, still is in fact. I'd just rather not tell him that since the man's ego is already the size of Laevaris.

Yes, I know underground fights are illegal in Laevaris. But it's literally the only outlet for me other than spending time in the forest during the day or tending to the animals in the stable, plus I get to see Vi in all his sweaty muscular shirtless glory. All these suffocating rules during the day and hiding my emotions around the nobility while playing politics really wears on a woman.

I am almost to the back door of the castle near the kitchens when I hear a muffled feminine yell and then a male grunt. Something topples off a table, and breaks on the ground. Closing my eyes and listening, I can tell it's coming from the castle's kitchen. Or pantry? For one second, I selfishly think, maybe I should just keep going and avoid anyone noticing me. Perhaps they are meeting up for a late-night tryst?

Damn it! I'm just not that kind of person. Also, I tend to be overly curious. I'll just take a quick peek to make sure everything's fine, and then I'll be on my way.

Back tracking to the kitchen, I lean around the corner and peek in. I can see a huge guardsman standing against one of the kitchen girls holding her against the wall leading into the pantry. Squinting a bit since he is slightly turned away from me, I can identify the guardsman as … Buck. Or as I tend to call him, dumb fuck! Standing almost seven feet tall like a giant and full of straight muscle, he's intimidating. He may be the largest of the guards, one of which Counselor Malphas uses to manhandle me from time to time, but he's also the dumbest of the bunch. Hence my nickname for him.

"Shut up, slut, and lift your skirt. I could see you were wanting it earlier when I was here for dinner. You're such a tease getting all the men to look at you then acting all innocent. But I can tell when a bitch is in heat. Now you're going to get what you wanted," he yells at her while holding one hand on her throat and the other fondling her breast through a ripped portion of her bodice.

She starts to whimper and struggle against his hand on her throat unable to get any words out. Then as his hand travels down pulling her skirt up and sliding up towards her privates, he whispers, "You're so fucking tight and wet. I'm going to enjoy this so much.

If you fight me, then I'll touch that precious little sister of yours too. You hear me?" She nods repeatedly while tears track down her face.

I can see now it's Isa, one of the younger kitchen staff. Ugh, disgusting prick! I think she's only seventeen or eighteen years old and her younger sister is thirteen working in laundry. He picks her up and lays her on a nearby table with her skirts pushed up.

It's the unzipping of his pants that propels me into action. Grabbing a dagger from my thigh sheath, I run up behind the idiot and hold it against his throat drawing a little blood.

"Put your undersized cock away and step back from the girl." His eyes widen suddenly when he feels my dagger on his throat and he steps back with his hands raised. Unfortunately, this makes his pants fall further down exposing his cock and ass. Have mercy on me, Patrov!

"That must be the most disgusting thing I've seen in all my years, also the smallest if I'm comparing to others. It's no wonder your muscles are so big, you're likely compensating for little Buck down there." I smirk with a chuckle.

"You prissy cunt! You're going to pay for your insults and for interrupting me! Maybe I should teach you some respect and just how big my cock is…"

"Oh please! No wonder you're so dumb, all you think with is your cock. We both know I can beat you in a fight any day, any time, honestly with my arms tied behind my back and a blind fold." I then forcefully state, "If you so much as look at this girl or her sister again, I will cut off your small dick and then forcefully shove it into your nose hoping to promote more blood flow towards your underdeveloped brain. Can you understand that or do I need to repeat it, slower?" While I'm talking, I hold another dagger to his cock, making me internally cringe. I'm going to have to thoroughly disinfect my poor dagger after this.

"I understand …" he slowly says flinching at the cold steel he likely feels down below.

"Now get out of here!" I say pushing him towards the door.

Nodding his head, he stumbles out the door naked from the waist down. Hopefully someone will see his embarrassingly little member on his walk to the barracks.

After the door shuts behind him, I look over to see a stunned Isa sitting up on the table. She's trembling slightly and holding her dress together on the top. At least her crying has stopped, I think to myself.

Holding a hand out to her I ask, "Are you injured, Isa? Did that imbecile do anything other than what I saw? I can go back out there and dismember him…"

"You know my name, princess? But, I'm just a kitchen girl! Also what are you doing down here?" she softly says.

"*Of course I know you!*" *I say patting her hand and smiling. "And your sister, and nearly all the other servant's names. I believe you're newer here? Yes? You came with your family about a month ago?"*

"*Yes, princess. I just wasn't aware … I thought all the nobility didn't really see us,*" *she says shyly looking down.*

"*Well, you may have not been paying enough attention, but the servants around here are more like extended family to me. They've helped me more times than I can count. I try to help out if I'm able to but… it's hard when my father's around. Please, whatever you do, avoid him and Counselor Malphas. Neither are good for you or your sister. They're … depraved. Also, as you've just realized, stay away from Buck and any of his cronies. They tend to favor Counselor Malphas more than they should.*"

"*Thank you, princess! I will try to keep my head down. I'll also make sure my sister is aware.*"

"*Please call me Solveig or Sol in private. I hate the formality, but I guess it's necessary around my father and the other nobility. I'll keep an eye out for you or your sister. Are you ok to make it back to your room?*"

"*Yes and thank you again!*" *She quickly races from the room holding her dress together.*

I turn towards the kitchen door but pause when I hear the voice that haunts me in my nightmares.

"*Well, well, well … what do we have here? Princess Solveig? Up late at night in the kitchen? Tsk, tsk.*" *His menacing voice echoes from the doorway. I suddenly get a deep sinking feeling in my stomach and then a full body tremor which I quickly try to suppress.*

"*Counselor Malphas. What are you doing up late at night? I didn't think you came into any areas the servants inhabit. Also, it's none of your business what I'm doing here,*" *I reply in a snarky tone and an arched eyebrow.*

He steps closer out of the shadowed door and then reaches out to flick open my cape revealing my low cut and tight black fighting outfit.

Fuck! I think to myself. He then runs a finger over my exposed collar bone and down my chest to the tops of my breasts. I'm really regretting wearing this outfit now.

"*Hmm. What is this outfit you are wearing? Definitely not appropriate for a princess. More for a whore in one of those fighting rings. And also how you speak to me is not very respectful.*" *Rolling his eyes, he says in a patronizing way, "We have gone over this, Solveig … you need to know your place. Silent. Beautiful. Respectful. Compliant.*"

"*Fuck you. I will not conform to your idealism of what a perfect woman should be. It's not as if I am under your authority. I am the Princess of Laevaris!*" *I shout back at him and reach up to slap him across the face. There're too many repercussions to pulling a dagger on him right now knowing my father trusts him more than myself. It would only add fuel to the fire that I'm too wild and out of control.*

He suddenly traps the wrist of the hand that I was going to slap him with and then grabs me around the throat lifting me in the air. Fuck! For such a weaselly tall man, he's surprisingly quite strong. Something about him brings out the worst in me since I was that grieving thirteen-year-old girl he preyed upon. Mostly weakness, fear, and terror. It's like … I can't control my actions around him. And instead of fighting, I become frozen with fear. My thoughts replay his "lessons" over and over in my head making me fear the repercussions of retaliating against him.

Yelling angrily in my face with spittle flying out of his mouth onto me, he states, "Quiet! Since you look like a whore and talk like a dirty street rat instead of a princess then I will treat you as one. You are temporarily under my authority until you can act appropriately per orders of your father. One day soon it will be a permanent arrangement." He then smiles maliciously. "I think we should try a new punishment tonight. Also, I don't think we kept you long enough in the dungeon for you to contemplate your actions fully. Perhaps more time down there will help persuade you to be a good little girl. Don't think I didn't see that little display you did with the guardsman. He was given permission by myself to take her as a reward from me whether she consented or not. If you fight me, I'll find every one of those pretty little servants you befriended and make sure the guardsman know they're fair game. I may even join myself. You hold no sway, no power over me, regardless of your royal blood. This castle is run by me, not you, and not your feeble-minded father."

At a loss for words now, which is uncommon for me, I can't help but dread what I know is coming. I also can't control the full body tremors his threat induced. I can't let him harm the servants or Isa. I've dealt with this before. I can endure it … I must. I just hope Vidarr doesn't wait for me. He's likely too busy and already started his fight to notice I'm not there.

Alone. I'm alone and on my own, again. Always will be …

Malphas drags me roughly down the stairs to the dungeon, which aren't far from the kitchen in the castle. Lucky me! I trip down the last stair, and he grabs the cape around my neck. Pulling sharply back, he rips the cape off me tearing it at my throat and making me choke for a second then grabs me again walking me into the dark dungeon.

"You know where to go. Good girl. Sit up on the table," he coos at me while manhandling me into the room of my nightmares.

He closes the door with a latch and then looks me over like I'm some prized piece of cattle. His gaze stops on my half-exposed chest and tight shirt. Breaths are heaving in and out of me rapidly since I am slowly starting to panic being in here. It's like I can't move, can't breathe, and my anxiety is holding me captive just as much as he is. Unfortunately, my rapid breathing is drawing more attention to my breasts spilling out of the low-cut shirt.

"Goddess Yasmil," he curses invoking the Goddess of beauty and staring creepily at my chest. "You are perfection in physical form. Beautiful. Except for those repulsive ears of yours." He walks pulling my hair out of my braid and covering my slightly pointed ears. He then grabs my breasts with both hands squeezing painfully to which I go to shove him away defensively. Quickly and catching me unaware, he rips down the front of my low-cut shirt fully exposing my breasts and then he cuffs me across the face with a hand. I'm a bit disoriented and punch out blindly in my panic. There's a satisfying crunch and gush of blood that tells me I broke his nose! Yes!

"Disrespectful whore!" he shouts at me and pushes me roughly onto my back. My head hits the table with a dull thud. This time I lose consciousness for what must only be seconds however it costs me. When I wake up, I can't move my arms since he restrained them in two iron cuffs near the top of the table. He is so focused on pulling off my leather pants and boots that I catch him unawares with a booted foot kicking right into his groin. Got you, cock-sucker! I internally cheer myself on.

"Ahh, you—ugh …" He moans while cupping his pants. Then, after a few minutes, he stands up straight dabbing at his nose with handkerchief. Looking me straight in the eye with a dead expressionless face he whispers, "You will pay for that little tantrum."

He reaches over to another table and grabbing a sharp hooked knife shaped as a "C", he swiftly walks over to me and looping it into my pants that are partially pulled down, he cuts through them like butter to my feet effectively removing them and my boots. Holding in my scream is an effort since he used the tip of the knife to cut a long line down my legs on both sides. Blood pouring out of the lacerations seems to only excite him more.

He then grabs my ankles, while I'm trying to mentally pull myself together, and snaps them into two more iron manacles. I'm now more vulnerable and exposed than I've ever been down here. Usually, he only removes one area of clothes for better ease of carving me with his knives, so I'm starting to truly panic that this is more than just the start of a bloody torture session.

As my legs start to go numb from the rather deep lacerations and blood loss, I try compartmentalizing my pain. My healing is very, very slow in this room given the lack *of sun and nature. Darkness starts to creep into my vision, as I give into panic. Shaking my head, I try to stay focused and realize he's speaking to me.*

"Now that is a sight for sore eyes! I want you naked and bleeding every time I see you from now on," he coos running his eyes over me on the table. "I have to thank you Solveig for causing such a disturbance tonight. I was worried I'd be bored tonight with nothing to play with until our next session. You made it so easy for me tonight. I'm starting to think you like our little punishment sessions … hmm?"

Still trying to battle my anxiety down, I can't really reply without whimpering so I stay quiet. I will not give him the satisfaction of hearing my shaky voice. Meanwhile, he walks over setting down the hooked knife and picks up a what looks like a thick neck cuff which he snaps around my neck tightly making it hard to swallow and my head feel full.

"Get the fuck off me. There's no way you can do this … I'll—" I try to forcefully say but the neck cuff makes it difficult to project more than a quiet, weak voice.

"Language, language, princess! Perhaps the neck cuff isn't tight enough. If you can curse me then it must not be fitted properly," he says while smiling and tightening the cuff. It starts to cuff off my air and I flail a bit feeling like I'm suffocating. "Oops! Too much?" He adjusts it to where I can rasp in a tiny amount of air but can't swallow. It's degrading and very uncomfortable to wear a collar of any sort. "You're going to learn how to speak respectfully to your betters or we will use this neck cuff more often."

Unable to focus on anything other than taking in shallow thin breaths, I miss that he grabbed a small knife and is reaching over my abdomen until I feel him start to carve around my right breast. Gritting my teeth, I bear through the pain.

"Hmmm … I wonder if this type of metal will leave a scar on this beautiful skin? We will just have to keep trying in the same spot. Perhaps repetition to the same area is the key? I've tried everything almost! Steel, silver, gold…I thought for sure iron would leave its mark on you given your pointed ears but no," he rambles to himself while grabbing different tools. "I do have a new knife that I obtained from the Beamus Kingdom …" He reaches over, flipping open a green velvet cloth, then he holds up a knife that appears almost made of glass but has a green tinge to it. I turn my head to the side to look at it. I've never seen anything like it in our kingdom.

"Interesting, isn't it? It's called Avralite. It's a crystal found near the border of Beamus and Avaria. The Beamulian jewelers form it into a knife and state it can be potentially very harmful to a certain type of people. I guess the cave it was found in was completely hidden away like someone was trying to hide it from existence."

Confused, I'm unsure who he thinks I am that I would be affected differently than himself. He then handles the new Avralite knife and begins to carve into my right hip causing me to scream out loudly regardless of the cuff around my neck. I can't help it. It's like burning fire coursing through the area. Sharp, piercing and burning pain travel deeper and outwards from wherever he touches me with the knife. I've never felt anything like this in all the years he or my father tortured me! I can barely stay conscious, and my brain feels groggy almost as if the knife has a more systemic effect on me.

"There it is! Finally, a reaction from you!" He stabs down with the knife in my right thigh causing my right leg to get a sharp electrical shooting pain down it. His other hand reaches into his pants and starts tugging on his cock making my mouth fill with bile. Then using his blood-coated hand he starts to fondle me and lean his head in towards my privates. He parts my folds and shoves two bloody fingers deeply into my slit causing me to shout out. I've never been touched this way before. The violation of his hands fill me with shame and disgust. After pumping those fingers in me a few times, he withdraws them and places them in his mouth sucking on them. Humiliation burns through me sharper than the knife he used to carve me with.

"You taste better than I imagine. Good girl. My wild princess." He starts to fondle my exposed breasts then sucks one into his mouth. Running his hand up and down his cock a few times he then reaches down pulling the knife out of my thigh. It causes me to loudly gasp from the pain and as much as I try not to, a single tear leaks out of the corner of my eye. "You liked that didn't you?" he whispers to me after popping his mouth off my breast.

All thoughts leave my head as he takes the knife and, stabbing into my abdomen, leaves it there. He repeats the sadistic process once more before I blissfully lose consciousness at that point.

"Solveig! Sol! Sunshine! Come back to me, sweetheart …" Snapping out of my flashbacks are always hard especially that one. But Vidarr's frantic whisper shouting does the trick.

It's then that I realize, he's holding me in his lap shaking me gently. *Wow, how long was I out of it?*

When I look up at him, he suddenly relaxes and starts to smooth the hair back from my face that came out of my braid. I look over to see the others trying not to stare at me and appearing slightly uncomfortable. Sindari is standing near us stomping his hoof and at my perusal of him he uses his nose to nudge my elbow. *Are you feeling better? Who can I crush with my hooves?* He projects into my mind with thoughts of trampling guardsmen.

"You with me now, sunshine? You slumped over on your horse," Vi asks me gently. "We need to get this done. I'm sorry to rush you but it's getting late—I mean early …" He looks around at encroaching dawn.

"Yeah, sorry! I'm fine. Just daydreaming for a while." I fake-smile and pat him on the shoulder then stand up. But I'm not fooling anyone including my myself. He shoots me a doubtful and concerned look.

"If that's a daydream, sunshine, then I'm scared to see one of your nightmares. I don't care what you say, Sol, we're having a talk once we get this over with."

"Let's just focus on hiding this iron and supplies right now. I'll … explain some things later."

"Fine. Darritt, we're following you from here."

Rolling into the sleepy town of Tillian, I notice most haven't started their day yet. Good. Less people to see three wagons traveling heavily into their town. Darritt pulls his wagon up to a small cottage on the other side of town near its edge. It's a small stone cottage, but well maintained and has a well-tended garden in the back with a small fence around it. He walks up the front porch and knocks on the door. All of us stay back with the wagons to avoid scaring his mother at such an early hour.

"Mother! Open up! It's your son, Darry!" He looks over his shoulders at us with a sheepish smile just as the front door opens and an older woman peeks out. She's short and rounded with brown hair piled into a bun.

"Darritt! What are you doing here? I know you like to get up early working in the smithy but this is a *bit* early for a surprise visit to your mother! Regardless, I'm glad to see you! You're lucky I made fresh bread last night. Come in and have breakfast with me." She speaks quickly while wrapping her arms around him. It makes me sad thinking about all the years I missed out on with my mother. These flashbacks I get sometimes must make me emotional afterwards. Taking a deep breath, I center myself again.

"Mother, I can't have breakfast with you yet. I need your help … you see …" He turns back towards us and gestures to the wagons. "I need to use your cellar under the house to store some things that need hidden from prying eyes, if you know what I mean." Darritt told us earlier that his mother is a supporter of the Rebellion just like her son.

"Oh! I see you brought friends! Of course, dear! Anything you need, that cellar's been empty for a while now except for a few bottles of wine. Just go around the back and unload those wagons. I'll get breakfast ready for you all to eat after you are done." She kisses him affectionately on the cheek and waddles back into her house closing the door.

After another half hour or so unloading the wagons, we all clean up in Darritt's old home. I must have looked a mess after the bloodbath we caused and then moving all that iron ore.

When I step into the living area, I realize I'm the last one. "Sorry to keep you waiting on me," I say to the woman as she hustles over to me. All the men are sitting around a larger wooden dining table.

She quickly throws her arms around my shoulders causing me to stiffen in response. Realizing she's just trying to hug me, I start to relax. "You must be Princess Solveig!" Grabbing my hand, she kisses the back of it. "Welcome to my home. I know it's not much but it's done me well over the years. I would kneel before you but these old knees don't like the hard floors."

Holding her hands gently in mine, I beg, "Please don't do that. I don't deserve you deferring to me or anyone for that matter. You've done us a massive favor by harboring our supplies. I'm very grateful to you and your service to our kingdom."

"Very well then. I guess you'll just have to get used to me hugging you. Come sit and eat before you go about your day. You seem so much sweeter and more mature than I thought. We hear a lot of rumors about you and King Batair here. Many are upset with the King's treatment of us but the people love you." Turning towards her son, she says, "I like her, Darritt. Bring her with you again next visit and I will make my famous berry tarts."

Smiling to myself at her quick acceptance of me, I walk over to the table and eat with the men who are now relaxed in their chairs discussing plans for the day. It's the most comfortable home I've ever been in. Feelings of contentment run through our group with full bellies and knowledge of a completed task for the Rebellion.

Noticing the sun rising outside, I hastily hop out of my chair stretching my sore muscles. "I have to get back to the castle before my father notices I was gone all night. I'll take one of the horses back." Turning to Darritt's mother, who I learned was named Esma, I warmly embrace her. "Thank you for your hospitality. I'll have to learn that recipe for the bread some-time. It was delicious."

"I'd love that, princess. You keep Darritt in line for me, will ya? I don't get to see him as much what with him living in the capital city."

"I'll try my best, Esma."

Everyone follows me outside, where I run my hands over Sindari, be-fore projecting my thoughts of him carrying me back to the castle with haste. He agrees and starts to kneel allowing me to hop on him bare-back again.

"Oh my! Did that horse just kneel for her? She doesn't need a bridle? How will she control that large animal? Darritt!" shouts a surprised Esma.

"Mother, *please*, she'll be fine. Sol is special and has a unique way with animals. It's one of the many reasons we're all in awe of her. You should see her fight. She can take on men twice her size. She's blessed with many gifts and will make a wonderful leader someday." Darritt smiles at me. "Don't worry about the other horses, Sol, we'll sell the ones we don't need. I also know a man here that will buy the wagons off us. Safe travels," he says to me with a wave.

"See you later, sunshine!" Vi salutes me with a smile. "I'll see you in a few nights for our designated fight night."

"Bye, princess!" shouts Finn earning him a hit to the back of the head by Darritt.

Turning Sin around, we start traveling with speed back to the castle. I can only hope I won't be too late.

SOLVEIG

Luckily, the ride back to Falal was uneventful and we made good time. Sindari truly is a treasure, and I intend to keep him with me at the castle stables. I just have to think of an excuse for why I'm unexpectedly bringing back such a beautiful horse.

Sin is hardly even panting as I dismount at the stables and ask him to follow me.

"Good morning, Princess Solveig!" says Josef, a stable boy with way too much exuberance for this early in the morning. "I didn't know you were out on an early morning ride." He then notices the large black gelding standing with me. I glance over to see a perturbed Sindari digging his hoof in the dirt.

"Ooh! Who's this handsome boy?" Josef asks excitedly.

"He was a gift from a neighboring royal. His name is Sindari. He's a bit haughty but makes up for it with his speed. Take care of him for me and give him a few extra carrots since he did earn it this morning."

Tipping his head to me in deference, Josef says, "No problem, princess. We all know how you like your animals cared for. No one knows 'em like you do. I'll inform the stable master of your new horse too."

"Thanks, Josef. Is Sigurd around?" I ask.

"I know he's awake, and I think he was doing his morning inspection of the stables."

"Very well. See you later!" I say with a nod while walking further into the barn. I want to talk with Sigurd directly about last night and the new horses we acquired. He's not only the castle's stable master and a close friend but he's also part of the Rebellion. Additionally, I want to see where Jorah, his son and my childhood friend, is hiding at this early hour. Trying to suppress a yawn from my lack of sleep, I blearily walk through the barns.

I don't have to search very far before the stable master calls out. "Solveig, what are you doing around the stable this early? I was told you have a royal event today and tonight?" Sigurd's deep raspy voice projects from the nearest horse stall startling me from my stupor. He walks up to the stall door and rests his large forearms on the door in a relaxed but curious pose.

"Well, good morning to you too, Sigurd!" I reply in a dry tone with a dramatic eye roll. "I wasn't aware you were my secretary. I was up late last night." Then leaning in closer to him I whisper, "We were very successful last night and managed to obtain the whole shipment. We repossessed several horses and wagons, which I think Darritt will be selling. You may see a new horse I brought back who I'm keeping." I try to make a stern face at him knowing he'll argue that I have too many animals already, especially horses. I think my horse tally is up to five at this point.

"Solveig! Really, another one? Goodness, child, we are going to have to expand the stables at the rate you collect animals." He states this with a paternal tone and a soft smile at me. Sigurd is the closest thing to a father figure for me growing up in the castle. He was always there to help me when I was upset, crying or injured. I remember I would run to the stables whenever something happened or if I needed anything. His knowledge on treating injuries and soothing me emotionally with his soft raspy voice was likely due to his years of experience dealing with horses. I always found him to be a safe place.

Jorah was another reason I usually sought him out. Jorah was similar in age to me living in the servant section of the castle, so it was natural for us to form a quick friendship. I didn't have any siblings to play with, but I could always count on Jorah to join in my games.

"I think the stables could use a little renovation and expansion. By the way—I missed you too," I say smiling warmly and walking around the stall door to get his signature hug. He embraces me gently at first since he was aware of my last "lesson" with Counselor Malphas. A lot of the servants were aware of it unfortunately. Smelling of hay and leather, Sigurd infuses me with a sense of calm after all the excitement of last night.

"Get going, Sol. You need to get cleaned up fast before you enter the castle, as I can see dried blood on your leathers. How's your back doing?" he asks then steps back to inspect me like one of his horses.

"Shoot, you're right. I'll sneak in the castle through the back servant door. As far as my back goes, I'm all healed up now. Any idea where Jorah is?"

He huffs and then looking up to the rafters he mutters, "You know that boy … he's likely already in the library with his face stuffed in a book. He went to see some other scholar about a book a few days ago. I swear on Avilt, that boy never stops reading! He *should* be in the stables learning our trade, and he needs to learn a skill more than just opening a book." He must be really vexed if he's cursing the God of Knowledge so early in the morning.

"Sigurd, you know Jorah loves reading and honestly, he doesn't have a passion for horses. We've gone over this. I think he's wanting to apprentice to the scholars here at the castle."

"No, that is not a respectable job for a man of his age. I won't discuss this right now, Solveig. On with you," he dismissively states with a shooing motion. "Don't forget you have that morning tea with the nobility and the royal ball tonight!"

"Ugh, don't remind me! And stop monitoring my schedule or I'll add more horses to your barn again! Bye!"

Rushing out of the stables, I look around trying to avoid anyone's notice. I must look a sight given our exploits last night. The courtyard is getting busy at this hour of the morning with people going about their morning business. This is why I wanted to get back sooner. The less that see me the less chance it will get back to my father. He does tend to enforce specific events (tea or breakfast with nobility, dinner, royal balls), but when it's my free time, I'm lucky because he doesn't monitor my activities at all. In fact, he blatantly shows disinterest or at least I think he does. I honestly don't know if he knows exactly *how* I spend most my time. So I use my free time to my advantage … which is getting out of the castle.

Quickly, I make it across the stone courtyard to the back servant entrance. Crossing the laundry room as I enter, several women look up at me. One gasps and all works stops. *Shoot! Real stealthy, Solveig.*

I look around and notice Isa's familiar face amongst them.

"Nothing to see here, girls. Just pretend I wasn't here," I state with a smile and a silly awkward wave. "Isa, can I speak with you for a moment?" I ask softly while she gapes at my appearance. She snaps her mouth shut then nods before following me to a corner of the room. "What are you doing in laundry? I thought you worked in the kitchens? Never mind, I need a favor if you're willing?"

"Anything for you, Princess Solveig. Are … are you okay? You look a mess and is that blood?" she says urgently then covers her mouth with a hand looking scared. "I'm so sorry, Princess Solveig! I didn't mean it that way … of course you always look beautiful …"

I wave my hand around and then grabbing both her upper arms I whisper, "Shush, don't worry about it and call me Sol in private. Remember? I know I look a mess, that's why I need a favor."

"Of course I'll help you Prin—I mean Sol! And I switched from the kitchens to laundry service to be closer to my younger sister after what happened with that guard. I want to keep a closer eye on her." Smiling, she goes on to say, "I'll never be able to repay you for what you did. How can I help?"

"Well, I need to sneak into my room. And … I need help with a bath and dressing for a formal tea party, which hopefully I won't be late for. Can you find the housekeeper, Marion, and send her to my room?"

"No problem, I got this! You can trust me, Prin—I mean Sol," she says rubbing her hands together and then clasping mine in her gentle hands. "I want you to know you can trust me with anything and have my family's loyalty. Nearly all the servants feel the same way. No one will report that you were sneaking in this morning. I'll make sure of it. I'll also make sure the way is clear ahead of you and then notify Marion about your needs. She can send up a maid to attend you while you bathe." Then sticking her head out into the hallway and walking like she's confidently going about her business, she turns her head and waves me subtly forward.

I start to quickly walk through the hallways a few paces behind Isa. *Thank Valirr I saw her in the laundry!* She takes the less traveled halls until we finally make it to my room. Then, winking at me in conspiratorial manner, she turns and struts down the hallway to find Marion.

Shedding my clothing and running the bath with a hurry, I jump in before it even has a chance to warm. The cold water wakes me up from my lack of sleep. I'm going to need my wits about me today to deal with the politics of the nobility. Sighing and relaxing back into the tub I let myself slide down under the water for a minute.

When I come up for air, I see Marion standing in the doorway. Squeaking loudly in surprise, which never happens, I then blush and quickly start scrubbing my mass of hair with shampoo to cover up my embarrassment.

"And just *where* have you been, Princess Solveig?" she says with a scolding tone while looking down at me with her arms crossed. "You are going to be late to your morning tea session with the ladies of the court." Marion then briskly walks to the tub and slapping my hands away from my hair, she finishes washing my hair for me.

"I was out late, Marion, which you very well know since you check on me at all hours of the day and night!" I reply in a snarky tone back to her. "Also, I don't particularly care if I'm late to some meaningless tea party! I can't comprehend why I have to do these every week. All those ninnies do the whole time is gossip about others."

Suddenly, cold water is dumped over my head making me sputter and turn my head around. Marion smiles at me innocently. "You know it's part of your duty to attend the ladies of the court regardless of your opinion of them." Then leaning in, she softly whispers with a concerned voice, "Also if your father, the King, hears you aren't going, he may decide to punish you again. Please behave, Solveig, and just go. I can't bear to see you injured." She begs me with tears pooling in her eyes.

Do you remember how I said Sigurd is the closest thing to a father figure to me? Well, Marion is what I consider the next closest thing to a mother figure since my own passed away. Her blonde hair is pulled back into a bun at her nape, and she's dressed plainly but well for her station in the castle. She's about my height with slightly more curves than me but is still considered beautiful for her age at forty-five years. She was my mother's hand maiden and close confidant to her when she was queen. She often says to me that she owes it to my mother to care for me.

"Fine. I'll go! But please, no frilly dresses!" I beg her trying to make my eyes appear bigger.

Chuckling softly, she helps me finish up my bath and then starts to work on my hair and makeup. With her help things move much faster and she pulls out a soft yellow A line dress with tight bodice and flowing half sleeves. There are small vines with flowers in cream along the waistline creeping down the dress. No lace or frills in sight, thank Valirr! Then stepping into the dress and with a nod to myself in the mirror, I pull on my "princess mask" which basically consists of a lack of facial expression and bored-like appearance. Kissing Marion on the cheek in thanks, I rush from my room to the castle's atrium.

Already running about five minutes late, I nearly fall over when I turn a corner and hit a hard wall of muscle. Two large hands grab my waist to prevent me from falling over causing me to stiffen in reaction. I'm not accustomed to casual touches since grabby hands are usually associated with nothing good in my experience.

Brushing the hands off, I straighten and mutter an apology, not really paying attention as I attempt to walk around the man. *I'm late, damn it!*

"Sorry about that, miss! Can I help you get somewhere?" He says in a deep, strong voice.

I look back and up into soft brown eyes. With a confused expression, I realize he called me miss instead of princess. I assumed he was a guard, but I don't recognize him and know nearly all of them that reside in the barracks at least.

"It's fine. I'm in a rush as you can see. Are you new here? I don't recognize you and I know everyone staying in the castle," I state with a curious look before I surreptitiously start to scan the rest of him. He stands well over six feet and towers above me with a muscular build that you would see on someone who knows how to handle a sword. *He must be a new guard.* I then peruse his *very* handsome face showcasing a perfectly straight nose and strong jaw. His hair is startlingly white! Like ... a very, very blonde-white hair which is spiked up and shaved rather close to his head. *Interesting. He must not be from Laevaris. I think most people with that shade of hair come from … hmm … the Kingdom of Gorva. Yes! That's right. At least all those tutors taught me something!* I ponder while looking over his body with interest. Then shaking my head, I look again into his brown gaze which now appears filled with heat after my lengthy perusal of his body.

"I am new here. And I'd love for you to get to know me …" he rasps out in a deep husky voice that instantly has heat pooling in my belly and a blush forming on my traitorous face. "I'm just getting settled in, miss …?"

"Solveig. Or most people just call me Sol for short. Nice to meet you. I should… be on my way. Right. Excuse me." I shake my head *again* and curse myself for procrastinating going to this idiotic tea gathering. Then walking quickly away before I can make a fool of myself anymore, I look over my shoulder at the last second and notice he's still standing there staring after me with a half-smile.

I can't help but stare after the girl … I mean *woman*, I think to myself, as she walks away out of my line of sight.

Wow. She's stunning. She's delicate and thin but with just enough curves a man can appreciate.

Like a ray of sunshine, she came barreling into me with that yellow dress. She was so light and petite, that I was surprised when I grabbed her, she was nearly all lean muscle under my hands. It was hard to restrain myself from touching her long brown hair that hung all the way to her waist where my hands were. I've never seen someone so beautiful in all of Gorva or for that matter in the Kingdom of Laevaris, which I now was. I internally groan and adjust myself in my pants.

It's too bad I'm here for a purpose. And that doesn't involve seducing a beautiful woman such as her. She must be of the nobility given her appearance. Best for me to avoid her in the future since she would tempt me too much.

"What was that about Prince Cadoc?" my best friend and personal guard, Eirik, asked as he stepped out of the shadows shortly after she disappeared. He tends to use my title when we're in a foreign place just in case someone hears us. There're spies everywhere in castles which I would know from experience.

"Something that's off limits, Eirik …" I reply glancing out of the corner of my eye at him. All he does in response is smirk back at me and shrug his hairy eyebrows up and down. "Don't even think about it. I mean it. We can't jeopardize this alliance."

"Ugh, you're no fun since we started this venture. Also, why all the secrecy with our arrival? I expected a nice big room with a warm willing woman waiting for me when I got here. But all I get is a tiny bare room with a cot in the barracks," Eirik whines to me while crossing his massive arms. "I'm going to sleep on the couch in your room. Might be comfier."

"Let's not discuss this again right now. We're too exposed in the hall. Come on, let's go back to my room." I say with an exasperated sigh.

Sometimes it's hard having the weight of responsibility on your shoulders, but once you make a choice you must accept the responsibility.

I came here for one purpose and one purpose only. To obtain an alliance with the Kingdom of Laevaris. I'm the crowned prince of the Kingdom of Gorva by right, and the leader of the Gorvian army by skill and hard work. I *will* convince King Batair that an alliance with the kingdom of Gorva is in his best interest, even if that means selling myself. And by selling myself, I mean I'm willing to offer my hand in marriage if necessary.

Of course, I would prefer not to since I'm very happy with my life and the occasional willing woman in my bed when needed. I don't like distractions. I prefer to focus on my future and taking care of my kingdom. I thrive on order, organization, and knowing the next step. Women are unpredictable and a definite distraction to my daily responsibilities.

Honestly, I do see the benefits of marriage though, just perhaps not for me. My parents had an arranged marriage but ended up falling in love. Their relationship set such a high standard I don't think I would ever be able to find that with a woman. They care for each other deeply and still seem so in love many years later. They also never put their marriage above the kingdom's needs which they ingrained into me.

Walking into my room and shutting the door behind Eirik, I turn around seeing him flop backwards onto the couch in a relaxed pose.

"Make yourself at home, Eirik." I say raising one eyebrow at him.

"Don't mind if I do!" He stretches his arms behind his head and looks over at me. "Ahh, so what *is* the plan? Also why the secrecy showing up at dawn without an announcement of our arrival?"

"Well, I wanted to show up quietly without all the royal fanfare to assess the situation before we are scheduled to meet with King Batair. There are several rumors I've been hearing from my spies in Laevaris," I say sitting across from him and resting my forearms on my knees. "They say there's unrest in the kingdom … possibly rebellion from the people. I've also heard that the king's counselor, I believe his name is Malphas, is gathering his own secretly loyal followers."

"What?" He says raising his voice and sitting up. "Well then, why do we want an alliance with them? Seems pointless if the unrest leads to new leadership … Cadoc, this is dangerous! Why didn't you let me bring more guards? We could be in the middle of a rebellion!"

"You know we need this alliance and not only that … my parents, your King and Queen, ordered me to do whatever it takes to get it. We need it for two reasons. One: the Kingdom of Jaarn is building an army and encroaching on our northern border. They have the weapons and plenty of iron to cause some serious damage to our kingdom. There's talk they hired mercenaries and are hiding their army in the mountains. Need I remind you of Sterling outpost in the North that was destroyed by those giant steel crossbows only six months ago? It took us a whole month to rebuild it and reinforce our borders. We need to prepare and have every alliance there is before war occurs. Two: the Laevarians have been testing our borders recently and there's talk they're considering an alliance with Jaarn. One of my spies told me that this Counselor Malphas has been slowly importing Jaarnian steel and iron ore into the kingdom."

I state in a serious tone: "We have to prevent Laevaris and Jaarn forming an alliance with each other, or they will make too big of an enemy for us to handle alone."

"But Cadoc, we have the largest army and the best trained warriors on the whole continent of Daelarias! Surely, we can deal with Jaarn ourselves."

"Eirik, sometimes when you lead you have to consider not just the end results but all the consequences of your decisions to get there. I don't want to lose men unnecessarily if we can prevent it. Yes, we are the largest and likely best army around, however those Jaarnian weapons will cause us serious losses." Looking out the window of my room, I think about my next step.

"You know I'm with you. I'll always have your back. Just tell me what we need to do."

"Well, tonight they're having a royal ball to celebrate Counselor Malpha's birthday. I say we attend but don't announce ourselves if possible. We will be just visiting nobles from Gorva here for the party. I want to observe and figure out the situation here more. Also if I can see or speak to the Princess Solveig, then I can gage if she is open to my attentions and possible marriage if it comes to that." I think rubbing the palm of my sword hand. I likely overdid sparing with Eirik the other day.

"Geesh, you make checking out a woman sound like a chore! For once in your life Cadoc, just think like a man and not a prince! Hopefully, this princess is as beautiful as they say and you may actually want her in your bed. When was the last time you got laid?"

"Eirik, let's not discuss this. It's not important." I say with a huff of anger and frustration. *It has been a long time... I may need to take care of that before tonight,* I think to myself.

"Okay... so I'll take that as too long ago. Come on let's go spar with the guardsmen in the training arena until we need to get ready. I saw it on our way in and you need to let out some of that long suppressed sexual frustration that's brewing."

CHAPTER

Eight

SOLVEIG

The tea party was a complete and utter waste of my time. I nearly ran from the atrium in my haste to get away from those harpies.

All those mindless ninnies talk about are other women and men's appearances. Complain. Complain. Complain. It's like they have nothing more important in life than to gossip about others.

Did you see her hair was all mussed up and cheeks flushed when she stepped into the dining hall with Duke Chervil? I can't believe she is such a trollop and flaunting it with a married man!

Did you see Evaline's dress? It was definitely past season, and I think I even saw her wear it a year ago! Scandalous!

These scones are disgusting! I swear the kitchen slaves must have made them last night, they taste stale! Don't you agree, Princess Solveig? Maybe you should punish the slaves, your food should always be freshly made.

You should consider wearing your hair up, princess. Your hair is very … wild being down … I mean … it's different that's for certain! Most women don't wear their hair down this season unless they're children or not one of the nobility. It's more fashionable to expose the neck, see? I like to pin it up and show off my latest necklace. It draws men's attention to my chest and a possible suitor which you should be doing now. Has your father, the King, arranged your marriage yet? You are nearly nineteen!

Trying to keep a straight emotionless face (my mask) while they gossiped was difficult. My fingers itched to palm my dagger and start throwing it at them. The Laevarian people are starving in the streets and these women were worried about what is fashionable, who is sleeping with whom, and stale scones.

I quickly change in my room to some leather pants and a looser shirt for sparring. Grabbing my twin katanas, harness, and a few daggers (just in case), I peek out the door and race to the training arena close to the barracks.

Since it's still morning, there are a few guardsmen training and sparring. I start my usual routine of warming up by running around the arena for a few laps then stretching. Looking over my shoulder, I see Captain Mavin talking to another guardsman nearby.

Captain Mavin walks over to me as I stand up from stretching. Smiling and with a nod I say, "Good morning, Captain. How are you?"

He bends at the waist bowing to me. " Solveig, glad to see you this morning. You missed a few days of our usual training last week. I expect hard work today." Mavin is always so stern and serious but after knowing him for years, I can interpret his subtle tells. Like the small twitch at the corner of his mouth that just appeared, indicating he's amused and happy to see me. He likes to keep appearances in public for the other guardsman and for propriety's sake, but I know he thinks of me as sort of a daughter. Even though he's the Captain of Laevaris' guard, he always found time to train me in secret since I was fourteen years old. I think of those early years with mixed emotions.

I just got dragged out of the dungeon by one of the guards … I forget his name, but he smells bad and has a strange look on his face as he stares at my body. This is my second "punishment" lesson for misbehaving around my father. Afterwards, they put me in a dark cell in the dungeon for the first time where they left me over night. It was scary, dark and cold. Now, I feel so weak and thirsty making it easy for the guardsman to drag me up the stairs. Luckily the four whip lashes on my back are already healing and nearly closed. The swelling on my cheek and cut on my lip are also better now.

Throwing me in heap on the top of the stairs he says, "Get back to your room and clean up child, or should I say woman? You seem to be maturing nicely over the past year.

Although, you look a mess…" Then covering his nose says, "… and smell. I'd be happy to assist you in your shower?" he then gives me a lecherous grin which is easier to interpret. Disgusting pig! I wonder what his wife would think of his insinuation. And—He thinks I smell? He's the one that smells like rotten cabbage.

Before I can reply to him to get lost, I hear a strong stern voice yell. "Billen! What's the meaning of this? What are you doing with this child?"

I look towards the voice and recognizing the Captain of the Guard, I start to shrink and cower towards the nearest wall. He's a big man and very intimidating. He likely hasn't recognized who I am yet or maybe doesn't care. I have never really interacted much with him around the castle so I'm not sure. Either way, I'm too weak to flee, so I slowly crawl trying to avoid any more notice. I just want a shower and to sleep in my bed without worry that someone will punish me for whimpering or simply for breathing too loud.

"Uhh … Sir! Well, you see…I am to assist her back to her room by order of King Batair," he stutters out appearing nervous and glances intermittently at me.

"Princess? Princess Solveig?" Captain Mavin shouts then squints over in my direction where I'm cowering away from his voice. "Where was she and why does she need assistance?" He then glances over Billen's shoulder towards the entrance to the dungeon stairs and I can see he finally puts the pieces together.

Quickly Captain Mavin's face transforms to anger and disgust. He then walks up to his guardsman and leaning into his face he softly says, "I see. Why then were you offering to shower the princess? Hmm?"

The guardsman starts to nervously shift on his feet while not making eye contact. "I was just offering to help her since her injuries have made her weak. I'll take her to her room and call a maid instead. Sir."

"You will do no such thing. You are on latrine duty starting now and restricted from even looking at the princess. If I find out that you have touched, talked, or even looked at the princess again, I will gut you myself." Captain Mavin states in a deadly serious voice. "You're excused."

The guardsman quickly scampers away like a dog with his tail between his legs mumbling a "yes sir". The Captain then looks over at me and briskly walking to where I'm cowering, he crouches down to eye level. After a few minutes of silence, I gain the courage to look up since I don't detect any movement.

He's inspecting me or more likely looking for any visible injuries. He seems to be a stern man which makes me nervous he could be similar to my father.

"Princess Solveig, please let me assist you back to your room. I swear on my honor that no harm will come to you in my presence, and I will get to the bottom of this mis-

treatment that has occurred. Your father will be informed of this…misdeed." He reaches a hand out to me slowly.

Flinching from his reaching hand, I look him in the eye directly and say, "Please don't mention it. He was there. It's a punishment lesson that my father and Counselor Malphas believe I need for poor behavior that's unbecoming of a lady. I don't want you to get in trouble too. I must have deserved it. My father says I'm a disappointment." Looking down in shame and biting my quivering lip, I then reach for his hand to pull myself up, but suddenly my legs collapse from weakness.

He supports me around the waist and holding me slowly starts to walk back towards my room. He looks at me out of the corner of his eye as he walks then softly says, "I'm sorry to hear that, princess. If this is true, there's not much I can do to prevent these 'lessons'. I am of course a subject of the King; however I find it hard to believe you would ever be a disappointment." Then he shakes his head sadly, "You're just a child … I don't understand what they feel would warrant a punishment fit for a traitor."

When we make it to my door, he turns towards me and holding both my hands in his he quietly says, "There may not be much I can do to prevent it, but … I could train you in secret on how to defend yourself and how to avoid worse injuries. You'd be able to stave off any guards that are disrespectful."

For the first time today, I feel a soft smile overtake my sore face. I think to myself it would be nice to have some control in my life by learning self-defense. Then standing up straight with effort I say, "I would like that very much. Thank you!"

He clears his throat and looking at me says, "Very well. How about before dawn the day after tomorrow? Hopefully by then you will be better enough to train." Then turning around, he starts to walk away but stops after a few steps and smiles to himself.

"You remind me of my daughter … Strong. Resilient. Just remember, princess, that we gain strength from the lessons we survive in life."

Snapping out of my memory, I hear Mavin shout, "Camaeron! Spar with Princess Solveig!"

Oh great! I think to myself. *Camaeron has to be rather unhappy with me after our last sparring session.* I mean I did dislocate his shoulder and then shove his face in the dirt, but he deserved it after pulling on my braid. He knows that makes me angry! No one should mess with a girl's hair!

I then walk to the right of the arena as there are a few other guardsmen training throughout the arena. I look around and notice a few ladies and new faces watching. Most of the ladies watching are whispering behind hands and wearing frilly dresses that are more appropriate for a lady.

I look down at myself with my pants and weapons then reach up to touch my pointed ears. Shaking my head, I think how I will never fit in with them no matter how I try. Bouncing in place I center myself and see Camaeron swaggering over to me.

"Solveig, I've been waiting for a rematch for the past month!" he says with a large grin and rubbing his hands together with glee. "You won't be so lucky this time. First person to draw blood wins?"

Nodding my head in agreement. "Luck has nothing to do with it, Camaeron. Skill and practice. I may need to report your laziness to Mavin, but I can tell he already wants me to wipe your ass with my katana." Then stepping back into a lazy pose like I have all the time in the world I wait for him.

As predicted, he rushes at me with a broad sword and a dagger. Mavin likes to pair us up for sparring because we both tend to dually wield when fighting. Camaeron also tends to be one of the better fighters in the guard, making it more fun for me. I wait till the last minute and then with speed not many men have I run towards him sliding between his legs then jumping up behind him and pulling my dual katanas. As he recovers from his lunge, I slice one katana forward to nick his chest but only catch his shirt since he arched his back and avoided the tip of my katana. My other katana blocks his dagger when he came around.

We then start our fight in earnest. Our moves so fast and precise many of the guardsmen stop their sparring to watch. I can tell we are drawing a crowd but don't have time to look. Camaeron starts to smile since he loves the attention, but I can see he is starting to tire by the sweat on his brow. That's why I don't like to use the broadsword, too heavy, more work. I prefer the sleek slicing of my katanas. I lean down with one hand and katana in the dirt while I kick my legs up to try and dislodge his hand from his sword, but he thrusts forward unpredictably causing me to roll and twist back like an acrobat onto my feet. We parry back and forth for a while and when he overextends to thrust at my side, I jump up with one foot off his bent knee shooting myself up and wrapping my legs around his neck to pull him down. He drops his sword to roll with me in close contact and I let one katana fall on purpose. Once on the ground, I continue to squeeze with my legs while he aims his dagger up but I'm able to block him with my longer katana. Pulling a small dagger from my left thigh I nick him on the chin.

He drops his dagger and holds his hands in the air so I release him from my choke hold. We are both panting on the ground a bit, but I don't feel tired, just invigorated. Being outside and using my strength to fight makes me feel in control of my body and *alive*. I get up from the ground quickly and reach a hand down to help Camaeron up but he hesitates.

"You are way too agile and flexible. It's like fighting a catchki! And I have no idea how you can do those fancy moves, it just seems impossible to have that much speed, almost like magic," he says frustratingly while running a hand over his chin where I cut him. "Tell me your secret, Sol."

Picking up my katanas from the ground and then placing them in my back harness, I then put my hands on my hips and stare down at him before speaking.

"Fight like its life. Like its survival. Because one day, it will be. Either yours or his," I try to say softly but I can tell some of the surrounding crowd can hear. Mavin told me those words one day when I was moving too slow in practice, and they stuck with me over the years. Camaeron looks at me with a squint and then nods. He reaches a hand out to me and allows me to then pull him up.

"Do I at least get a kiss on the cheek for my wound? You damaged my best feature! Now the ladies will never take me home! Perhaps … you'll keep me company?" he says with a pout and then a wink.

I walk over and throw an arm around him then kiss his cheek. Noticing that even though he's a big jokester and a known ladies' man, he still blushes prettily. "I'll tell you what, Camaeron … I'll buy you a drink tonight at the tavern instead."

"Deal!" he says with a tug on the end of my long braid causing me to angrily look at him. All the guardsmen around us to hoot with laughter. They know I love my long hair and am sensitive to people touching it.

"Alright, children! Calm down, let's focus," shouts Captain Mavin while clapping his hands together to get attention. He then turns his focus on me saying, "Since Princess Solveig here doesn't seem winded enough from her fight, let's make it a bit more challenging this time. Princess let's see you take on two opponents at once. I have a new guard here that needs a good workout and let's see … Lanief may give you enough fight. Also let's make this hand-to-hand combat. No weapons." Several guardsmen cheer at that.

Lanief steps up to the area where I'm standing while I unhook my harness and katanas. He's a big guy made up of all muscle and standing nearly a foot over me. Half his face is covered in a tattoo with daggers crossing a rose that I know he got when his young daughter died two years ago. He must be the second biggest man in the guard other than that dumb fuck Buck. However, I know Lanief. We love to fight in the underground street fights on and off together for fun. He's also part of the Rebellion and contradictory to his intimidating size he's one of the biggest, sweetest men I know. He looks at me and nods with a soft smile for me.

A younger guard similar to my age steps up. He must be only eighteen at most. He looks lean and trim. And as I stand there observing him, I notice his posture is leaning slightly to the right, favoring his right leg. I mentally catalog the possible weakness for later use in the fight. I'm guessing he's the trickier of the two and possibly more flexible which should present more of a challenge.

"Princess Solveig, this is Nivael. He was just recruited recently to the guard for his skills," says Mavin cryptically. "Let's begin!"

After observing my opponents, I decide to take more of an offensive start and assess the new guard's reaction. I run towards Nivael and swing up my right leg for a downward roundhouse kick aiming for the soft spot between his neck and shoulder. He swiftly tilts sideways to avoid the kick and getting lower to the ground tries to do a leg sweep. He's fast … I'll give him that! But he doesn't know my fighting style and just how agile I am. I can see in my peripheral vision Lanief coming up behind me, so I do a quick backwards bend avoiding the leg sweep. Using the momentum as I bring my feet over, I kick out with both feet directly into Lanief's chest knocking him over onto his back. He tries to roll over, but I end up straddling him and punch him in the jaw, hard.

Nivael comes out of nowhere doing a kick to my head rolling me off Lanief and making my vision lose focus for a second. Thank Valirr, god of all Gods, for my quick healing powers! Suddenly, I realize Nivael put me in a triangle choke hold with my arm up by my head. Laughing to myself when I realize I'm having fun working against an opponent that is somewhat agile compared to all these bulky slow men, I perform a quick counter maneuver. I angle my body towards his knees and push my chest forcefully into his thigh then bringing my left leg up my body in a very flexible way I break his hold on me. I then start delivering a series of punches to his head that knocks him out cold. *One down. One to go.*

Lanief reaches down and with one hand manages to grab my entire throat blocking my air and pulling my back up against his front. He uses his other hand to punch me in the right flank twice. *Ouch!*

Tightening my belly muscles, I bring my right leg straight up at a speed so quick many couldn't see coming and knock him directly in the nose. *Crunch ... Oops! Might have broken his nose again!* His hand that is choking me loosens up some after that hit and I immediately slip my left arm up then bring my elbow down on his inner elbow to break his hold on me.

We turn to each other facing off. He's angry now but smiling through the blood dripping down his face. "Sol! You vicious demon! My nose again? I just got it re-aligned!"

Instead of answering, I run in swiftly and trying my luck again do a perfect roundhouse kick to his head snapping his chin up which he didn't see coming. He falls to the ground with heavy thump that I swear shakes the ground.

Okay, now I'm breathing heavy! Finally, I look around at my surroundings now that the fight is over and see Captain Mavin smiling snuggly with his arms crossed over his chest against the barracks. There are several ladies with looks of shock on their face and guardsmen exchanging coins subtly. A few shout out "congratulations!" and "never doubted you, princess!"

Leaning down, I help Nivael up and pat him on the back. He quietly says, "Thanks, princess. See you next time!" When I turn back around, Lanief is already up and sharply pulls his nose back in place.

"I expect a rematch one on one tonight or a few drinks on you since you broke my nose!" Lanief says when he walks by me towards the barracks. At the last second, he reaches out and tugs on my braid, but I manage to swipe his hand away.

"What is it with you men and tugging on my braid?" I say in exasperation while rolling my eyes skyward. Everyone starts laughing loudly.

"Well, you see, princess ... some women prefer when a man stimulates them by pulling on their hair as they—" one of the guardsmen, I think his name is Fallon, cuts off when Captain Mavin slaps him upside the head.

"Alright, everyone back sparring. Fallon, run four laps around the arena. Nivael and Lanief pair off against Camaeron and Finn." Captain Mavin then looks at me and continues: "Princess Solveig, ten laps around the arena for letting yourself get into that triangle chokehold. You know better. Then get out of here. I believe you have a ball to prepare for?"

Those ten laps took longer than I expected after my two sparring matches. Using legs feeling wobbly like a baby lamb, I eventually make it back to my room and prepare for a night of being silent but pretty.

CHAPTER
Nine

CADOC

After warming up by running around the training arena and racing Eirik a few times, we decided to work on our swordsmanship. It was only about ten minutes into our sparring, when we both heard the commotion and cheering. Eirik called a pause to our fight and we both rested our swords down while we listened the gossip of two guards around us.

Ten to one he beats her.

Oh please! You've never fought against her before.

She's amazing! I think she was trained by the Captain.

But I hear he's fast, maybe fast enough for the princess.

Their voices fade as they walk towards the commotion.

"Come on. We should check this out. It could be good for us to get news on the princess from the sounds of it. What do you think he meant by fast enough for the princess? Maybe she's watching some men spar?" Eirik says to me tugging on my arm.

"I'm not sure. I don't know much about the princess except her name and that she's supposed to be a great beauty," I respond while we walk towards the crowd gathered around a corner of the arena. "I was supposed to meet her when we were younger," I say trying to remember. "My father and I traveled to meet King Batair to promote trade between Laevaris and Gorva but when we got here, the king said his daughter was indisposed. I'm assuming she was ill, so I never got to meet her. I think she was around fourteen or fifteen years old at the time. Perhaps, she is of a weaker disposition. I heard some guards talking at the last tavern we stayed at that she is frequently indisposed and sometimes weak for several days before she is better."

"I also heard that most of the guard and even the army here are very loyal to her. Likely most of those men are smitten with her due to her looks," Eirik states as we walk up to the crowd of guards, soldiers, and gawking nobility.

Who is that? My gaze instantly focuses on the woman standing in tight breeches with twin katanas. *She's beautiful.* I think as I look her over. She stands with confidence and strength holding those weapons like they are an extension of her body. Her long dark brown hair is wild with strands falling out of a complicated long braid down her back. She looks strangely similar to that girl I ran into earlier in the hallway. I then notice her ears which are partially covered by her hair—*they're pointed at the tip!* I've never seen such a feature in a person, but it seems to just enhance her natural beauty. The rest of her features with her ears are delicate and sharp with full lips and long eyelashes. But her best feature by far is the piercing blue sapphire eyes that almost seem to glow. *She's exquisite. Exotic.* And those leather pants are so tight they display all her womanly curves, making me adjust myself with a groan.

At this point, I am totally captivated by her. It's like my surroundings have completely faded and all I can focus on is her. Eirik says something to me, but it takes me a few seconds to process his words.

"Bless you, Yasmil!" he says invoking the Goddess of Beauty and not taking his eyes off the woman either. He must be just as captivated as I am which makes me slightly irritable for some reason causing me to shove him on the shoulder. "What was that for?" he says with narrowed eyes. "I'm going to find out who she is! Do you see those curves? And that hair? It's like she was made for my pleasure," he rambles on closing his eyes with a moan.

We then walk a little closer to hear what the surrounding guardsmen are saying and notice she starts to spar with a much larger guardsman.

Camaeron is going to get his ass kicked again!

No he's not, I heard he was training more often since she beat him a month ago. His shoulder is all better ...

No way, shoulder dislocations take a while to heal and can pop back out easily.

He looks like he's holding his own.

My focus returns to the sparring match going on and I can't help but feel like the woman is holding back some. She is definitely the superior fighter and could probably end the match within a few moves of those katanas. However, I notice she's smiling and trading friendly insults with this Camaeron. They must know each other well. Again, I feel that sudden irritation and irrational anger that someone knows her better than me which is confounding. I don't even know her, and I've never been so interested in a woman before. Well—maybe that woman I ran into in the hallway.

The fight ends when she pulls a flexible and advanced move then drawing blood from a cut to his chin. As several guardsmen cheer and clap, I lean over and ask one of them who the woman is.

He stares back at me with confusion and then his face turns slightly wary and almost protective. He crosses his arms over his chest and tries to stare me down but that doesn't work too well for him since I am at least four inches taller than him. "I don't recognize you...Who are you and why do you want to know?"

"Just a visiting Lord's son from Gorva, my friends call me Cad," I say nodding my head. "I'm only here for the next week. I thought I'd train with my friend, and we saw the match. The girl is very skilled and we're interested in who she is."

He relaxes his pose some at hearing who I am but then smirks at me. "That *girl*, as you call her, is none other than Princess Solveig. She's one of the best fighters here and trained by none other than our Captain," he states proudly puffing his chest out a bit. "You'd do best to stay away from her. Everyone here would take a sword wound for that *woman* and she would do the same for us. So, watch your back."

I barely catch the last part of his sentence due to my utter shock. *That's the princess!* I look over at Eirik who's listening in and see a dumbfounded look on his face as well.

Eirik recovers from his shock faster than me and leaning in whispers to me, "No wonder the guards and army are loyal to her if she fights like that. She trains with them!? A princess? I've never seen the like …" he says shaking his head.

"Me either. Training with the men makes her more approachable as a royal and builds camaraderie between her and the men. Just like I do. I've never seen a princess though that fights like that or even dresses like that. I mean … look around. All the women here are wearing frilly dresses and prefer stitching. She's a rarity," I quietly say to Eirik while my eyes track the princess.

"You lucky bastard!" Eirik says shoving me in the shoulder with a smirk. Then he whispers, "It's not such a chore or obligation now to consider her for a political marriage, eh?"

"No, it definitely isn't," I whisper. We then hear the supposed Captain Mavin shouting about another match. Two men step up to face off with the princess. I watch as a giant of a man steps up cracking his knuckles in anticipation and smiling down at the princess. "What are they thinking putting her against two men?" I yell into Eirik's ear since the crowd is suddenly yelling bets and cheering in excitement for the upcoming sparring match.

"This is crazy! That one guardsman has to be the biggest man in their entire army!" Eirik replies.

Suddenly, she runs towards the smaller of her opponents performing a perfect downward roundhouse kick that would knock most men on their ass. The guardsman astonishingly avoids the kick in a flexible move that no one expected then tries to sweep the princess off her feet, and not in a good way. Watching her move, she displays a grace and agility that many can't obtain even with extensive training. She is also unusually fast. Some of her kicks and twists are nearly so fast it's hard to see. My admiration for her grows the longer I watch her.

The fight ends after the princess breaks the giant's nose and swiftly knocks him out with a kick to the head. Everyone is cheering and clapping. I glance around and notice the smug look on the Captain's face. *Interesting. He looks like he expected this result. Perhaps that guard is right and the Captain does train her.*

Smiling, I clap Eirik on the shoulder and he grins back at me. Both of us strangely proud of the princess and her unusual skills. We then unintentionally hear some of the ladies closest to us gossiping.

Honestly, Dara … she is an embarrassment to women!

So unbecoming of a lady of her station! Look at her clothes! Pants! They're so tight they're indecent! And she is filthy rolling around in the dirt with two men where everyone can see…

Shhh Eva! Don't let anyone hear you! Can't you see the men adore her.

Probably because she's so masculine and fights like them. I wonder what King Batair will do to her when he hears about this? Perhaps he will punish her. This woman Eva says with a malicious grin.

I saw her once after one of her "punishment lessons" don't tell anyone. Counselor Malphas was dragging her back to her room …

Confused, I look at Eirik and he nods his head away from the crowd indicating we should go. We walk back to my room in silence, both of us trying to process that woman's words.

Once the door closes behind Eirik, I ask, "What do you think she meant? Is she just starting a rumor or is it true?" I feel angry and concerned for Princess Solveig based on what those women were saying.

"I don't know …" Eirik responds while collapsing on the couch in my room. "However, I'm sure her choices in wardrobe and fighting with the men doesn't sit well with the king. He doesn't seem like someone who would be proud of a woman with independence or debasing herself by fighting with common guards. He's too arrogant for that."

Rubbing a hand over my face to clear my thoughts I say, "We will have to be cautious tonight at the ball. See how the king interacts with his daughter and also who this Counselor Malphas is to her. I've heard nothing but bad things about him." Then after sticking my head into the hallway to let a servant know to bring us something to eat, I go to bathe and prepare for the night ahead.

CHAPTER

Ten

SOLVEIG

Feeling energized and content after my sparring, I nearly skip down the hall towards my room.

Nothing's better than the gratification you feel after winning a fight, I hum to myself as I enter my room. It almost feels like lightening is running through my veins, similar to how I felt after the fight with Vidarr to obtain that shipment. I've been experiencing that energized sensation more and more after sparring since I turned eighteen last year. I then recall that my nineteenth birthday is only about two weeks away.

Suddenly, I feel a hot burning pain on my right upper outer thigh. *Ahhh!* I yell to myself throwing a hand over the area.

I quickly run into my en-suite bathroom and struggle to strip off my leather pants as fast as I can. *Maybe I got a wound from the fight that I was unaware of?* It's difficult to get my pants off quickly … tight leather plus sweat, not always a good combination, but eventually I'm free. I look down and see a strange symbol on the skin there. It's then that I notice the pain was gone by the time I got my pants off.

I reach down and touch the skin marking. It's smooth and all black like a tattoo. Only about the size of my hand in size, it's still noticeable against my golden skin.

What the hell? How could this—

It now feels tingly and cool. I also notice that energized feeling is gone almost as if it was building up to this symbol's appearance. *What does it mean?*

The sound of my bedroom door opening and shutting startles me out of my tumbling thoughts.

"Princess Sol! It's Isa! Marion sent me up to assist you with preparing for the ball tonight! May I come in?" I hear her yell and footsteps approaching the bathroom.

I panic. I don't know what to do about the tattoo-like symbol. I decide to keep it to myself for now and look around for something to hide myself with. "Just a minute!" I shout in reply. Then I see the bath already filled with steaming water and jump in with my shirt still on, splashing water over the edge just as Isa enters the bathroom.

She gives me a strange look eyeing my shirt. "I didn't take you for someone that is concerned for modesty Princ—Sol," she says. "You're going to have to take it off in order to get clean. I heard you put on quite a show this morning. Several guardsmen were gossiping as they dropped off their sweaty shirts. Also, you're covered in dirt. Here, let's undo your braid and I will wash your hair." She chatters while grabbing bottles and rummaging about the room.

Throwing my wet shirt off and into a heap on the floor, we then start the slow process of transforming me from warrior into a princess. I make sure to keep my new tattoo below the water to avoid her notice and when dressing I kept a towel around my waist hiding it from her gaze. She likely assumes I'm shy or again modest, which couldn't be farther from the truth.

We finish with my hair that is half up half down in a complicated braided crown circling my head while the rest of my hair curls down my back. It unfortunately exposes my pointed ears to everyone which I tend to avoid. They only add to my discomfort that I'm different from everyone here.

"All done! You look beautiful, Sol! So, why do you suddenly seem so uncomfortable and sad?" Isa says and tilts her head around to look my face.

"It's just … my ears. I usually cover them with my hair. Father hates them and most people find them repulsive," I tell her softly looking down in shame. I actually like my features normally but when I'm in the public eye, I tend to get very self-conscious about my unusual ears. I don't mention to her that they are a large part of why my father punishes me. He says they embarrass and bring shame upon him. He would frequently say that it's all my mother's fault for mutating his one and only child.

"Oh please! You have to be joking … you're stunning! I think they give you an exotic and distinctive look. Honestly. No one else looks like you in all of Laevaris which is a good thing," she says with a soft smile and direct look into my eyes. Then she surprisingly gives me the same advice my mother used to say to me when I'd cry as a child over my appearance: "Be calm and know yourself." She rubs me on the shoulder and then walks over to the wardrobe pulling out a silky dress my father had sent up for tonight.

Be calm and know yourself. I repeat like a mantra in my head and center myself.

I step into the dress she holds out while putting my back to her to hide the tattoo on my leg. Once it's fastened and the complicated straps are arranged, I step up to the mirror.

The dress is possibly the nicest and uncomfortably the sexiest I've ever worn. I'm trying to understand why my father would have given me this dress to wear tonight since it's so revealing. It's a dark sapphire blue gown that matches my eyes. It's long and formal with a high slit up the left leg all the way to my hip! *Goodness!* I guess I can't wear any underwear with this one. I've never worn something so revealing. *Thank Yasmil the slit is on the left side and not on the right or my new tattoo would show!* I mentally thank the goddess.

It's silky and light in texture laying against all my curves and leaving little to the imagination. The bodice and over my chest is a series of complicated straps that cross over my shoulders and chest with a deep V revealing my moderate sized cleavage. As I turn around and look over my shoulder, I see the back of the dress is completely open down to the curve of my ass. *Luckily the only scars I have are hidden under the dress.* The whip lacerations are nowhere to be seen due to my rapid healing leaving smooth skin on my back.

"Wow!" Isa says staring at me with her hands clasped under her chin. Then shaking her head, she claps her hands and starts to push me towards the door all while sliding delicate slippers on my feet. "Your escort is here. I just heard him knock. Out you go, princess!"

I don't even have time to respond before she pulls the door open revealing … "Jorah?" I blurt out loudly in my shock in a very unbecoming way.

He has this huge-eyed nervous look with his mouth hanging open and his hand in the air like he was about to knock on the door again. Slowly his eyes travel down the length of my body and his cheeks instantly turns red.

"Uhh … umm …wow … I … ahem," he mumbles out then clearing his throat and looking at the floor. "You look breathtaking, Sol," he whispers and then peeks up into my eyes. If I didn't know him better, I would think that he has a heated look of appreciation in his gaze. "I'm sorry I haven't seen you in a few days. I did miss you! I went to a neighboring town to discuss a book on the Lost lands and only got back two days ago. I couldn't put it down … did you know it mentions a different race of people that lived in the Elaritian Forest by us? It was fascinating! I couldn't find any literature on the Elaritian forest or this former race of people in our library! It's weird you know? I mean why wouldn't we have even one book about the forest our capital city abuts to?" He rambles on like he usually does when excited about a subject.

Smiling at him, I reach forward and pull him into a hug. Then stepping back, I place my forehead against his with my right hand embracing the back of his head that he mirrors in our signature greeting. "I missed you too, Jorah."

I've known Jorah since I was around eight years old. He moved here with his mother and father at that time. We became fast friends and sidekicks playing around the castle fighting imaginary dragons and since we were both the same age it just made sense that we should play together. His mother works as a maid in the castle and his father worked his way up to stable master. My mother at the time never once discouraged the friendship but I could see she was nervous for my father to see how close we became.

As we became older, Jorah started to become more protective over me. Always trying to tell me to be more careful. I will admit I was a bit reckless, still am if I'm honest. He tends to be more on the introverted side spending his time in the library reading or when forced to out in the stables doing chores.

One night I got pulled into Counselor Malpha's office for talking back to him and he forgot to fully close the door. I think I was around fifteen at the time. I shouted out when he backhanded me and pushed me onto the desk grabbing a whip he kept there. My yell must have been heard by Jorah, who was walking down the hall and saw the door cracked open, for the next thing I remember is Jorah standing in front shielding me from the whip as it came down. Somehow, we made it out of that room but Jorah still carries the scar from that whip diagonally across his chest.

He steps back from our embrace and holds out his left forearm like a gentleman then with a smile he states, "May I escort you, princess?"

I take my time perusing his form like I'm thinking about it before haughtily saying, "I suppose you shall do, good sir." Chuckling, I grab his left forearm and allow him to escort me.

Out of the corner of my eye I look him over while we walk to the ball-room. He's grown into a tall man nearly six foot three however it's not as noticeable since he tends to be usually slouching over a book. Mostly lean and with large hands, I've heard many of the servant girls gossiping about how handsome they find him to be. He nervously runs his other hand through his hair and glances over at me noticing my perusal of his body. I look at his messy blonde hair and emerald, green eyes asking myself why he never looks at me as more than a friend.

Clearing his throat, he says, "What? Do I have ink on my face?"

I laugh and reach up with a hand to mess his hair up more. Its adorable. "Nothing. Let's go or I'll be late." He nods and we walk swiftly in companionable silence the rest of the way.

When we get to the upper door entrance to the ballroom he steps back and bowing at the waist says, "See you soon, Sol." He steps back and then enters the ballroom at a difference entrance. Unfortunately, he can't be seen escorting me into the ballroom since he isn't nobility. No need to draw unwanted attention to him or to myself for that matter. I have enough to deal with.

Taking a deep breath, I repeat my mother's saying: *be calm and know yourself.* I nod to the guards at the door who smile at me in acknowledgement while opening the doors in synchrony. As I pass, one of the guard's whispers, "Nice sparring match today, princess."

I grin over at him and then step through the doors changing my face to an expressionless mask. *Time to play politics, Sol.*

SOLVEIG

"**L**adies and Lords, may I present … Princess Solveig." The herald (and also the steward) proudly announces to everyone when I start to descend the stairs towards the ballroom. Holding my head up and trying not to show my discomfort at the initial silence after that announcement, I continue to walk gracefully towards the raised dais at the opposite end of the ballroom.

Slowly conversation starts back up again, and I relax a fraction until I look around and see several noblemen ogling my body and cleavage. *I knew this dress was too revealing!* I feel so exposed now and realize all the other noblewomen are wearing conservative ballgowns frowning and whispering behind hands while staring at me. The only skin exposure is their arms and necks. I nearly stumble when one nobleman steps closer and subtly runs his hand up my exposed leg through the slit of my dress chuckling and whispering, *whore.*

I start to pause and look to him, but he's already camouflaged back into the crowd of pretentious nobles. The nobles of the royal court have never respected me. Sniveling for position with my father, they take their cues from him and prefer to flatter him hoping for a higher position. Since I don't play their political games, they usually dismiss me. I've never fit into their world in the past, why start now.

Be calm and know yourself.

Don't punch any asshole nobles in the face.

Father's watching.

Taking another deep breath, I make sure my face is expressionless before I continue walking. Finally making my way over to the raised dais where my father, King Batair, stands arrogantly, I curtsey low with my head down submissively and wait.

After a long pause to where I wonder if my cleavage is in full view or he just forgot about me, he finally states, "You're late, Solveig. Rise and join us."

I look up and see my father frowning down at me. Then I see Counselor Malphas to his right blatantly staring at my nearly exposed breasts in this position. *Damn this dress!*

Taking a seat at the table to the left of my father, I feel warm breath on the back of my neck making me break out in goosebumps. "I see you got the dress I sent up for you," Malphas whispers in my ear causing me to shutter while he runs his hand over my exposed back. "It looks perfect on your body as I knew it would. No one compares to you in this room, princess. I do so hope that you misbehave so we can have more time together later."

I keep my back straight and my gaze forward somehow maintaining my composure by a thread. His whispered words make me feel dirty and more exposed than I already am. I thought my father sent the dress for me to wear. I would have thrown it in the trash if I knew Malphas had sent it to me and expected me to wear it. My father seems to be giving him more and more control over me as I get older which makes me nervous.

"Hmm, no response for me? You must be learning well then in your lessons. Silent. Beautiful …" He runs his hand down my back towards my ass where no one can see due to the table in the front. "Respectful. Compliant." Then after grabbing a handful of my ass, he stands up and smiles. He then more loudly says, "Oh, Princess Solveig, you can have my attention anytime! Save a dance for me?"

Staring up at him with a blank face, I don't acknowledge him with a response which I know will anger him later. *Fucking disgusting chauvinistic pig!* Hopefully my eyes give away my revulsion to him.

After he walks away, I subtly relax back into my chair and scan the crowd of nobles. My father is talking with his advisors and several Dukes laughing while drinking wine. I do a double take when I see a familiar face with a hooked nose, dirty blonde hair combed back and light blue-grey eyes glancing my way and winking. Shaking my head and chuckling to myself, I half-smile at him and then notice Vidarr's in servant attire serving drinks around the room. *Hmm ... must be doing some eavesdropping to gather intel for the Rebellion then.*

I stand up from the table and walk down the dais planning to bump into him and lighten my mood. Unfortunately, as soon as I step from the dais, as horde of noblemen swarm me asking for a dance. This is the part of being a princess that I hate. Wearing a cold expressionless mask, I calmly accept one dance after another. I try to ignore their grabby hands and accidental touches when dancing, but it becomes exhausting. *Honestly, you'd think Malphas was trying to sell me or something by dressing me so scandalous.* I decide halfway through the ball that I'm going to emulate Vidarr and gather info for the Rebellion. Surely these noblemen know something interesting.

After my fifth dance, I step into a traditional Laevarian waltz with Duke Havass. He runs a large region of the kingdom in the north along the border of Jaarn and abutting Counselor Malphas's region. He gives off a sinister aura similar to Counselor Malphas. I always tried to avoid him in the past and usually he's not at court given the distance to the capital.

"Princess Solveig, it's a pleasure to see you again. You look ravishing tonight and much more ... mature since the last time I saw you," he says with a lecherous gaze down my bodice. He then gracefully spins me around the dance floor. "You know your exotic features are very unique however I have seen them before."

He suddenly captures my attention with his words more than his wandering hands do. "What do you mean?" I ask.

"Well, my dear princess, I'm not sure it's appropriate discussion for your delicate disposition as a lady but since no one has told you ... I feel like it's my responsibility to educate you," he says with a condescending tone. "In my region of the kingdom, we have many ... I guess you could call them *camps*, for lack of a better word, where we keep criminals and lowlifes away from the more respectable population." He stops dancing as the song ends and reaches up to run a finger over one of my pointed ears making me flinch unconsciously. "You see, I've seen these particular features many times before, although it's now becoming rarer. I see these repulsive ears on several of the slaving criminals in our camps. They help with the mining and forestry jobs that help serve our great kingdom. Perhaps one day I will show you if you wish to visit with me? Or, you can join me tonight and I may tell you more ... Enjoy the ball, princess." He smirks and then bows walking away before I can respond.

I'm shocked. No one --and I mean no one-- has ever told me there were others with similar features to me. What are these camps? I wasn't aware we had camps for criminals. My father definitely wouldn't deign to answer any questions I have since he thinks it's not my place as a woman. I'll have to ask Vidarr, I think, while looking around.

Not paying much attention after that shocking revelation, I accidentally run into a large muscular wall nearly stumbling backwards.

Hands grab my waist to support me before I fall over and a deep voice says, "I feel we always meet under these circumstances."

I look up into the handsome smiling face of the man I ran into earlier today. Unable to control the blush from my clumsiness and also due to his attractiveness, I throw my hands up to my cheeks to cool them.

"I'm so sorry! Sir ..." I state while trying to gain his name.

"Please call me Cadoc," he says with a smile and bow. "It's a pleasure to meet you, Princess Solveig. You look stunning tonight although I also prefer seeing you in your fighting leathers and dirt in your hair." He winks at me! Me! *Oh shit! He must have seen me earlier! There's no way father won't hear of it.*

Huffing out some air and blowing a piece of hair out my face, I respond: "I'm assuming you saw me sparring this morning Cadoc?" Fanning my face and trying to recover from his sinful wink at me I look over and notice a grinning man standing at his side.

Cadoc must notice my gaze as he says, "Yes, we saw your skills this morning. Please excuse my manners. This is my best friend and travel companion, Eirik."

"Well met, Eirik," I say while he bows over my hand kissing the back of it. *Goodness! Does everyone look so attractive where they come from?* "Where are you both from? I haven't seen you around the castle other than the one time we ran into each other."

"We are both noblemen from the Kingdom of Gorva, at your service, Princess Solveig."

"Ahh, hopefully you brought my father some of your famous wine? Although," I say grimacing and looking over my shoulder towards the dais where my father is laughing loudly and spilling wine in his hand, "he looks as if he's already had too much."

"Of course! Who doesn't like a well-seasoned Gorvian wine?" Eirik says smiling.

During the conversation, I become aware Cadoc hasn't removed one of his hands at my waist and shifts it possessively to the small of my back. "Let me get you a drink, princess." He waves down a servant, and I happen to look up into the eyes of Vidarr.

"Here you go, Princess Solveig," Vidarr (the pretend servant) says with strained smile. "And may I say you look beautiful tonight." This makes both Cadoc and Eirik frown since its unusual talk for a servant to address royalty so familiarly. I try to stare at Vi and make him understand that I need to talk with him, but he just looks down at Cadoc's hand on my waist with frown and walks away.

"Well … may I have this dance, princess?" Cadoc asks me after I take a few sips of the, shockingly, Gorvian wine. *How ironic.*

"Please call me Solveig or Sol. And yes," I respond before he leads me back onto the dance floor.

CADOC

Seeing Princess Solveig, I mean Sol, up close is much more breathtaking than it was in the training arena.

She feels like she's meant to be in my arms. Her waist is so tiny in my hands, and she looks so delicate that it's hard to believe so much power and strength is wrapped up in such a small package.

When I saw her walking down the stairs into the ballroom after her entrance, I felt like I was under her spell. However, looking around I did notice most of the men in the room probably felt the same way. She has this grace about her and the way she moves it's very sensual and, unintentionally on her part, extremely sexual. Seeing her in that scrap of a dress clinging to all her curves made me instantly hard. If the Goddess of Beauty, Yasmil, had a body it would be in the form of Princess Solveig without a doubt. That dress should be outlawed on her since it exposes nearly all of her left leg when she steps forward and then leaning down her generous breasts are almost exposed. I wonder why her father allowed her to wear it.

"So, how do you like Laevaris so far Cadoc?" she asks while we travel around the dance floor. It takes an iron strength of will not to look too far down into her exposed cleavage and keep eye contact with her. She's so distracting.

"It's beautiful," I respond while looking directly into her sapphire blue eyes. I can tell she gets my double meaning when she blushes prettily and looks away. *Ahh. So she can be humble when not sparring.*

Feeling the smooth exposed skin on her back, I run my thumb back and forth which elicits a soft moan from her that I can tell she didn't mean to do. *So responsive.* I twirl her away from me to avoid her noticing my hard as hell cock that is in total agreement with me that she's ours.

She smiles and curtsies to me when the song ends and I can't help but appreciate her curves or the position this puts her in. Imagining seeing her on her knees in front of me with those full lips and big eyes in a different situation makes me instantly hard again. *Damn! What am I a horny teenage boy again?*

The herald calls out loudly to gain everyone's attention and interrupting my thoughts.

"Nice to meet you, Cadoc, and tell your friend I said bye. I enjoyed my dance with you and will try to avoid running into you next time! I have to go ..." she says while swiftly walking away before I can respond.

Eirik walks up to me and clasps a hand on my shoulder while I stare longingly after Solveig. "Damn. She is something special ... too bad I didn't get a turn. Come on, Cadoc, you look like someone just took your favorite pastry from you," he teases while leading me off the dance floor to await this anticipated announcement.

Walking briskly back up to the dais, I can't help but smile thinking about my dance with Cadoc.

He has this strong protective presence to him. *It also helps that he's gorgeous!* I think to myself. That white-blonde hair slightly mussed up and spiky on the top paired with his soft brown eyes made me nearly speechless the whole dance. Or it could have been his strong hand touching me gently on my low back. The feel of his callused fingers running over the exposed skin there made me embarrassingly moan into his chest. Hopefully he didn't notice!

When I make it back up on the dais where my father and Counselor Malphas are standing, the herald calls for silence. A hush falls over the assembled crowd with anticipation buzzing through the area. I look over to my father with curiosity wondering what this big announcement will be and suddenly get tense when I see Malphas smugly smiling to himself with his hands clasped behind his back.

"Today is a special day!" King Batair announces loudly while raising his drink. "Thank you for celebrating our fine and noble Counselor Malphas who has assisted me well for these past many years as a trusted advisor. As a reward for his service to me and also a present for his birthday, I have decided to grant him approval for my daughter's hand in marriage." He pauses for effect with an eager smile. Suddenly my world falls apart and I break into a cold sweat. It feels as if the floor has collapsed beneath me. "As you know, she will turn nineteen in a few weeks, and I feel it is well past time for her to yield her wild ways to a husband and provide an heir. "

After his speech, Counselor Malphas steps forward with a nod and a wave expecting applause. Most of the nobles nod their head in agreement and clap as expected. However, all the servants in attendance and guards scattered throughout the ball room stare in somber silence.

Once the initial shock clears out of my system, burning rage takes its place. *How dare my father give me to him like cattle! A present! To that monster! I'll show him wild!* I think gritting my teeth together and hearing my heart beat loudly in my ears.

I step forward angrily and feel my expressionless mask crack. I want to punch or stab someone, particularly my father at the moment.

"Over my dead body will I marry that disgusting pig! He is nothing but a plague on our kingdom!" I shout loudly at my father and point to Malphas.

I look up to see the strain in my father's neck and growing flush of anger creep up to his face. Faster than I thought possible, he backhands me causing me to fall backwards off the raised dais and hitting my head on the stone floor with a dull thump. Shocked silence reins throughout the ballroom except for a slight ringing, oh wait … that's probably in my head. My father jumps down from the dais standing over me and seeing me still conscious grabs me by arm and spits in my face.

"Never insult me in front of my subjects! And *never* disobey me again. You have learned nothing from your lessons! Perhaps it is a good thing I am giving you to Malphas since he will be most qualified to help break this spirit you seem unable to control," he says in a soft but malicious voice. Then raising his voice louder, he says to the nearest guard, "Please assist the princess to her room, she seems to have fallen and needs time to compose herself. "

Two guards step forward to hold my upper arms and walk me out of the ballroom of whispering gossip. I can barely keep consciousness and definitely can't walk by myself since the room is spinning. *Must have a concussion.*

Once the doors to the ballroom shut, I sag in the guards' arms and let them drag me. I only make it to the hallway by the kitchen before I lose consciousness. *Blissful darkness.*

I wake up to nearly a full room of servants fluttering over me in the kitchen. Marion is speaking to me in a soft voice, running a cool damp cloth over my forehead and holding a towel to the back of my head but I can't focus on her words yet. *Hmm … when did I lay down? Why am I in the kitchen?*

"Solveig! Princess!" She frantically says, "Please keep your eyes open … there you go. Can you hear me now?" She says with a tearful voice.

Croaking out a reply I say, "Marion, stop fussing so much. I'm sure you are a busy woman. I'll be fine in a few hours. Just another day in my miserable life."

Marion's face transforms to anger, though I don't think it's directed at me. "Stop *fussing!*" she says, reiterating my words. "You have a concussion most likely and a serious head injury that's bleeding all over the kitchen! I swear … that horrible man! Why I could … I could …" She rambles on until someone makes a loud shushing noise. I think it's one of the many kitchen servants. The guards are standing awkwardly behind the cluster of servants that are trying to soothe me on the kitchen floor.

"Let us carry you to your room, Princess Sol? We have already sent a runner for Liv to look at your head once you are back in your room," one of the guards asks somberly.

"Fine. But then I just want to be alone," I say to the guards. Then I whisper to Marion, who's leaning over me, "I can't do it anymore. I can't— not Malphas." Tears run silently down the sides of my face.

"I know, child … but when things go wrong, we must hold on to the belief that there's more to come," she says running a soft hand over my face to wipe the tears away. I hear a few sniffles behind her.

"Based on what my father said earlier, there won't be *more to come.* Only darkness." Then the guards come over and gently lift me to carry me back to my room.

CADOC

"... As a reward for his service to me and also a present for his birthday, I have decided to grant him approval for my daughter's hand in marriage," I hear King Batair announce and the rest of his speech is ignored due to the pounding of my heart and my sudden anxiety. *This can't be happening! Not now!*

Lost in my thoughts, I miss Solveig yelling at her father in an uncharacteristic display of emotion. I look up to the dais when I hear the shocked gasps of the surrounding nobles nearest to me and see the King backhand his daughter causing her to career off that stupid dais.

I'm floored with horror and then sudden anger at his treatment of his only daughter. I make to step forward, but a heavy hand lands on my shoulder. Turning my head to look over my shoulder, Eirik shakes his head with a conflicted expression and whispers, "Are you sure?"

Nodding my head to him, I shove my way through the crowd to the front of the ballroom and notice Eirik assisting me. I make it in front of the dais just as Solveig is being dragged away by the guards and see a small amount of blood on the stone floor.

I take a deep breath trying to control the raging anger that floods through my system and center myself. Standing up straight and putting on my "prince" expression of cool disregard, I loudly project my voice to the king, "King Batair. May I please introduce myself to you and your court? I am Prince Cadoc Arigari Desmond, the crowned heir to the Kingdom of Gorva and appointed leader of the largest known and may I say best army in the five kingdoms." I nod my head to King Batair. "I wish to discuss a potential alliance through a betrothal to the Princess Solveig."

"What is this?" the king states looking at his advisors on the dais and stumbling a bit spilling red wine on his tunic. *Disgusting drunk. It's embarrassing that he would allow himself to be so inebriated in front of his subjects,* I think to myself.

He continues speaking as though he didn't just make a mess all over himself: "I was unaware of your arrival and was told it wouldn't be for another three or four days at least."

"You are correct, your majesty, however me and my royal guard just arrived earlier than planned and were notified of the ball tonight. I thought … given the circumstances of your recent announcement … I would introduce myself and request an early audience with you."

"Very well, welcome, Prince Cadoc of Gorva. I will notify you tomorrow of an appropriate time for our meeting. As you can see, this celebration is for my counselor and we will not be discussing business tonight. Please enjoy yourself," he says with a nod of arrogant dismissal and then turns to this counselor that everyone keeps talking about. I notice the counselor is eyeing me with distrust and irritation.

Eirik and I turn and head back over to the side doors. I want to check on the princess after seeing the blood on the stone floor. Sneaking into the hallway, we notice two servants whispering angrily and waving their hands towards the kitchen. I decide that must have been where they took her.

We walk on silent feet down the hallways, and I look into the kitchen seeing several servants crowding over a form on the floor. Also several guards are turned towards the still form of the princess. No one notices me and Eirik as we eavesdrop on what is being whispered by the guards.

He could have killed her!

This has to be stopped.

That man will break her if we let him marry her.

Someone needs to get word to the Rebellion and Vidarr.

I can just barely hear the soft words of Princess Solveig. "I can't do it anymore." I swear those words break something inside me when I connect her connotation that this is a regular occurrence.

I back away from the crowd of guards and servants knowing she is in good hands that obviously care for her. Tilting my head to Eirik, we silently walk back to my room. *Time to plan.*

CHAPTER
Thirteen

JORAH

After having left the ridiculous ball early, I meandered back to my usual comfort zone. The library. I mean … I only stayed long enough to eat and then snuck out the back.

I *hate* crowds of people, and I especially hate dressing formally. I only attended because my father told me I could go in his place and escort Solveig to the entrance.

I would have thought it was a waste of time but that would be a lie since I got to see Solveig. Anytime alone with her is special to me. *And seeing her in that dress!* I groan to myself, wiggling in my chair by the library's fireplace.

Opening my newest book on the Elaritian Forest (or as most people around here call it the Broken Forest), I settle in ready to spend a long night of reading. But for some reason, I can't keep my thoughts from straying to her. *Solveig. My Sol,* I internally think.

She's not only my best friend; she's my only friend! I don't tend to socialize much making it hard to meet people. I know I'm a tall somewhat attractive man (per some of the other servants) but to me that seems to be an annoyance as it draws attention to me when I want to be left alone. I sometimes hear the younger maids around the castle whispering about me but all it does is make me flush with embarrassment. I guess that makes me shy or awkward however you want to interpret it.

But Solveig ... she understands me and puts me at ease. Tonight, when I looked her in that dress, I tried to convey that I have other thoughts about her which go beyond friendship. Indecent thoughts. Manly thoughts. And I wanted something other than a book for companionship late at night.

She doesn't seem to notice me as a *man* though. Particularly, a man with carnal wants and needs. She still looks at me as the boy who kept her secrets and played around the castle with her. Somehow, I need to make her see me as *more*. I think as I run my hands through my hair and try to focus on the book in front of me.

Solveig

I wake up alone in my room nearly a full day later from the head injury. Wondering what woke me up, I then feel it ... a searing pain in my upper back just below my neck. *Maybe I injured my back from the fall?*

Trying to remember what happened and grimacing through the pain in my upper back, I snap out of my thoughts when the pain miraculously disappears to be replaced by a cool tingling sensation. *Oh no, not again!*

I scramble out of the bed noticing someone changed me into a light shift for sleeping and make my way to the large mirror in the room.

First, I see a white bandage wrapped around my head which I remove quickly seeing dried blood on the back part of the bandage. I feel around the back of my head and notice it's all healed up. Then I turn my back to the mirror and glance over my shoulder. Confirming my suspicion, I see a rather large black symbol overlying my spine peeking up over my sleeping gown. I pull my gown over my head quickly to see the full tattoo. Starting at the base of my neck extending to the bottom of my shoulder blades is a large intricate tattoo, I can't help by wonder what this means.

Just as I have these thoughts, and while trying to rub a hand over the tattoo, I get the inkling on what it means.

I feel invigorated. Honestly, I feel the best I've felt in a long time.

I notice the sun outside the window and assume it's late afternoon based on its position. I decide to spend some time in my favorite place with my favorite companions.

Sneaking out of the castle in pants and with a long bow over my shoulders is easy given that usually the castle is quiet after a big party. Everyone can still be seen hung over and walking around bleary eyed for a few days.

I make it to the stables without anyone noticing me. Entering, I breathe in the scent of horses and hay, hints of leather, which reminds me of a time when I met a visiting young girl, one of the nobility whom I befriended.

It was the year before my mother died and I was just entering into adolescence. I snuck out to the stable after a party just like today wanting to get some alone time when I came across a young girl that was the same age as me stroking *my* horse's nose.

She was garbed in stableboy clothes with loose pants, boots and a shirt that was nicer than most servants. I would have mistaken her for a boy if it weren't for the long red braid falling down her back. I hadn't had much chance to interact with most kids my age given that I was a princess, and my father restricted my activities back then. Most of the visiting nobles also didn't let their children travel with them for security reasons.

"Who are you?" I ask her. "That's my horse, she's pretty, no? Better yet—she can jump over creeks in the forest."

The young red-headed girl turns around scrunching up her nose and looking at me. "I'm Cassia and my horse at home can do that too. But—I will admit she is pretty."

I walk up to her and hold my hand out to shake. "I'm Solveig. You look like a stableboy, no offense. But you talk like a noble. I wish I was allowed to dress like that but my mother says I need to act like a lady," I state grabbing the skirt of my dress and pulling it away from my legs like it's gross. Maybe I should steal some pants from the stableboys?

"Hello. Nope," she says popping the "p" in nope. "I'm not a stableboy just pretending. I'm actually from the Kingdom of Beamus visiting your parents with mine. I was bored and decided to sneak out using one of our servant's clothes." She pauses looking at her fingernails on one hand and putting the other on her hip while she stands with attitude. "He likes me … so I can usually talk him into doing things. Boys are so strange." Then she looks up at me with a genuine smile. "Maybe we can be friends. I don't have many that like animals or hang out in a stable like you."

"Okay. Want me to show you some of my other animals?" I ask her excited for something to do. "Wait, your parents—are they the King and Queen of Beamus? I know there's a few other nobles with them from Beamus but you said both …"

She smirks and then grabs my hand, pulling me through the stables. "Yeah, yeah …
I'm Princess Cassia. But today, we are just two stableboys finding some adventure and
playing with animals. Come on—let's find you some better clothes to play in."

I smirk to myself thinking about Cassia and our first time hanging out
as two kids. We were able to stay in contact on and off over the years but
our communication kind of fell off for a while after my mother died. She
visited once after with her parents, but it was short. I wonder how she's doing … I heard she was engaged to another noble from her kingdom. Maybe, I should write to her—ask her if she's going to wear stableboy clothes
to her wedding. Chuckling to myself, I walk past a few friendly stablehands.

Sindari's intense gaze is already tracking me as I walk towards him.
He projects a thought of running with me on his back laughing and then
quickly changes it to me feeding him a bucket of carrots. I laugh out loud
at his antics. I project back to him, *I missed you friend. Want to take a ride?*

He yinnies in agreement and stomps his foot anxiously as I unlatch the
stall door. I reach in and rub his forelock with a hand and pull out a carrot
from my back pocket that I snatched from the garden on my way out the
back door. He munches on this happily while he follows me out into the
sunlight.

Just as I swing myself up onto his bare back, Sigurd walks out of the
stable behind us with his arms crossed.

"That horse is spoiled and a pain in my ass. Take him for a good long
ride and bring him back tired for me, you hear!" he says with a narrowed
gaze at Sindari. I chuckle and pat his neck.

"Yes sir! I think we both need a good long run!" I respond.

"Oh, and Sol?" he starts and then rubbing the back of his neck he
says, "I heard what happened at the ball. This is getting out of hand. You
need to be more careful. I don't want to see you hurt anymore sweetheart."
Smiling sadly at me, he then says, "Vi contacted me. I guess he was there
last night, and he says to meet him tonight. There's an underground fight
going on at the Hidden Dagger Tavern if you are up for it."

Nodding my head that I heard him, I then start to nudge Sindari away
from the stables. I wave over my shoulder and say, "Don't worry, Sigurd.
I'll be fine. "

Sindari and I race out of Falal and leaving behind the city walls, we
head for the Broken Forest. I let out a deep sigh once we get under the

heavy branches and then take a deep breath smelling the earthy clean scent of nature. I throw my arms out and my head back before projecting a thought of racing through the trees to Sindari. He instantly agrees taking off running and weaving through the forest while I relax for the first time in a while.

Most people who live in Falal and even throughout the Kingdom of Laevaris, tend to avoid this forest. They fear it, most people whispering its cursed. No one knows it's true history or why it's thought to be cursed. Some say it will trap you, others that it makes you confused and lost, and others … that there are creatures and even ghosts that will tear you apart.

Ca—kek-kek!Kek-kek! shrieks out my friend, Tyr, in his excitement while he swoops down in front of me. It's been a few days since I saw him last, and he must have missed me. Although the surly Goshawk would never admit it!

Tyr flies abreast to us as we race through the forest for a while. The two of them projecting competitive thoughts back and forth.

Slow-hooved mule! You could barely make it over that log back there! Tyr says to Sindari. Then Sindari throws his head in the air and his mane hits my face. He abruptly jumps over a large creek nearly in one leap catching me by surprise.

Take that you, pesky bird! I think you're getting slower in your old age.

I can't help but chuckle at their antics and feel a true bond with the forest at times like these. I project to Sin that I want to slow down and dismount which he does instantly.

I walk back towards the creek we just jumped and meander through the forest for a time lost in my thoughts. As I walk, I place my hand on the surrounding trees feeling their energy and life course through my body. *This is where I belong.* I close my eyes in contentment for a second just soaking in the forest. Branches start to shift to follow me and gently touch my sides as I walk. I don't notice as I walk that flowers bloom near my footsteps along the path I take. A small green snake with a red stripe down its back slithers across the path ahead and when I step closer it travels up my leg twisting and turning until I see its keyhole shaped eyes in front of my face. It projects easily to me a warm greeting of friendship and thoughts of hunting small birds together.

Hello friend. I project to her, and yes I mean a female, which I can instinctually know. *You want to hunt?* The small green snake nuzzles my face and slithers around my neck like a fitted necklace. *I'll take that as a yes.* I smirk thinking to myself as I scan the area.

Looking up to the branches, I try to see if Tyr is around since I don't want him to ruin my new friend's hunt. Not seeing him or Sindari at the moment. I think to the little snake. *What should I call you little huntress?*

She instantly projects an image of a green stone. *Jade?* I ask. Then I feel her nuzzle my neck again in agreement. *Very pretty I think to myself.*

Silently moving through the forest, I spend the next half hour or so looking for a small animal or bird fit for a meal to please my friend. I crawl through the dirt and overlook a shallow pool branching off the creek where I see a tiny bird hopping around trying to grab insects off its surface. I pull a small dagger from my belt that is thin and sharp. Throwing it swiftly and with deadly accuracy, I hit my target instantly killing it. Jade slithers down my body as I walk towards the tiny bird. I say a small prayer to Patrov, God of self-reflection and patience, before removing my dagger and smiling at Jade.

While Jade happily consumes her meal and promptly projects a satisfied farewell, I look to the sky and notice it's getting closer to the evening. I start to walk South in the direction of the city and instantly become alert when I hear a shifting of feet. Its subtle. But with my exceptional hearing and awareness of the forest, it sounds like a blaring alarm to my system that someone is following me. Drawing a larger dagger from my hip sheath since I left my katanas back at the castle, I slowly turn in the direction of the noise.

CHAPTER
Fourteen

SOLVEIG

What I see next … it's hard to comprehend.

I thought last night when my father announced my betrothal to Counselor Malphas that I was shocked. Well, I was wrong.

This is shocking.

I stare at the man walking towards me with complete silence and a dumbfounded expression. I must look ridiculous with my mouth open and my eyes wide! The dagger I have held in my hand drops to the forest floor in my shock and I place a hand to the nearest tree to support my weight since I suddenly feel like I'm going to pass out.

"What? Who are you?" I sputter out unintelligently.

The man approaches me with head tilted to the side and a look of curiosity on his face. He has this presence about him that I inherently sense—powerful and ancient. He has long silver hair flowing down his back and perfect sharp features with almond shaped eyes that demonstrate amusement. I notice very subtle wrinkling of the skin near the corner of his eyes as the only indication that he may be older than he appears. My gaze then travels over his long dark green robe and ends at his … ears! They are sharply pointed similar to mine but almost more pronounced than mine are. I've never seen their like other than on myself.

"No, my dear. Who are you? That is the true question …" he responds running his gaze over me.

I instinctively know this man is someone important, someone powerful. Bowing my head to him I say, "My name is Solveig Andraevian."

He smiles at me then gracefully placing a hand over his heart bowing his head in greeting, "Well met, Solveig Andraevian. My name is Aren Floraevial, I am an elder of the Elarians and caretaker of the Elaritian Forest. May I enquire towards your parentage, you have a similarity to someone I knew many years ago."

"Well … I—" I stumble over my words, trying to think how much I should tell him. He's obviously not from the city and I've never, *and I mean never*, seen someone in this forest.

Then, before I can finish what I was saying, Tyr flies in with a *kak-kak* and lands on my left shoulder surprising me once again.

He is Elder. Friend, Tyr projects directly to me. Elder Aren tilts his head at this and smiles at my goshawk.

You know him!? Why have I never heard of people living in this forest before? I yell back at Tyr.

You never ask. Assumed you knew. They watch you sometimes, Tyr responds and then with a rustle of feathers flies off into the branches.

Huffing to myself in annoyance. I turn to respond to my new acquaintance, "That was Tyr, my friendly goshawk. Sorry. You were asking about my parents … well … my father is King Batair, ruler of Laevaris, and my mother was Queen Vivian Andraevian. Why? Do you know them? I'm sorry but I've never seen anyone who lives in the Broken Forest nevertheless travels through it but me."

"May we please sit, Princess Solveig? My old legs sometimes tire," he says while lowering himself onto a nearby log covered in moss. I look at him doubtful since he doesn't seem "old" to me, more like early forties. I sit a few spaces down from him and turn towards him.

"You must be mistaken, child. Hasn't your mother ever told you? You have the same face and same blue eyes as your father, Lochlann. Not this false king, King Batair," he says with sympathy and then disgust. "I knew your real father, Lochlann, it's where you got your strong Elarian features from and I suspect your powers? How old are you now?" he asks with that eery head tilt.

"No, I think you are mistaken, Elder Aren. I've never met this, Lochlann!" I state confused. "My mother passed away when I was thirteen and was married to my father, King Batair. He calls me his daughter, and no one has ever disclaimed this. I'm nearly nineteen in two weeks," I reply feeling my heart race as I think back to the last time my mother spoke to me from her sickbed.

"Sol, my heart, come here," she whispers softly before getting a coughing spell. "I want you to know that I love you more than anything. You're special dear and not just to me," she says while putting my hair behind my ears and then running a finger around the shell of my pointed ear. "Batair ... he doesn't understand you and whatever he doesn't understand, dear, he tends to fear."

"Okay, mommy," I say holding one of her hands that's resting on the bed. "Whatever you say. I just want you to get better. I can't be without you. I have no one! Other than Jorah that is."

"You have more people that care than you know. There are people ... a person ... who would have loved you more than you'll ever know ... he ..." She stops talking as a single tear falls down her cheek. Then she goes into a coughing fit again gasping for breath afterwards. "He never got to know you ... would have loved you more than ..." she mumbles to herself with her eyes now closed appearing pale and exhausted.

"Sure, momma. I love you. Get some rest for me," I say to her and leaving the room don't realize that was my last moment speaking to her before she died.

Looking back now, I start to wonder who she was referring to. I never got to find out. I assumed it was maybe a grandfather I never met. Or an uncle? Not ... a father.

"Solveig. Lochlann was your father. I'm as sure of it as I am that the moon rises at night. Your mother was also half Elarian however she didn't carry enough of the heritage in her blood to possess our features or power. Your father on the other hand, well, you see child ... he—he was my son," he starts to say with a nervous, but hopeful look my way.

"Say I believed you, even though I don't. Where is my supposed father, Lochlann? Why did he never know about me?" I ask confused.

"Your father, my son, was our ruler and King of Elaria which was in the Elaritian Forest or as you probably know it, the Broken Forest. He was nearing two hundred years old which is an age of maturity in Elarians. We, Elarians, can sometimes live nearly up to a thousand years depending on our power level. The forest helps sustain our health as well so many survive longer if living in our homeland."

He pauses thinking about his next words.

"About a hundred or so years ago, King Gaargon, who was Batair's father and ruler of Laevaris at the time, mounted an attack on Elaria catching us by surprise. He was a greedy ruler and wanted to expand the Kingdom of Laevaris into our forest. He met with us under the false pretense that he wanted to harvest timber for new houses in Laevaris and was willing to trade for our coveted ancient trees. We obviously denied him access to our trees since they help sustain our lives and are our basis for our culture. He was not happy, but we left the meeting on civil terms. The attack came at night a few days after the meeting. He would have never won if it weren't for his allies in Jaarn. They surrounded us and lit half the forest on fire which weakened us. Most of our forest burnt to the ground. Nearly all were slaughtered brutally, women were raped, and a quarter of the Elarians were unaccounted for. We couldn't find them. The Elaritian Forest ceased to exist and became the Broken Forest after that. Only Lochlann, myself and two dozen others were alive after the attack. We decided we needed to find the unaccounted for Elarians. Where did they go? We spent years trying to find them but with no luck. Meanwhile, the King of Laevaris decided to remove any history of us and forbid his people from mentioning us. We couldn't return to Elaria as there was something strange preventing us from entering so we lived off the forest in scattered camps. Life was difficult and we lost a few to grief during that time."

He pauses again and takes a deep breath.

"Then about twenty years ago, your father decided to go on a journey into the forest for solitude and to see if he could find any leads on our missing people. He was overcome with grief, we all were. We were losing hope of ever returning home and finding our people. It was during that trip that your father met your mother, Vivian, near the border of the Elaritian Forest and Avaria. Your mother was an Avarian before she married King Batair, no?" He pauses while I nod my head. "Well, I never met your mother, but when Lochlann returned later than he promised, he told me of a beautiful kind woman he had fell in love with. He said she was part Elarian on her mother's side. They had been together for most of his stay in the forest, but she was betrothed to a man in Laevaris and she was willing to cancel the betrothal and leave Avaria for him. But she said she wanted to speak to her parents and end any attachments to the betrothed. He agreed since she was his mate and the desire of his heart. He would give her anything. But he never mentioned the possibility of a child to me. I had told him that if this woman is the desire of his heart and his mate, then he should have brought her home and never left her side. He said he wasn't thinking straight since he was upset that he could find no word about the missing Elarians." He shakes his head sadly.

Continuing he says, "Unfortunately, another attack occurred three days after he returned to me. Lochlann never made it back to your mother and never found out that she was very early in her pregnancy with you. Your mother had sent an immediate message through pigeon to King Batair cancelling the betrothal stating she found her love in the Elaritian Forest." Aren then rubs his hand over his eyes. "King Batair was obviously furious and confused as his father had told him the story us being deceiving greedy Elarians that he decimated about one hundred years prior. Batair was told no Elarians were left alive free in the forest. So, he mounted a raid on the area surrounding Elaria after finding out his betrothed had been deceived and tricked by an Elarian. We were only few in number and they captured Zxian with a knife to his throat. The raiders said they would let us all go if the one who stole Batair's betrothed turned himself over. Lochlann sacrificed himself for us and we will forever wish we stopped him. They killed most of us that day despite their promises and several were captured. I found out later he was taken to a special work camp hidden in the mountains on the border Laevaris and Jaarn. I never saw my son again after that."

Looking up with a tear running down his cheek, he says, "I heard reports he died last year in one of those camps. I … lost nearly all hope for our people and myself after that. Until now, meeting you."

"Why did you never save him? Couldn't you break into these camps? Why did I never hear of these camps? Why have I never heard of the Elarians or the Elaritian Forest for that matter." I ramble out questions in an angry voice. "All our history books call it the Broken Forest. It's complete genocide! You can't kill an entire race for greed!"

"Most of this occurred over a hundred years ago. King Gaargon had the history wiped out, burned any books containing information about us and the forest. He had anyone killed that knew about Elarians or mentioned them. They prevented talk about Elaria in the schools, so no one ever learned about it. We are a broken people or a forgotten kingdom if you want to put a name to it," he states sitting up straighter and looking me in the eye. "I was unable to save my son, I know. I used all of my powers at my disposal but still it wasn't enough, and I will forever live with that knowledge. I would have broken into the camps to save my people and my son but only two other men survived the last attack twenty years ago. It wasn't enough manpower to achieve the impossible. Those camps are heavily fortified and located under mountains. And I only know of the location of one. He could have been taken to any of them."

CHAPTER

Fifteen

SOLVEIG

"Where are these other men?" I ask looking around the forest.

"Here, Princess Solveig," I hear spoken next to me as a man suddenly appears out of the surrounding forest five feet away causing me to squeak in surprise (and embarrassment) loudly. "It's an honor to meet Lochlann's daughter. I'm Zxian."

He literally came out of thin air. I know for a fact that I didn't see anyone there a few minutes ago. "Whe—where did you come from? I didn't see or hear you! Were you there the whole time?" I ask while looking him over. He's definitely a warrior with a strong body packed full of muscle and standing almost seven feet in size. He has two swords sticking up over his shoulders similar to me and an axe at his hip. His hair is so dark brown its nearly black and his skin is a dark golden color. There's a small scar running through his right eye that breaks up his handsome face and makes him look more intimidating.

Chuckling to himself and providing a half smile, he says, "I have a rune for camouflage, Princess Solveig."

Confused I squint my eyes at him and then look at Elder Aren for an explanation. "Rune? What does he mean?"

"All Elarians usually develop a rune or sometimes in the more powerful warriors several runes, around the age of nineteen or after. They are symbols or markings on the skin that develop when that person has found a need for it. It indicates a power that the person can utilize. Zxian has the rune for camouflage. It is very useful as a warrior in the forest when trying to sneak up on enemies or in this case a certain unsuspecting princess," Elder Aren explains holding back a smile and looking at me with a raised eyebrow. "It's unlikely that you have any runes yet since you aren't yet nineteen."

I must look almost comical to them with my large, surprised eyes once I realize he is talking about the tattoos that recently appeared.

Then confused again, I ask, "I *have* seen them before ... on myself. It only just happened recently! But I'm not yet nineteen for another two weeks! Why do I have them already?"

"Already? Hmm ... Excuse me, Solveig, but I thought I heard you say *them?* Meaning you have more than one? You are likely very powerful if you are already developing your runes before nineteen." Aren discusses while rubbing a hand over his jaw in contemplation. "Your father was the same way. He had three runes which is nearly unheard of. Most have one or two runes on their skin."

"Yes, I have two runes already. One on my upper back and another on my right thigh. Can you tell me what they mean?"

Elder Aren stands up and walks slowly towards me before sitting on the log next to me. "May I see the one on your back, child?" I nod my head and turn my back to him so he can lift the back of my shirt and see the large rune. I hear Zxian shift so he can see my back as well, then he whistles loudly in appreciation.

"Is that a healing rune, Elder?" Zxian asks quietly and when I look over my shoulder at him, he almost looks sad.

"What happened to you, child, that you needed such a large and powerful healing rune? I only know of one other Elarian in our history that had a healing rune." Aren says looking me over with a serious expression. "She had a near death experience before gaining it. She was not only able to heal herself but also others."

"Well, yes. I mean, I guess I have had a lot of injuries and ever since I was a child, I always had more accelerated healing than others." I say trying to avoid his direct questions and looking at the ground.

"Very well. But let me know if you need anything. I can help you harness your power to heal others which usually takes training. But beware … if you heal others in the future it won't come without great cost to yourself. Supposedly, the prior healer that had this rune would siphon the wound or injury into herself before healing the injury as if it was her own. It was very painful and dangerous for the healer depending on the severity of the injury. You understand?"

"Yes, Elder. I would appreciate your help in learning anything I can. Should I show you the other rune?"

"No," he says grabbing a small stick from the ground. "Draw it for me in the dirt given where it is on your skin."

I draw out the rune from my right upper thigh carefully in the dirt already knowing it from memory. I see Elder Aren and Zxian exchange a glance and a shared smile.

"This rune is more common than the healing rune. It stands for agility and speed. It's very useful in battle. Your father had the same rune on his wrist," he says fondly to me.

"Your father was a great warrior, Princess Solveig. I was proud to fight alongside him and guard his back," states Zxian.

"Where is the other surviving Elarian you told me about Elder Aren?" I ask while looking around.

"Ahh. He was told to scout the area while we talked and to make sure we weren't heard by anyone." As he says this, an arrow shoots into the dirt piercing the center of the rune I just drew surprising me. I stand up suddenly drawing a dagger on my thigh.

"No need for that princess. Yaeril is just showing off," chuckles Zxian looking up toward a branch nearby.

A shorter (and by short, I mean only six feet compared to all the other men I've met) lean man drops from the tree twenty feet away and comes walking towards me with a bow in his hand.

He's smiling and drops to a knee before me, then placing a hand over his heart says, "Well met, princess. I'm Yaeril. I was also a warrior who knew your father well. I'm honored to serve him again by protecting his daughter."

"Well met Yaeril. I'm assuming you have a rune for weapons? Or accuracy?"

He smiles with eyebrows raised. "Yes, very good. Not only beautiful but smart. Lochlann would be proud," he says this towards Elder Aren before turning back towards me. "I actually have two runes though, one is for accuracy as you said, and the other is for climbing."

"Wow. That's helpful." I smile and nod while wondering how he ended up getting those when he was younger. "Camouflage is also very helpful. But please both of you call me Solveig or Sol for short."

They both smile at this and nod. Then Aren looks up at the sky as it starts to darken with the evening and states, "Best make your journey back home before dark. The Catchki will be out hunting soon. We can meet again and will be watching for you next time you come to the forest. Your goshawk friend, Tyr, usually alerts us to your presence anyways."

He's correct. I've lost track of time and need to get back for dinner then slip out to the city. I make a short whistle sound indicating to Sindari that we need to leave. I'm supposed to meet with Vidarr for a fight tonight.

Thinking about all I've learned in such a short amount of time, I can't help but be amazed and for the first time in my life … truly happy. I've found my people! People who are similar to me in not only appearance but understanding. I'm not alone for the first time in my life and have answers to some of my questions. It's starting to make sense why my father doesn't treat me as he should.

"Wait … does my fath— I mean King Batair know that I'm not his daughter?" I ask Aren.

"I'm not sure, child, but I would suspect that he may. Only you can find out that answer. Be careful Solveig and return to see me soon. If you need one of us just send Tyr. 'Til my heart greets you again … grand-daughter," he says this with a hand to his heart and a tear in his eye.

Overcome with sudden emotion that I have family who cares for me, I rush forward and throw my arms around him. Stepping back, I feel Sindari nudge me with his nose and I hop onto his back. I wave back at Zxian and Yaeril who nod and then I race back to the castle.

CHAPTER

Sixteen

CADOC

Where has she been all day? Is she okay? Were her injuries worse than I was told by that servant? I ponder in the barrack mess hall. I was eating dinner with Eirik when he had to get up and use the restroom.

Tapping my fingers on the table waiting, I suddenly feel antsy.

Eirik comes back heading towards me at a brisk walk and a look on his face. "What is it?" I ask.

"I saw a woman sneaking out through the back entrance of the castle." Eirik whispers to me and nodding towards the door to me. Following his lead, I get up and walk with him casually out the door into the courtyard.

"So …?" I ask.

"Well, the woman was all in black fighting leathers with a hood covering her hair," he says raising his eyebrows. "And she had twin katanas on her back," he finishes with a smirk.

"Solveig? Where do you think she's going?" I ask checking my weapons and briskly walking with him towards the castle walls.

"That's your girl. She looked ready to fight heading toward the city. Let's go." Eirik says with a grin and rubbing his hands together like an excited kid.

We briskly walk out of the barracks trying not to attract any unwanted attention. The sun had set making it more difficult to see anything but after we make it closer to the gate, I could see her. She's talking to the guard at the gate who glances both ways before waving her through. Eirik and I step out of the shadows toward the gate after a brief pause, but the guard blocks our way.

"Where are you two soldiers off to? Its rather late…" the guard states crossing his arms over his chest.

Eirik's quick thinking saves us when he throws one arm over my shoulder laughing good naturedly.

"We're getting a drink in the city and meeting some of the serving girls. My friend here needs to let off some steam. Don't worry, we're off for the night." Eirik smoothly lies.

The guard's suspicious expression changes to own of disinterest before he nods and moves out of the way.

Eirik and I quickly walk through the gate frantically trying to catch back up to Solveig.

Patrov must be smiling down us since I see a glimpse of a black cape disappear down an alley to the right. Nudging Eirik silently, I tilt my chin towards the alley before we run after her. I notice less and less people the closer we get. There's also fewer lanterns lining the street and more trash in this part of the city making me more apprehensive of our surroundings. I swear I can feel eyes watching me as we head there.

When we reach the alley she ran into, there's no sign of her. There is however only one door. The Hidden Dagger tavern.

SOLVEIG

ONCE I MADE IT BACK TO THE CASTLE, I ATE QUICKLY AND CHANGED INTO MY tight black leather pants and fighting gear. The top showed off a decent amount of cleavage since it was low cut and I threw a cape with a hood over my hair to prevent recognition. My twin katanas were in place and

I prayed to Faktirnor, God of war and strength, that Counselor Malphas doesn't come across me again on my way out of the castle.

I quickly run through the city indirectly to the Hidden Dagger tavern so no one can follow me. As soon as I enter, all heads turn to assess the new intruder but after seeing my katanas they quickly return to their drinking. I catch the eye of the barkeeper who nods his head to the left of the bar where a small door blends into the wall.

Walking confidently to the door and closing it behind me, I then follow more steps down underground. I can now here the distant sounds of fighting, yelling and weapons banging as I approach another door at the base of the stairs.

Knocking once with my knuckles then once with my fist followed by two knuckles and then a fist again. A man opens the door and looks me over.

Karltin smiles at me with that signature gap in his front teeth and a crooked nose on his face. "Sol! Glad I am to see you! It's been a bit since your last fight. Vidarr's been in a foul mood all night and beating everyone to pulp since you didn't show up an hour ago." He ushers me through the door locking it behind him.

Feeling excited about my upcoming fight, I start to bounce on my toes and look around the underground bar and central fight arena. It's so loud down here with all the cheering that I can't hear what Karltin says next. He nods his chin towards the bar to the right and I see Vidarr.

I run my gaze over his muscular form hungrily as if I haven't seen him in months. *Goodness! How long has it been?* Maybe only a week but it feels longer. He's beautiful in a rough and dangerous way.

He's leaning his elbow on the bar with a bloody hand wrapped around his beer. Covered in tattoos and powerful in his own way, I can't help but think of him dominating me in the bedroom with his tattooed arms around me and those calloused hands running over my breasts.

Down girl! Feeling my underthings start to get damp with my dirty thoughts, I start to shake my head to clear them. *He thinks of you like a sister, get your mind out of the alley gutter, Sol!*

He must feel my heated stare because in the next second, he turns his gaze towards me and smiles releasing some of the tension I didn't know he was carrying. Grey-blue eyes look back and he assesses me from head to toe, most likely looking for injuries. He sets his drink on the bar and runs a hand through his dirty blonde hair that falls over his eyes.

I walk over to him, and may have added a little hip sway, while pulling my hood down. He reaches forward and tugs on the end of my braid that's hanging over my shoulder and says, "Hey, sunshine! I didn't think you were gunna show up tonight. I was worried about you and didn't know if I had to break into the castle or not." I swat at him to let go of my braid, but he tugs it again quickly before kissing me on my cheek surprising me.

Before I can get over my shock at the sign of affection he just gave out like it's nothing, he pulls me towards his stool at the bar and tugs me onto his lap.

"What are you doing, Vi?" I ask him suspiciously. "Are you drunk?" he throws his head back and laughs loudly making several rebels at the bar turn their head and smile.

"I just missed you and I need to absorb my sunshine as much as I can while I got you," he says into my ear and then rubs his nose into my hair smelling me softly. *He must be drunk.* Meanwhile, his hand on my left hip is rubbing soft circles on the exposed skin between my pants and shirt making me break out in goosebumps.

"Alright only water for you," I say with a smile and a pat on his head. "I missed you too. I wanted to talk to you after the ball but … well … you know." I cough trying to cover up my discomfort. His expression changes quickly from a sweet to downright murderous when I mention the ball.

"That piece of shit… fucking cock-sucker laid his hands on you. You could have died Sol! I heard your head hit the ground, and I nearly lost it! I pulled a dagger and was almost to the dais when Darritt grabbed me from behind and forced me out," he says breathing heavily. "Has he been hurting you? He's your father, Sol! God fucking damn it! That's why you were injured last time I saw you in the forest? I'm going to kill him." He rambles, putting the pieces together. Then, he whispers, "What has he been doing, Sol?"

I turn his head and put my hands on his cheeks pulling his face towards me. Then I do what I've wanted to for a long time. I kiss him with total abandon. Like the world around us is nothing and we are everything. After a second of surprise, he then starts to kiss me back and damn, it was worth the wait! *I knew he cared for me.* I could see glimpses of it before but to hear him so concerned for me and that he nearly attacked the king for me. I think, oh no … I'm definitely falling for this man.

He gets over his shock at my forwardness and immediately takes over the kiss with dominance. He grabs my braid and, pulling back with a tiny tinge of pain in my scalp, attacks my lips. I open for him, and our tongues entwine dancing around each other. I shift position to straddle him on the stool. I nip his lower lip causing him to groan and thrust his pelvis up into me. He's hard beneath me and I swear my underwear is soaked at this point.

He works his mouth down from my lips to the exposed column of my throat while he has my hair pulled back in his fist. After kissing me repeatedly on my neck, and likely leaving a visible mark there, he says, "I've been wanting to do that for the past year. Fucking Patrov has been testing my patience for sure!" After cursing the god of patience, he straightens up and lets go of my braid. Looking me in the eye he says, "I care for you, sunshine. I just didn't know how you felt about me before now." He rests his forehead against mine and then with a calculating heated smirk he softly says, "All bets are off now. You won't be able to get rid of me."

"Maybe I don't want to get *rid* of you. And I care for you too Vi," I say sincerely while looking into his blue-grey eyes. "Also if you're going to pull my hair, make sure you do it in a bedroom next time. I have to keep up appearances and you know how no one's allowed to touch it. It's my favorite part," I say sassily with a smile.

"Sunshine, I'm going to show you that you have way more favorite parts than your hair that you haven't realized…" He winks at me then says, "Come on I signed you up for a fight with Lanief and then some new guy." He tugs me towards one end of the arena where all the illegal street fights occur.

"Okay but I have some things I really need to tell you. I learned something important about where missing people from the city could be." I start to remove my cape and check my weapons then stretch a bit while they call my opponent over. Vidarr's gaze drops to my outfit, and he whistles in appreciation.

"Damn, sunshine! That shirt …" Vi says shaking his head with a smile.

Bets are being placed on us from the surrounding seats when I see Lanief walk up smiling. He chugs the rest of his beer down and then belches loudly. "Solveig, my feisty little tiger, you are going to regret that performance the other day. Get ready for a broken nose!"

"Drinking before a fight? Tsk, tsk, Lan! This will be easier than that fight we had a year ago where I cracked your kneecap and you fell face first into some horse dung!!" I yell laughing.

We start to circle each other in the area as the announcer yells to begin.

"You have a sick memory, Sol. I swear you only remember the fights you win and all the injuries you inflict on people. I happen to recall a fight four months ago where I knocked your feet out from under you and you fell onto your ass cracking your tail bone with a girly squeal!" he says grinning and then rushing at me.

These fights are no holds barred and lack any rules other than you stop when the other submits or is mortally injured. Lanief and I tend to want to crush each other with our fists most of the time, in a friendly sort of way.

He gets a quick punch to my face, but it glances off my cheekbone luckily when I turn my head with the punch. I swing my left leg up and bend at the knee grabbing his right arm at the elbow and locking it down with my knee. I throw a roundhouse punch to right eye and … *Bam! That's going to leave a mark.* Hopefully, I won't have a black eye tomorrow like he will. I grin since I always enjoy our sparring. We wrestle around on the ground for a while with both of us gaining dominance of each other back and forth. Eventually I put him in a head lock and wrap my legs around his waist. He taps the ground submitting to me and then spits up a tooth with blood when he gets up smiling. We laugh and pat each other on the back before going to the bar for a drink.

"I guess I owe you a drink this time since you lost a tooth," I say.

"No, you owe me two drinks since you broke my nose last time and now my tooth!" Lanief says. He turns his attention elsewhere when a pretty scantily clad tavern wench runs her fingers over his eye and they meander off to a back room.

Vi walks over putting an arm over my shoulder and ordering me a drink. "Nice punch. I was always surprised how much power you pack in those arms of yours," he says squeezing me a bit. "Sit with me before your next match. I don't think I have any more tonight."

We get to talking and laughing about some of our prior fights. Reminiscing with Vidarr makes me feel relaxed and at home. Shortly after my break, I have another fight with a new guy carrying a long thin katana. We nod at each other in respect of our choice in weapon before starting. The fight is short, but he does have skill. Unfortunately for him, I have more speed and not many people are a match for me with my twin katanas once I'm in a certain mindset. I win a small sum of money by having Vidarr bet on me.

We are at the bar again laughing with a few other Rebellion members when Vidarr throws a tattooed arm around my waist. It's natural and feels good so I lean in a bit never having felt this sense of comfort or affection from a man before. Then, I get this feeling that someone is watching me from the shadows. Looking around I don't see anyone and Vi notices my concern.

"Tell me about what you learned at the ball," Vi asks me and the other Rebellion members quiet instantly leaning in.

I then tell them at length about what that creepy Duke Havaas insinuated. How there are secret work camps in his land near Jaarn. How they keep criminals and "lowlifes" there and I discuss that I am concerned the guards may be taking people from Laevaris there. That I suspect not all the people that go missing from these "purges" are dead. Our missing people could be slaves in a secret work camp! I also then tell them about how the duke reported he's seen people with my distinctive features in those camps and they have been slaves there for many years. I tell them about the genocide of the Elarian people and how King Batair's father wiped out evidence of an entire kingdom years ago. How if we could free the Elarians from these camps they could be allies for the Rebellion.

I finish talking and notice I withheld my meeting with Elder Aren. I just … I'm not quite ready to let others know about this yet. It could endanger them without knowing completely who to trust and it almost feels too personal. It has more to do with my heritage than it does for the Rebellion. Everyone's faces including Vidarr's are deeply troubled and shocked when I look around our group. Some look uncertain and doubtful. Several voice denials that these camps could exist, and no one would know. But eventually everyone said they would bring this up at the next gathering for the Rebellion in a few days' time. We also discuss what to do with the shipment that we have hidden.

I eventually say my goodbyes and start to tug Vidarr towards the door, hoping to get a quick kiss before heading back to the castle. In my haste, I don't look forward and run straight into a brick wall of muscle. *Not again!*

I look up into soft brown eyes and a handsome face that is scowling down at me. His strong jaw and straight nose are protruding somewhat from his hood that's covering his distinctive white-blonde hair. I look over his shoulder and see Eirik standing behind Cadoc as usual.

Just as I say, "What are you doing here?" Vidarr pulls me behind him and puffs his chest out in an age-old dance of male dominance. Both Cadoc and Vidarr square off in a stare match.

"Well … Solveig. That seems to be the question of the night. I followed you here and am wondering what a woman of your standing is doing in such a back alley disreputable tavern," he says without taking his eyes off Vi.

"She's here with me. And it's none of your business where she goes, mister," Vi angrily says, shoving Cadoc with his tattooed arms. Suddenly the bar chatter silences and nearly every man stands up looking over with arms crossed at Cadoc.

You see, the Hidden Dagger is really an established rebellion member meeting place. Nearly everyone in the bar tonight is someone that is part of the Rebellion or somehow related to someone trustworthy.

Cadoc glances up and realizes something has changed in the air. He takes a step back and runs a hand through his hair pushing his hood back then looks at Vi.

"Name is Cadoc and I'm a friend of Solveig's. Look, I just wanted to make sure she was okay. She was in rough shape last time I saw her after that horrid ball. We'll leave as soon as she's ready. Can I walk you home, Sol?" he says with an eager look my way.

"Sure," I say trying to diffuse the situation quickly, then I pat Vi on the chest to let him know I'll be fine. I push up on my tip toes and kiss his cheek near the corner of his mouth and smile shyly. "See you soon, Vi? Also, no more Aruvian liquor for you!" Winking, I turn around and grab Cadoc's arm to lead him out trying to avoid confrontation.

"Name's Vidarr! Don't forget it Cad-dick! If you lay a hand on her, I'll mangle that pretty boy face you got there," I hear over my shoulder just before we make it out the door. I turn my head with a scowl at Vi and see him wink and smirk at Cadoc who looks furious but continues out the door.

CADOC

EIRIK AND I WALK INTO THAT DILAPIDATED UNDERGROUND BAR AFTER WHAT feels like an hour of hassling we got from the bartender upstairs. I knock on the underground door and after the fifth attempt, a gap-toothed door-man sticks his head out angrily and says *"wrong"*. It isn't until I mention Sol that he seems intrigued and lets us in with a few questions but watches us suspiciously.

Immediately, I see her. She's radiant. Somehow, she draws all the light and attention to herself. At the moment, she's laughing at something a man is saying next to her and looking happier than I've ever seen her before. It's breath taking, but then my breath stops in my lungs when I see that man put his arm around her waist and leave it there. He looks down at her and squeezes said waist before pulling her closer. The group of rough looking men around them all don't seem too surprised in their casual affection.

I get a deep burning pain in my chest and feel my face flush with jealousy seeing them from a distance. *Who is he? How does he know her so casually?* I think to myself when Eirik says, "Who's that?"

"I don't know, and I don't like this. The air feels charged down here like a fight's ready to start. We need to approach with caution," I quietly say to him. We then notice the small fighting arena to the left where two men are wrestling and bloody on the ground while several men hold up money and shout out bets.

The rough group Solveig is with are leaning together in corner of the bar talking animatedly about something serious based on their facial expressions. Eirik and I watch them for a few more minutes. Then thankfully, Solveig and the handsy man with her, start to approach the exit where we're leaning in the shadows. I go to step forward and greet her when she turns around and bumps straight into my chest. *This seems to be a regular occurrence with her.*

SOLVEIG

"WHAT WERE YOU THINKING? THAT *ESTABLISHMENT* HAS TO BE A HOT HOUSE for all sorts of criminals! You shouldn't be wandering around in the middle of the night without anyone to watch your back!" Cadoc starts yelling at me once we are back out in the alley. He sends Eirik ahead of us back towards the castle obviously preparing to reprimand me.

How dare he! I meet him twice and suddenly he feels he has a say in where I can go? As if I'm some weak damsel that needs protecting. Fah! I think to myself and decide he doesn't deserve an answer. So, I briskly start to walk back to the castle. I hear a sharp releasing of breath and then his following footsteps trying to catch up.

"Look, I'm sorry! It's just that's not exactly what I thought I'd see when I followed you." He rubs the back of his neck in discomfort. "I've just never met a lady or for that matter a princess like you." He pauses then says, "You don't exactly fit the normal expectations for a princess."

"Apology accepted. And for your information—no man controls me. Perhaps one day I'll find a partner that respects my decisions as an equal and strengthens me instead of holding me back. But until that day, no one, and I mean no one, dictates where I go and who I see. Bigger men have tried," then looking him in the eye before we enter the castle courtyard, I say, "Don't ever follow me again. You could have been seen by my father's men."

He nods his head but looks at me with a firm mouth and perhaps a bit of resistance. "So that man with you tonight … is he such a partner to you?" he hesitantly asks with his arms crossed.

"That man tonight is one of the few people who has my back, no questions asked. And yes, he respects and strengthens me in most circumstances. I trust him with my life. He's dangerous for a noble like you and you would do well to avoid him in the future." I state defensively. "Rest well tonight, Cadoc." Nodding goodnight to him, I walk into the castle ending our first…argument.

CADOC

"WELL *SHIT* ... THAT ALTERS OUR PLANS A BIT. DO WE TELL HER FATHER ABOUT her secret rendezvous with this Vidarr character?" Eirik says once we are alone walking to my room.

"No, we don't tell anyone. Something else is going on there and not just teenage infatuation. That man radiates secrets and danger and I suspect he could be part of that rebellion group we heard whispers about. You saw how all those men in the bar seemed to back him up? Well, I think he could be somewhat important. Now, why Solveig is involved is beyond me. Let's get some sleep and consider this in the daylight." I say kicking my boots off in my bedroom. It doesn't take long before I'm already passed out and dreaming of a feisty brunette with full lips.

CHAPTER
Seventeen

SOLVEIG

O ver a week goes by without much excitement since the night of the fight, or should I say the night of my kiss with Vidarr.

I haven't heard from him which is strange. Although, I have been rather busy with "princess" things. I've had meetings, formal tea, lunches with the nobility, dinners and other boring events that I was forced to attend by order of my father. He says I need to be more present given my recent engagement. Rolling my eyes and thinking about his lecture to which the housekeeper and steward were there, I realize I'm not paying much attention to my surroundings.

Suddenly, a strong firm hand grabs me around the waist and puts another hand over my mouth silencing me. I have a small dagger already out and slice his arm drawing blood. Unfortunately, this only angers him into kneeing me in the abdomen and hitting my wrist against the wall making me drop the dagger. At least, I smile in satisfaction, I marked Counselor Malphas with a deep cut on his forearm dripping blood.

He laughs at my violence then pushes me into a small hidden alcove in the hallway. He moves his hand from my mouth down to my throat, when

I bite said hand, and squeezes my throat in retribution. "My, my, princess. Feisty today, aren't we? I missed my betrothed and feel as though I have been remiss in my attention towards you. Don't worry I will schedule some alone time for us soon. For now, I just want a small taste," He says with a malicious grin.

Keeping one hand on my throat the other travels down from my chest and dips into my bodice squeezing my left breast. A full body shiver takes over my body and I stare blankly ahead knowing what's coming. Many would judge a woman who doesn't fight back all the time, but I've learned to pick my battles and do what I must to survive. Sometimes you have to shut down your emotions and not let them hurt you where it hurts the most … in your mind. Malphas gets sick enjoyment off of my reactions and by not giving him one I can usually avoid more confrontation.

He's whispering to me even though I block out most of it.

"… You're such a dirty whore of a princess, just like your mother. I can feel you shaking from your eagerness to be with me. I like your fire princess, but I like seeing it put out much more. Let me feel how wet you are for me. Just one taste and then I have to go …"

He says this while running his right hand down my dress and bunching it up. I start to thrash a bit at this and scratch his arms, but he squeezes harder on my throat making me nearly pass out as he pushes his body against mine. His hand travels to my inner thigh and pushing aside my undergarments pushes two fingers into me. I freeze up in terror and repulsion. He's getting bolder doing this in a nearly public area which makes me break out in a sweat and nearly vomit my last meal up. His actions make me wince at the discomfort. After pulling his hand away from me, he puts those fingers in his mouth moaning. "You taste like musk and honey. Be a good, good girl, Solveig, and I may give you a taste tonight."

He starts to walk away at last releasing my throat and causing me to gasp in much-needed air. I slide to the floor in a puddle once he's out of sight. Seeing no one around and feeling more alone than ever, I let myself fall into the darkness I know so well and cry for my broken self. *I can spare one moment of pity for myself, can't I? What am I going to do?*

JORAH

Walking from my room down the hall, I realize I forgot to grab an open book I left out in the library. It's one of the books that talks about the Elaritian Forest and I don't want King Batair to know I have it. I'm in rush already trying to make it to the stables since my father needs help saddling the horses for a hunt that's occurring this evening.

I make it to the library and see the book out on a table in the corner where I left it. *Thank Avilt!*

I rush out again and am nearly running at this point when I hear someone's deep breathing down a hall to the right in a dark alcove. I slow and squint into the darkness noticing a golden leg partly exposed with a slippered foot. Realizing something must have happened to the woman, I loudly walk over so as not to startle her and crouch down.

Seeing red rimmed piercing sapphire eyes, I startle realizing I'm looking at a very vulnerable Solveig, *my Solveig*. I've never seen her upset like this especially in a slightly exposed place such as a hallway, so it has me doubly concerned something horrible occurred.

"Sweetheart. Sol. Please tell me what's wrong? Did someone hurt you?" I ask frantically looking her over and realizing how disheveled she looks. She continues to stare blankly ahead taking deep breaths. Her dress is scrunched up on the side nearly to her upper thigh and I see a black mark peeking out over golden skin. Also the bodice of her dress seems pulled rather low and with abrupt clarity I know what happened. *Fuck!* I immediately flush with anger, shaking with the force of it. I try to calm myself to provide her reassurance.

Leaning forward, I throw my arms around her and hold her, but I can feel the initial flinch she makes which only adds to my anger. Not at her but at whoever did this.

"Please tell me, Sol. Let me help you. You know I can take it, give me your trust and your pain," I whisper in her ear. I can feel the moment she comes back to awareness. She nuzzles her face into my chest and quiets.

"I wasn't paying attention! It's my fault!" she says softly, angry at herself. "He cornered me and he touched me, Jorah, more than he usually has in the past. I think he's getting worse since he has a claim on me now. I'm—" she says with a choked off breath. "I'm scared ... but there's nothing anyone can do about it. Father gave him approval."

Sucking in a sharp breath, I realize she's talking about Counselor Malphas. She must be since she said King Batair gave him a claim and she was recently betrothed to him. Then realizing she was alluding that some sort of torture has been occurring prior to this, I ask, "He's still been punishing you, Sol? All these years?" She nods her head in my chest quieting. "Why did you never tell me! I thought it was just that one time when you were younger!" I say more loudly. Angry at that pathetic excuse for a man, angry at myself for not noticing, angry at King Batair, and most of all hurt that Solveig felt she couldn't trust me with her secret.

"I do trust you, Jorah. You're my best friend, honestly one of my only friends. You've always been there for me," she says into my chest and then looking up. Huh, I must have spoken my last words aloud.

"You should have told me, Sol."

"You couldn't have done anything. It doesn't matter. No one can help me," she says with a sad shake of her head and then looking blankly at the wall. "If you would have known, you would have done something to get yourself hurt or even killed. I can't live with myself if something would have happened to you ... like last time." She says this while lifting a hand under my shirt and then running it over the deep scar on my chest. Her hand on my bare skin, *goddess*, feels like utter bliss.

Closing my eyes and enjoying the skin-to-skin contact, I grab her wrist when she starts to pull away and say, "Don't. I like you touching me." Then I look her directly in the eye and say, "I would do it again, and again, and again if it would protect you. This scar is worth it, you are worth it. I care for you, Solveig, more than I should. More than a simple stableman and scholar should. You shouldn't have to handle this yourself. Let me help you. Or at least, let me take care of you," I beg her and place a hand on her cheek then wipe away the tear with my thumb that falls from the corner of her eye.

SOLVEIG

JORAH HELPS WALK ME BACK TO MY ROOM AFTER FIXING MY DRESS AND MAKING me look less disheveled. *Goodness! I must have looked a mess!* He checks the hallways before me to make sure no one sees us.

What must he think of me now? I can't help but feel embarrassment that he saw me that way. He knows my darkest secret now. He should be repulsed by me and yet … he told me he cares for me and he likes me touching him. I'm confused. Did he mean as a friend? Or as a man? Either way, I don't see how he could be attracted to me. I feel so *dirty.* The thought of Malphas's hands on me makes me shudder and want to wash it all off.

Once we make it into the room and the door is shut, I turn around and see a nervous Jorah looking around. He's wringing his hands in a nervous way and then runs them through his hair so he has something to do with them. It almost, *almost,* makes me smile but then I'm reminded of what just happened in the hallway. Jorah really is handsome with his tall stature and messy blonde hair. He has this caring energy to him that makes me feel he would take all my problems away if I let him. Looking back down to his big hands, I see some ink on several fingers while he nervously twists them around.

"What's wrong, Jorah?" I ask.

"I … is it okay if I'm in your room? I haven't been in here in a few years," Jorah says while nervously looking over at me. Then taking a deep breath he says, "I'm going to take care of you then we will talk."

"I need to bathe … the thought of his hands on me." Closing my eyes and taking a shuttering breath I say, "I feel dirty and I can't do anything until I do that."

He nods his head and visibly swallowing starts to walk into my en-suite and run a bath. He walks back to me and grabs my hand. Then, looking into my eyes to make sure I'm okay with it, he starts to slowly undress me. He struggles a bit with the laces in the back but eventually my dress pools in a heap on the floor and I'm in my lace underwear with only a dagger strapped to my left thigh. Why did I forget about the dagger being there?

My only excuse is that when Malphas is involved, all rational thoughts scatter.

Jorah groans making me look over my shoulder and I recognize the look in eyes, could it be … *desire?*

Then he shifts his heated gaze up from my ass and runs it over my body- slowly. I've never had a man look at me unclothed before other than—*never mind.* I can see the moment he observes the rune on my upper back. He takes a step forward and places his hand on it saying, "I didn't realize you got a tattoo, Sol? You've been keeping a lot of secrets from me." I can see him mentally trying to decipher the meaning of the tattoo.

"It's not necessarily a secret from you, Jorah. It's complicated. I'll tell you after my bath," I say with a tired expression.

He walks around to the front of me and kneels down, unstrapping my dagger. Slowly perusing my body from below, he notices the other tattoo on my right upper thigh. Then he shifts his gaze to my long golden legs, up to my lace covered pussy, and further up to my heaving breasts. For some reason, I can't suppress the raging arousal that hits me when I see him looking over my body while he's kneeled down in front of me. Almost like he worships me. Like he finds me desirable and not some broken piece of trash that Counselor Malphas makes me feel like.

Knowing I'm embarrassing myself with my damp underwear, I step forward into the bath. I'll remove my undergarments once I'm safely under the water. I look at him when he stands and say, "Are you going to stay? I'll be quick." I dunk my head under the water quickly getting my hair wet. Then pulling my undergarments off and into a wet pile by the bathtub I look for the soap.

Instead of answering me, he grabs a stool and sits on it at the head of the bath. Then squirting some shampoo in his hands grabs my hair and starts to scrub with those big gentle hands of his. He honestly has the best hands. I moan unintentionally while leaning back. Closing my eyes, I don't see the heated look that Jorah flashes when my breasts get exposed from arching my back to allow him access to my hair. He finishes with my hair and has me rinse it out by dunking it. Then soaps up his hands and starts to clean my arms and upper chest. He pauses just above my breasts and then smoothes along the sides, running his fingers along the edges of my breasts driving me crazy with need. Good thing he can't see I'm wet in more ways than one due to the water. He hands me the soap after cleaning my back and clearing his throat says, "Maybe you should finish the rest."

"Thanks, Jorah," I say shyly. "You're pretty good at this you know? Maybe you should be a maid instead of a librarian. Put those nice hands to use." I tease, trying to create some levity to the tension in the room.

He chuffs a soft surprised laugh into his hand and smiles. Then with a smirk and an eyebrow raise says, "I'd be even better with some instruction. You know how much I like to learn, Sol. Just say the word." Then without waiting for my reaction, he walks out the bathroom and grabs a towel before coming back.

My shock must still show on my face when he returns. He's never talked like that to me. I can't tell if he's serious or joking. If he's making an innuendo or not? *I'm confused. Is he flirting with me?*

He smiles looking at the floor and holds the towel out. When I step out and put the towel around myself, I say, "I'm good. Give me a minute to get dressed and I'll be out."

I take a moment to gather my thoughts on what just happened and come up short. Was the whole bath thing his way of saying, "I'm attracted to you?" I'm too scared to ask and potentially ruin our friendship. I get dressed in a simple violet tunic and soft brown leather pants. He's sitting by the fireplace in my sitting room with a book on his lap. However instead of reading it, he's staring into the fire.

I go to sit by him so I can brush and style my unruly long hair when he comes out of his thoughts.

"Here. Give me that." He reaches over and plucks the brush from my hands before I can argue. "I've always wanted to run my hands through your hair. You'll be doing me a favor. Come here."

Rolling my eyes but again internally confused, I get up and sit in front of him on the floor. While he's brushing my hair gently, he then says, "Tell me everything, Sol. Give me your trust and faith that I will help shoulder this burden you carry. Maybe we can come up with a plan to prevent this ridiculous betrothal."

I take a deep breath and tell him everything. Ignoring my embarrassment, I tell him about my father and Counselor Malphas, about their "punishment lessons", and about my fears for the betrothal. I skip over the gruesome details but give him the basics of how often and where they occur. We share a few tears and take a moment with our foreheads together for comfort after that. Then, I tell him about my training with Captain Mavin secretly, about my underground fights, and about my involvement in the Rebellion. I can tell he's really shocked when I tell him about the runes and meeting Elder Aren.

He pauses his brushing and runs his fingers over my pointed ears reverently saying, "I always knew you were special, Solveig. You're meant for great things." Then as he continues his brushing he says, "I'm going to help you research everything I can about Elarians and the Elaritian Forest. I'll pull up some maps and information about the mountains and surrounding areas that could be a location for these *camps*. If there's one thing I'm good at, it's finding information and research."

I turn around and climb up into his lap just like when we were children. We snuggle together in the big chair with his arms holding me tightly and I relax into the safety of his arms. I feel a small weight lifted off my chest at the knowledge that someone else knows everything about me. And I think to myself, maybe, just maybe I'm not so alone.

CHAPTER

Eighteen

SOLVEIG

It's only two days until my nineteenth birthday and I've been spending way too much time lately confined in the castle library.

Of course, it's not so bad since I've been spending more time with Jorah. But I miss the open air! We have been diligently trying to research everything we can about Elarians and the possible location for the work camps. He's showed me the book he obtained about the Elaritian Forest which has been enlightening. Otherwise, we've pulled up a few maps showing the Northern Traverian Mountain range which is likely the location of the camps. Unfortunately, that mountain range is spanning a rather large area.

"I need a break. It's still early. I'm going to grab an early lunch and spend some time in the forest. I'll see you later?" I ask Jorah.

It takes him a second to look up since he finishes what he's currently reading before doing so. "Sounds good, Sol! See you later. Be careful and let me know if you need me. Also say hello to your new friends if you see them." Jorah says before going right back to reading his book.

I quickly go to my room to change into navy pants with a sky-blue blouse and harness my weapons in place then stop at the kitchens to pack a lunch. To save time, I decide to eat it while walking to the stables.

Entering the royal stables, I smell the signature hay and leather scent. I distantly hear a few stable boys joking while cleaning horse stalls and a quiet scuffle further back. Lately, I've noticed my hearing has been more enhanced and wonder if this is due to my approaching birthday. Elder Aren did mention nineteen is a big day for an Elarian. While I'm contemplating this, I turn a corner and see Victor with his pants down rubbing against a terrified kitchen girl that he has pinned to the wall with his body.

She looks to be about twenty and was likely delivering lunch to Sigurd given the discarded food basket on the ground nearby. She's silently crying and shaking in terror. Standing only ten feet away I start munching loudly on my apple and leaning against the wall, I scowl disgustingly at Victor. He hears me munching away, turns his head and smirks at me.

"Like the show, princess? Maybe I should charge you for watching? Hmm … Oh wait! I know… you can pay me back by showing me that golden pussy you reportedly have. Go ahead … Tami won't mind will you, sweet cheeks?" he says and then licks the poor girl on the side of her face. *Yuk!*

I chuck the half-eaten apple right at his head and hit him directly in the eye. *Bulls-eye bitch!* He flinches back letting go of the girl and holds his right eye. She scampers away with a grateful look to me and runs straight into Sigurd who arrives on the other side of us and is holding a long heavy broadsword in his hands which he quickly deflects from the girl. Not wanting to miss an opportunity to damage Victor in the family jewels I hop forward and kick him right in the dick. He drops to the floor. Leaning over him, I punch his face blackening his left eye to match the apple one, before I bring my booted foot down painfully onto his unprotected dick. While he's howling in pain, I say, "Stop touching things that aren't yours or I'll cut off what's left of your dick and shove it into your disgusting mouth."

"Cold bitch," he whispers through gritted teeth then rolls over to the fetal position and sees Sigurd with his sword aimed at his face. Viktor pales instantly looking up.

"Get out of my barn. If I see you in here without my express permission, I will finish Princess Solveig's promise and then report you to your commander." Sigurd states in a strong serious voice.

Viktor scurries off like a rat with a limp and looks over his shoulder with a promise of retribution that should concern me but *doesn't*. I have bigger problems.

Sigurd sheaths his sword at his hip and then walks up and hugs me warmly. "Thanks Solveig. Tami's a sweet girl. I'm sure you'll have a few more grateful admirers in the kitchen come morning. Most of the servants adore you for your selflessness in defending them you know?" he says stepping back and then looking me over. Then with a grin says, "That part with the apple was priceless." We share a chuckle and then he asks, "Going for a ride? Let me help you."

"Thanks, Sigurd. How have you been? Jorah told me you've been rather busy with all the nobility since the announcement of my … betrothal," I say walking to Sindari's stall.

"I'm fine. Busy. But fine. Don't worry about me, Sol. These old bones can still care for the animals. However, there is a new filly we obtained. She seems off and I'd like you to take a look at her. I've tried everything and we all know you have the best bond with animals …" He rubs the back of his neck then says, "I'm not sure what the issue is. She's just not responding to commands and seems to spook more than the usual filly or foal. She needs to be broke to ride soon or the noble we obtained her for will terminate her."

Concerned I look over at him and open Sindari's stall door. "How long has she been acting strange?" I ask and then notice Sin standing statue-still while focusing on what Sigurd was saying.

What? I project to Sin.

I may know what's wrong with the young filly. Let us go and visit her then run free in the forest, yes? he demands into my mind.

"She's been here for almost two months, and no one has gotten anywhere with her. She's in the back paddock. I'll walk with you. I'm guessing no bridle or saddle for our dear Sindari?" Sigurd says while walking out of the barn.

"Sindari has a mind of his own and has made it clear to me that those things are unnecessary. Let's go."

We approach the back paddock, and I can see a beautiful palomino grazing. She's stalky and already rather muscular. But has a beautiful long blonde nearly white mane and tail. She has two front white leg stalkings and a white stripe down her face.

"How old is the filly, she looks nearly four? She hasn't been broken to ride yet! She's nearly a mare!" I state concerned. Sindari is a quiet presence behind me and rests his head on my right shoulder nibbling at my braid that's laying there.

"Yes, she's almost four and we were hoping to have made progress." He whistles loudly trying to get the filly to come over but she doesn't even flinch and continues to munch happily on the grass.

I try to project my thoughts to her but it's like there's a fog in her mind. Reaching up and pulling my braid out of Sindari's mouth, I then project to him: *Stop chewing on my hair, you mangy beast. Can you reach her mind?*

He projects back *no*, so I ask him then to go in the paddock to bring her over to me which he agrees.

"Well, what do you think?" Sigurd asks then stops when he sees me walking over and opening the paddock to let Sindari in. "Wait! Sol! What are you doing, don't let that gelding in there with her!"

"Patience, Sigurd," I say smiling at him. "Trust me."

With narrowed eyes, Sigurd tracks Sindari as he trots through the paddock towards the filly. The palomino filly doesn't even notice Sindari until he moves into her eyesight. Her head flicks up and she bounces back with her head thrown up. He then preens a bit and trots in a circle with his tail fluffed out and his neck arched before nudging her behind towards us.

She trots over to us with a heavy gait and leans her head over the fence. Sindari comes over and stands by her then projects to me: *She says I have the nicest tail and smoothest black coat she's ever seen.* He jauntily reports with a yinnie afterwards.

I chuckle and then ask him: *Can you please find out some useful information? Also tell her to let me speak with her.*

Sindari nudges her neck with his nose then reports to me: *Her name is Brienne. She says she likes it here, but she has a sore spot under her right flank that's bothering her. Some guy used these metal contraptions on his boot and stabbed her there with it. She was trying to roll in the dirt to relieve the irritation after the injury but it doesn't seem to be getting better. She asked me to lick it?* He projects and I swear if a horse's eyebrow could raise, then Sindari's would definitely be raised after that last comment.

I walk around and let myself into the paddock. Then approaching Brienne cautiously I place a hand on her neck and say, "Well met, Brienne, welcome to Falal. I'm Solveig and this over here is Sigurd but I'm sure you already met him. Can I take a look?"

Brienne looks at me and tilts her head slightly. Sindari projects to me instantly: *She says she can't hear you? She knows you are talking but cannot hear anything.*

Is she deaf? I ask Sindari strongly, perhaps too strongly because I must have projected my thoughts to both Sindari and Brienne.

She responds: *Yes! I have been deaf since I was born. I've been traded around since birth as I couldn't understand my masters' commands. The same is occurring here. I am glad to meet you though.*

Finally understanding the main issue here, I project back to Brienne: *My name is Solveig and this man over here is Sigurd. He is a good man and the stable master here. You can trust him. Please let him work with you to be ridden or else they may trade you or worse. Can I see the injury you spoke of to Sindari?*

She responds in the affirmative and rubs her head into my hand. *My lady. I trust you*, she projects happily.

"Come here, Sigurd," I state, then once he is by me and Brienne I say, "Two issues here. One, Brienne is deaf and therefore cannot hear any commands you are teaching her, so she has only been learning from hand signals and body language. This is why she doesn't come when you whistle for her or call her name. Secondly, she has some sort of injury near her right flank that is irritating her." I run my hand just under her right flank as I talk. "Might have been from a spur or something. Let's have a look." Sigurd looks the area over and we see a small red irritated wound that's trying to heal but appears infected.

"I can't even begin to guess how you figured out she's deaf, but it does make complete sense. That horse trader was a lying thief and I'll have to inform him we are no longer doing business with him." He says to me then turns to Brienne and in a soft voice says, "There there, girl. Brienne, what a pretty name. I'll come up with some hand signals for you," he says running his hands gently over her neck which she leans into. Next, he asks me awkwardly, "How do you know her name is Brienne? The boys have been calling her Shimmer for her white mane."

"I—well … you see … it just seems to fit her better," I stutter not having a good answer for him. He would likely think I'm crazy if I told him I could talk to animals.

"Thanks, Solveig. I'll take good care of her now that we understand each other. I'll clean and get a paste on that wound. It should heal up easily and I'll make sure none of the boys use spurs on her. You think she will be ok for the boys to ride now?" he asks me.

Sigurd wants to clean your wound on your flank and then one of the stable boys is going to work on riding with you. Will you be okay, Brienne? I project to her. She projects the feeling of gratefulness back to me and Sindari then: *Yes Solveig. Thank you again, my lady.*

"You are good to go, she seems to be in agreement with you and her first riding lesson. See you later, Sigurd," I say to an amazed and perplexed Sigurd. Then I turn running up to Sindari and mount his back. Sigurd waves after opening the paddock to let us out.

Sindari and I just enter the Elaritian Forest when I get that strange searing hot pain on my right inner wrist. It lasts nearly a whole minute or two and then completely resolves.

Knowing what the sensation means now, I tell Sindari to slow down to a walk and then pull back my right sleeve. A new detailed rune can be seen covering the inside of my right wrist. It looks as though there is a tree at the top and a soaring bird in the center. Perhaps this is related to my connection with animals and the forest?

I really need to talk with Elder Aren again. Sindari and I walk through the forest for some time before I hear a fluttering of feathers and a change in the air. I look up and see Tyr swooping down so I wait while he lands on my left shoulder. Luckily, I had my back harness fitted with a firm leather piece that he can land on without tearing my shoulder.

Hello, Solveig! I've missed you the past few turnings of the sun! I recently caught a large rabbit that was quite a difficult catch, required a significant amount of skill might I say. Just thought you should know, Tyr starts to tell me haughtily while puffing his chest feathers out and preening a bit.

Good afternoon, Tyr. Well met. I missed you as well and am very impressed with your prowess as a hunter. Any news from the forest? I ask him.

None in these parts. However last turning of the sun, I noted movement up near the mountains in the forest. I flew further north and spoke with a rather beautiful female hawk named Allira. She told me that several two-legged creatures were moving around more than usual, some bleeding onto the ground. She also told me she saw some fires in the forest. I wanted to spend more time with her so I asked her to show me. I did several dives from the sky and did an impressive barrel roll that she found very attractive as we traveled, Tyr informs me. *I saw a few humans traveling from the mountain with wagons but not much else. It was difficult to see more from above. I mated with the female and then traveled back to discuss this with you. I would like to travel back to my mate soon, Solveig.*

Deeply troubled by what he said, I feel my heart race. It sounds as though they are moving one of the camps or possibly hurt some of the slaves. *You did well my friend! Thank you for keeping an eye on the sky and coming back. I know it must be hard to leave your mate so soon. Can you wait a bit longer? I need you to inform Elder Aren or one of the guards I'm here and need to talk,* I ask him while petting his neck. He makes a *cak-cak* in agreement then flies off.

I dismount from Sindari and walk through the forest deep in thought.

Unexpectedly, I hear soft footsteps walking in time with me and look over to my left seeing Zxian walking next to me as if he came out of thin air. He's smiling at me and keeps walking with his hands clasped behind his back. Once he sees I notice him, he starts whistling a jaunty tune like we are out together for an evening stroll in a garden.

I can't help but chuckle and then say, "That really is an impressive skill. Almost like invisibility. Well met, Zxian."

He stops and turns towards me bowing formally at the waist with a hand over his heart. "Well met, Solveig. I'm glad to see you again. Elder Aren needs to speak with you urgently."

"Lead the way! I'm assuming Yaeril is with him? I have some important information as well," I say starting run alongside Zxian who is rather fast.

"Yes, Solveig. We will have a meeting and trade information. You are nearly nineteen, yes? Yaeril and I have a surprise for you," he says while running swiftly and smiling.

We are nearly silent as we run our way through the forest. Branches and roots seem to move out of our way to make the path easier. *Wow. Maybe my powers are progressing.*

I enter a small clearing in the forest where several ancient trees are bent inwards and have intertwining branches nearly making a roof for which provide coverage. Elder Aren sits patiently on a moss-covered, large boulder while Yaeril can be seen sitting on a larger branch adjacent to him both looking our direction as we enter the clearing.

"Greetings, Granddaughter!" Elder Aren says with a fond smile. "I'm relieved to see you again. I have much to discuss and need your help," he continues with a concerned look.

"Well met, Elder Aren, I mean … Grandfather," I say hesitantly with a soft smile. "I have some news too that Tyr imparted to me."

"I did see your goshawk but cannot understand all his signals. His presence let us know you were coming, and I'm interested to hear your news." He pauses in thought then more seriously he says, "We scouted the camp I knew the location of not long after we met with you. You have given us new hope that we may be able to help at least some of our people, so we decided to start preparing and gather more information. Zxian, here, was able to get rather close due to his camouflage rune. He was able to scout some areas outside the mountain. Also, he overheard the guards near the mining entrance that they're going to lessen the numbers in the camp by weeding out the weaker and older slaves before moving to combine with another camp."

Zxian interrupts, then animatedly says to me. "It seemed as though this could occur in a couple days' time based on what I overheard. We must act soon or more of our people could die."

"We need more men to help us. We have no idea how many soldiers they have inside the mountain. There's only one way in and one way out that we know of." Yaeril contributes to our conversation from his perch in a nearby tree. "We also don't know the location of the other camps."

"It will be a difficult fight to gain entrance to the mountain since they have the advantage of a defensive position. It will be a bottleneck battling our way in and out," says Zxian contemplating.

"Yes, these are all the reasons we haven't been able to do anything in the past years. Now that we have you, Solveig, we may stand more of a chance. I am deeply concerned there is going to be a shift in power soon. I foresee war coming," My grandfather says with a far off look in his eyes. He then looks at me and seeing my disbelieving expression he pulls his shirt collar down exposing his right upper chest and a large black rune there. "I have the gift of foresight, Granddaughter. Although sometimes it can be a curse. I knew I would meet you at some point but didn't know when. Just as I can feel that war is coming with many deaths, but I have no way of predicting exactly when. You are the answer, child, and we need your guidance on our next step. "

"Let me think about this. I have been researching and planning as well. My friend Jorah knows about you and the camps. He favors knowledge and is helping me obtain maps as well as any possible locations for these camps in the mountains. I have a few questions for you, Grandfather …" I ask hesitantly then once receiving a nod from him I continue, "A new rune appeared today on my wrist…" I pull back my sleeve and show him.

He stares at my wrist for a for a few seconds before his surprised gaze meets mine and I ask, "What do you think it means?"

"Three…I can't believe it." My grandfather chuffs in disbelief shaking his head to himself. Then he says, "This is a rune I've seen a few times. It is a rune connected to nature and if I had to guess… animals as well. You have a natural affinity for the forest being an Elarian but this rune enhances your connection with nature. You may find nature will assist you when needed, provide for you when you think about what you desire. Plants could grow easily for you. Animals will respond to you and calm in your presence. You may even find that you can read an animals emotions allowing you to interpret their behaviors. However, you seem to have stronger than usual communication with animals, this was never seen in the past with this rune. Can you actually speak mind to mind with animals?" When I hesitantly nod to this question he says, "I suspect… never mind, it would be nearly impossible as we have never seen another Elarian with more than three natural runes. I suppose only time will tell. I know you will do great things for our people, I've seen it."

"I assumed that was the rune's meaning. As for my connection to animals, it's not so much that I can speak to them … it's more like a thought projection," I say hesitating and trying to figure out how to explain. "Umm … this is hard to put in words … It's like talking without speaking. But not all animals are able to do so, some I can only get emotions or feelings," I say and then look over at Zxian and Yaeril when I hear nothing but silence. They both have looks of awe on their faces and a hand over their hearts.

"You must be truly blessed by Valirr, Granddaughter." Aren says with a proud look. "You're already so powerful for one so young. I have my suspicions on what this could mean but you're outside the realm of normalcy for an Elarian already. Your birthday is in two days? Yes? As you now know, this is when most Elarians get all their runes." Then pulling out a small leaf wrapped package that he hands to me, he says, "This is for you, Granddaughter. Blessed early birthday."

Zxian and Yaeril walk over as well and hand me another leaf wrapped package. "Blessed birthday, Solveig," they say smiling and then sit on a nearby rock watching with anticipation.

"I—I don't know what to say. I haven't gotten a birthday gift since I was twelve!" I stutter out in surprise. I immediately walk over and throw myself at my grandfather hugging him with sob and then pulling Zxian and Yaeril in for some affection too which makes them shift with awkwardness. They both gently pat me on the back while I quiet my tears of happiness. My grandfather places both hands on my shoulders and looks me in the eyes smiling.

"We are family, Solveig; not only in blood but in heritage deeply rooted in the forest. Glad I am to have met you at last child. You are more than I ever envisioned. We," Aren says, looking at the other two men, "will strengthen you and uphold you when you feel weak or lost. You are no longer alone, Granddaughter."

I feel the darkness and hollowness in my chest start to lessen with his words. It's been so hard to stay strong the past six years since my mother passed away. I now have a family again and I intend to make that family larger very soon by living up to their expectations and helping free more Elarians. These work camps or should I say slave camps *must* be stopped.

Taking a deep breath, I look down at my lap and open the gifts they gave me. I start with my grandfather's gift and open it to find a small delicate sapphire ring with scrolling silver around it and tiny leaves around the band.

"It was your grandmothers ring and your father, Lochlann, was going to give it to your mother as a mate gift to signify their bond together. Unfortunately, he never had the chance to show your mother but I was able to find it after the raid where they took your father. It's yours now, Solveig," he says with a fond tearful smile. "It matches your eyes beautifully."

"Thank you, Grandfather." I say placing the ring on my left middle finger. Then I start to open the other gift and see an intricately carved wooden medallion on a silver chain.

I look up and smile at Zxian and Yaeril who smile back at me looking relieved that I like it. "You like it Solveig?" Yaeril asks me. "I carved the medallion from a fallen branch of a very ancient oak tree in the forest. It's the symbol of home, Elaria. Zxian obtained the silver chain and helped me with the idea," he says looking over at Zxian.

The medallion is beautifully carved showing a symbol similar to a narrowed eye in the center with branches bending over and around it.

I place the chain with the medallion over my head and it settles against my chest almost as if it belongs anchored there. Then, I tell them both my thanks.

"We need to obtain trained men for infiltrating that work camp before it's too late. There's a meeting for the Rebellion in the city that's tonight. I can appeal to them and see if any men are willing to assist us. I'm not sure if they'll help since they have their own battle to fight but—they have noticed people missing from the city that disappear and never return. We assumed they were killed by the King's guards during the purges in the city. But now knowing about these work camps, we may want to reconsider their disappearances." I state confidently while playing with the medallion on my chest.

"Very well. Make sure these people are trustworthy that you gather. We don't need the King aware of our plans. If these rebels won't help, we can come up with a plan ourselves. Zxian knows a few mercenaries we could pay to help but it would take more time, time we don't have. We should meet back here tomorrow before dusk if you can. It will take at least an hour or more of travel to the camp on horseback." I nod my head in agreement before he says in parting, "Oh and Solveig. Don't let anyone see that medallion. Some may still remember Elaria. Especially don't let your father see it. Be well, child."

Zxian and Yaeril both nod and wave goodbye before fading off into the forest with Aren. I whistle for Sindari who trots up and nudges me with a wet nose.

I'm going to need your help, friend. It may require your ... particular communication skills. Should fit with your personality perfectly. You up for a challenge? I project to Sindari after mounting him and riding swiftly back to the stables. *I'll have Tyr help you as well since I know you both just love working together,* I think with a chuckle.

I accept your challenge. No need to involve the bird. Sindari doesn't need help. You need horses for your quest, no? I'll get you the best ones, he projects back surprising me with his intuition.

Alright, ride on, my noble steed. I say with a smile to him projecting an image of him in full battle armor rearing up. He ninnies loudly in response as we make it back to the castle.

CHAPTER

Nineteen

SOLVEIG

I sneak back up to my room to find Marion pacing anxiously.

"There you are, Princess Solveig! I was waiting for you. Your father, the king, wants your attendance at a formal dinner tonight in an hour. I tried to cover for you as long as possible knowing you were having some time in the forest as you enjoy. But I started to worry you wouldn't make it back in time and now we barely have any time to prepare!" she yells nervously throwing her hands in the air.

Before I can even get a word out, she shushes me and has me stripped bare in the steaming bathtub. I turn around once I hear her gasp worried that she injured herself on one of my knives which she helped me remove.

She has her hands over her mouth and is staring at my upper back while I'm sitting in the tub. I instantly pale and realize she's seen the runes on my skin in our haste to get ready.

She slowly reaches a hand out and touches one saying, "Oh dear, do they hurt? Why did you do this to your beautiful skin?"

"It's complicated, Marion, but it wasn't necessarily by choice, and I have two others., I say looking her in the eye and grabbing her hand. With a strong commanding voice, I then order, "You must never say anything. It could mean your death or mine should someone hear you." Then I say easing up on my tone, "I trust you. It's just some of these are related to my heritage and knowledge of them getting to the wrong ears could lead to many others being injured."

She breaks out of her shock and picking up some lavender soap starts to scrub me clean. She asks, "Tell me what they mean at least. Also, what is the medallion you are wearing and a new ring? I've never seen that symbol before."

"The runes are symbols of power each meaning something different. The medallion and ring are presents from some friends for my birthday. I need to hide them given the symbol on the medallion."

She finishes with my bath and grabs a towel walking me towards the fire to brush and style my hair. "Here give me the medallion. We can place it in your trunk at the end of the bed. I think you have a small pouch here …" she says while taking the chain and burrowing into the storage chest pulling out a purple velvet pouch. She puts the medallion in there and then hides it under some of my undergarments.

She takes extra effort to style my hair into an up do that creates a crown of hair around my head and small tendrils curling down. She then picks up a dark purple velvet A line gown with long sleeves that flare at the wrist and a deep V neckline. It's beautiful but heavier in material than I'm used to. I tend to like the lighter fabrics that move easier. Once the dress is on, I notice a high slit up the left leg again that prevents me from wearing undergarments similar to the dress from the ball. *At least all my runes are covered in this dress.* The dress has a fully covered back so I don't have to worry there.

I ask Marion, "Who sent the dress?" feeling a sinking feeling in my gut.

"You're betrothed, dear," she says with a sad pitying smile. "Counselor Malphas delivered it this afternoon looking for you. And he also left these." She pulls out a box with a necklace sporting several large deep purple amethyst gems one of which falls into the deep V of my neckline. There's also matching earrings that dangle. Rolling my eyes at the waste of wealth, I still allow her to put them on me knowing he would only hurt Marion for not following orders if I'm not wearing them. I have to get through the dinner quickly so I can make it to the Rebellion meeting tonight.

I walk into the formal dining room just as my father reaches his chair. He looks over at me with a shrewd gaze almost as if he knows I was up to something earlier. I start to feel a light sweat down my back from anxiety or maybe it's from this darn dress. *Damn dress is so heavy.* I make sure I have my emotions locked deep down and my "princess mask" in place ready to play politics.

I stand at my chair to the left of my father and wait staring straight ahead and a blank expression until he sits. My focus shifts for a second as Counselor Malphas walks in the door and smirks at me. He walks over to the seat on my father's right. My father nods to him sitting down.

Then while everyone is in the process of sitting, Malphas clears his throat loudly and asks my father, "King Batair, if I may graciously ask, could Princess Solveig, my lovely betrothed, sit next to me instead of her normal position? Especially since this is a small gathering and I have missed her greatly this past week. You have been keeping me so busy with the kingdom that she has not been well tended to and may need my attentions."

I freeze up in a half-bent position about to take my seat and feel a trickle of sweat down my back under the dress at his loudly announced words. Several noble ladies at the table swoon at his theatrics. And many noblemen nod their heads then look leeringly at me.

My father replies, "Of course, Malphas, she is your betrothed after all. You may do as you please with her. It will be good for her to have someone such as you to tend to her wild ways." Then looking at me as he raises a goblet of wine to his lips, he says, "On with you, girl, listen to your future husband." He turns away from me as if the issue is done and tells the noblemen to shift down. Servants scurry to assist in the new seating arrangement. As I nervously walk around the table to my new seat, I try to suppress the shaking in my hands that Malphas tends to incite in me. I take a seat at his side and look up seeing Duke Havass take my spot across the table.

Counselor Malphas leans over to whisper in my ear, "You have been avoiding me, Solveig, since our little interlude in the hallway. I'm disappointed and missed your whimpering." He then places a hand on the bare skin of my left thigh where the dress has fallen open from the high slit. I try to hastily pull the fabric together while looking straight ahead. He knocks my hand away and slides his hand up to my inner thigh near my nether regions but not fully touching them. He then says, "You look stunning in the dress and jewels I sent you. Like a present ready to be opened just for me. Your birthday is the day after tomorrow is it not?" He waits for my nod. "Well, I have a present for you to celebrate."

"I don't like gaudy jewels and fancy fabrics. You need not give me gifts or pretend to care for me. I know who you are. This sham of a betrothal will never happen," I whisper to him while smiling at some nobles down the table, trying to act as though I'm calm, when really I'm panicking with his hand rubbing on my inner thigh.

He squeezes my thigh roughly under the table and smiles. "Your present isn't only jewelry or clothing, princess. You'll see. And I am well aware of your proclivities with lowlifes and taste in men's fashion. You've never quite learned to behave after all these years. Don't worry we will have all the time in the world to work on this once married."

He then turns away from our whispered conversation to address my father and says, "Trade has been good lately, your majesty. Several shipments from the coast of Jaarn and a few from Beamus have arrived. Only one shipment never crossed but it was a smaller one and we have soldiers looking into the issue. With my marriage to the princess, we will secure more trade through my associates and create a more secure Laevaris."

"Very good, Malphas. I'm pleased with the progress of the Jaarnian steel and iron ore shipments. Our blacksmiths informed me they would be working on weapons soon. We need more iron harvested from the quarries and mines. We may need to obtain more workers to speed along our mining efforts at the Duke's reform camps. I need more weapons for our growing army yesterday. War is looming and I to be the one to come out on top," he states drinking already his third glass of wine.

"The reform camps were genius, sire. Instead of the lowlifes and criminals scouring the streets we have reformed the useful ones into structured work slaves that contribute to our great kingdom. I have at least three such camps right now helping to obtain you more iron and steel replicating the system that the Jaarnians started. They were very helpful in showing us how they run the camps and gave us various techniques on how to *persuade* the slaves into compliance," Duke Havass states proudly with a smug face that I want to punch. However, I don't move and stare at my plate of broiled fish trying to soak up any information I can gather.

"Yes, yes, Jaarn is useful as of now but may not be in the future. For now, we will keep them as allies. I want you to clean up some of those camps and get rid of the useless slaves since food is scarce there and I will have to cut your rations in nearly half," King Batair states nonchalantly with a wave of his hand spilling some wine on the table.

"Yes, your majesty, I was already given these orders a few days ago. May I suggest—" Duke Havass starts to say only to be interrupted again by an inebriated King.

"You may not suggest! Dinner as not the appropriate time for such talk of business. Let us talk of other more interesting topics. Also where is the entertainment?" King Batair says in a loud voice.

I see a woman similar to my age stumble into the room wearing a provocative red sheath dress that's nearly sheer. She has long perfectly curled blonde hair and a large chest. She stumbles over to my father and drops to her knees with her head lowered demurely saying, "My liege. I'm sorry for the delay. I didn't want to interrupt your conversations."

"We will discuss your tardiness later alone. For now, keep me entertained. I am bored of business," he says then tilts his wine goblet to pour wine into her open mouth. I see her quickly shift her gaze to me and then back before swallowing.

A world of shame and hopelessness can be seen in her gaze. I've seen her before and also another girl around my father. He's been flaunting whores around for the past two or three years at the endorsement of Counselor Malphas. It's disgusting to see him openly degrade and fondle women similar to my age. After some investigating, I came to find out they are slaves to some of the brothels in the city and also one of them a known Rebellion spy.

My father is shoving the woman's head under the table and reaching to adjust himself while he carries on conversation with Duke Havass as if nothing is remiss. *Fucking shameless.* I feel nausea and my stomach churning before I have to look away and become aware of my own situation.

Malphas and several other noblemen are enjoying the show my father is putting on now that dinner is done. Most of the nobles are drunk on wine at this point and I can see several noblemen lead their wives or mistresses back to their room. My attention is brought back to my father gripping the girl's hair when he speaks in our direction.

"So Malphas, Ah, when are you planning the wedding? I need an heir soon. Or perhaps I may make my own tonight before you can plant your own seed …" He cuts off laughing while the girl beneath the table chokes and he moans.

Poor girl. Maybe I can find a way to help her.

Disgustingly several noblemen chuckle and rub their pants but I can't even notice as my heart stalls in my chest waiting on Malphas's answer.

"I would like to have the wedding one month from the princess's nineteenth birthday. Several Jaarnian nobles whom we are trading with will be able to attend at that time and we need time to prepare. If that's agreeable to you, your majesty?" asks Malphas with a raised eyebrow and running his fingers from my thigh up under my underwear making me flinch.

King Batair doesn't answer at first instead groaning and likely finding his release. He then grabs the slave from under the table and pulls her to straddle his lap. He says to Malphas then, "Fine. Whatever you want Malphas. Just don't screw up our deal with Jaarn." Then he pushes down the girl's dress, exposing her chest for him to fondle. "Oh, don't forget I have a meeting tomorrow with Prince Cadoc about his silly proposal. I'll have to somehow deal with that."

Malphas instantly stiffens up at the mention of Prince Cadoc and says, "Just get rid of him. Those arrogant self-righteous Gorvians. The only thing they're good for is their wine. Let me know how it goes. I have plans for tomorrow night during your meeting." He reaches with his fingers and runs them over my underwear making me shake with disgust.

Nausea rises up in me at his words and when he starts to push his fingers in a bit, I jump out of my chair and say, "Excuse me, I don't feel well and must go to my room." I rush from the room before anyone can answer. Doesn't matter as my father has his face in that slave's naked chest. I can hear Counselor Malphas's mocking laughter down the hallway as I retreat back to my room.

CHAPTER
Twenty

SOLVEIG

Faktirnor! *Please, give me strength!* I race back to my room burning with shame. Shame for what I saw my father doing at dinner. Shame for how the nobles of this kingdom act with their carelessness for wealth and their demeaning leers. Shame for that woman, that slave, and what she is forced to endure! Shame for how I allow Malphas to treat me, for what he does to me. Shame for how Malphas makes me into a weak scared and trembling woman!

Back in my room, I lay on my bed for several moments staring at the ceiling. Trying and failing to center myself, I repeat my mother's phrase: *grin and bear it, but don't share it.* No need to tell anyone about my darkness. Suppress it, Sol. Keep those dark memories locked deep down. Put on your mask and get things done. .*No time like the present*, I think to myself.

I glance out the window and realize I was wallowing in self-pity for far too long. It's nearly midnight and I need to get going if I want to be at the Rebellion meeting. I change out of that heavy and now sweaty dress donning black pants and a tunic with sturdy boots.

I quietly make it out of the castle and check that I don't see anyone following this time before I make my way into the inner city of Falal. Our capital city is truly beautiful during the day, but it's my favorite at night. Streetlights line nearly every road and flower boxes line many a window with stone buildings intermixed with timber structures seen. Most of the roads are stone lined making the city much cleaner. Nighttime is the best to see the city though. There are no expectations. No one's looking at you for your station in the nobility or gossiping behind your back that you're deformed with your pointed ears. There's no judgement at night and if there is, well, then those people tend to get a dagger in their back. People tend to ignore things at night either from lack of interest or being too drunk to notice. I supposed I like nighttime in the city because I relish the shadows and the darkness. It hides my insecurities. It helps to hide what I feel under my emotionless mask which I have to don during the day but can reveal at night.

Creeping up to the back of a large warehouse where cheese is made, of all things, I sneak into the door and make it a few steps before someone roughly pulls back my hood to look at my face. I feel a dagger against my throat as I look up into the eyes of Darritt.

"Greetings, Sol! I missed ya, sweetheart," Darritt says tucking away his dagger and giving me a side hug. "They're about to start."

Hugging him back I whisper, "Well met, Darritt, see you in there." I swiftly walk in the central room trying to ignore the lingering scent of stinky cheese and lean against the back wall with a leg propped up.

Vidarr is at the front of the room on a chair speaking when he glances up at me entering. He cuts off his words mid-sentence and smiles warmly. He nods his head to the front of the room to which I shake my head. I really don't feel like being the center of attention after the dinner I just had to endure with King Batair and his followers.

He continues to talk about certain Rebellion missions and on-goings in the city. They then discuss and come up with a plan for using the iron ore and silver we obtained. Food has been bought and is being distributed tomorrow to any needy families in the city which makes me smile, feeling like I made a difference helping my people for once. My smile quickly dissipates when I think about that slave girl and the many other slaves that are still being suppressed in our kingdom. It makes me sick. We need change but even I know change takes time.

Once all their business is discussed, Vidarr calls order and asks for any new business. I stand up straight and walk towards the front which makes everyone turn and quiet their conversations. I suppose I can't hide in the back forever.

"Something to say, Sol?" Vi asks with a grin then waves his hand to the chair he was standing on.

I look at him with a serious face and nod making his expression sober quickly, then propping my boot up on the chair, I tell them about the "work" camps that are supposed to reform criminals and lowlifes that the guards deem necessary. I tell them about how the King and Duke Havass and likely Counselor Malphas are plucking these people off our streets never to be seen again and relocating them as slaves into these mines. I then explain briefly there used to be a people like myself with similar traits that lived as its own kingdom in the Broken Forest, once called the Elaritian Forest. But after a genocide enacted by the late King, those Elarians are now dead or held as slaves in one of those camps. I explain to the rebels that there will be a shift in one of the camps in a few days where more will die or be moved to another more secure camp and we only have a small window of opportunity to act on this. I lastly plead to the rebels to help me infiltrate the slave camp and rescue as many of our people as we can before it's too late.

Silence reins in the echoey warehouse room when I'm done speaking, then a sudden cacophony of voices start to shout out at the same time with questions and yelling their opinions.

Where is this camp?

Why didn't we know about it?

It's not our problem! We have too much to deal with already!

You're telling me there's more freaks like you out there?

We don't need another race of people returning and taking our jobs! Keep the pointed eared freaks in the forest and camps.

Did they take my Jaenne to that camp?

Could my Heroldin still be alive?

How many men do you need?

We need to focus on undermining the King before taking this on!

We need to stop slavery in our kingdom!

A shrill whistle cuts through all the voices, then Vidarr states, "One question at a time! And don't insult Sol again! If I hear murmurs slandering her, I'll personally meet you in the back alley afterwards for a lesson in respect. She's one of us and we should hear her out. She went at great risk to herself to get us information and also help us obtain that food that sits in your belly, and the iron ore we obtained." Several faces nod and others look down in shame.

A hand raises then after Vi nods a woman says, "I'll help, Sol. You know I can keep up with you. I owe you one after helping me get rid of those guards hounding my mother's business."

I gratefully smile at Kira, a woman only a few years older than me and rather skilled at being a spy for the Rebellion in the city. She's also very fast and knows how to handle a dagger in a tight situation. Several others start to volunteer to help including Darritt and of course Vidarr himself.

We end up with seven rebels volunteering before Vidarr says, "Alright if that's all, we will meet again in one week. Oh and Darritt? You still got one of those wagons we stole? Might need it for this journey." Darritt nods in reply and Vi continues, "Keep things on the down low people. Stay in groups of two or three at night in case of another purge. Dismissed."

VIDARR

EVERY TIME I SEE HER, SHE STEALS MY BREATH AWAY. IT'S CRAZY.

I call her sunshine just to irritate her, but in truth, she *is* like the sun to me. Brilliant and lighting up the room when she enters. I'm like a moth drawn to a flame as they always say. I've known her since she sixteen and you'd think I would still see her as that dirt covered scrawny girl and lose interest but no. The more time I spend with her the more I love how she's grown into the woman she is today.

Unfortunately, tonight she doesn't seem to be bright and shining as she usually is. She seems somber and dare I say dark, like I feel deep down sometimes after thinking about my sister and my family. My sunshine looks like she's battling her own shadows tonight and struggles to keep her mask in place. That look in her eyes when she came up to the front of the meeting nearly gutted me. The last time I saw her look at me like that was when I found her in that alley nearly three years ago and I swore to myself she would never feel that way again.

I follow her out into the alley near the warehouse. Everyone quickly cleared out after the meeting through different exits to avoid attention that a large gathering would attract.

Grabbing her arm gently, I swing her around to look at me and then place a finger under her chin tilting her head up to look at me. "What's wrong, Sol?" I ask trying to get her to meet my eyes. "You seem sad … and don't tell me it's only because of that shocking revelation involving the slave camps and finding out about Elarians. That's sad enough in itself, but I know you. I know there's something else."

When she finally makes eye contact, I rock back my heels with a jolt. *Shame. Despair. Anguish.* I see all those emotions and more in her gaze making me deeply disturbed. Sol always keeps her emotions locked down tight except when she's sparring with me or running wild in the forest which she tends to enjoy.

"I'm worried, Vi," she says looking down again as if it's hard to keep eye contact and discuss this. "I—I'm not sure what to do."

"Shh, come on," I say running a hand over her hair smoothing it down her back and pulling her into a comforting embrace. "Have a nightcap with me at my place before you head back. We can talk there." She nods into my chest so I grab her hand and we jog back to my apartment sneaking in the shadows to avoid notice.

I take her upstairs into my small *very* minimal one room apartment that sits above a tailor's business off one of the main streets in the city. I don't have much being an orphan but being a leader in the Rebellion does have its perks since I know just about everyone in the city. They like to gain favor or some just seem to want to care for me by giving me things. At least I have a roof over my head and food to eat, it's all I need. Also I get nice well maintained clothes from the elderly couple that owns the store below me.

Once she sits on the bed in my apartment, she immediately leans forward putting her hands over her face then sits in silence. Usually having a beautiful woman on my bed incites a different reaction in me, especially Sol, but right now all I feel is concern. I ask, "Tell me, Sol. You're starting to scare me."

I pour a finger of Avarian liquor, cheaper stuff, into two glasses drinking mine immediately then bring the other glass to her and sit on the bed. She takes the drink down in one swallow, setting the glass aside and then puts her hands over her face again. I reach over grabbing her hands and trying to pull them from her face, that's when I notice the edge of a tattoo on her right wrist where her sleeve got pulled back some. I have a lot of tattoos covering my body, some more meaningful than others and some just because I liked them, however I've never seen a tattoo that looked like what's on her wrist. I stare at it for a second and wait. I start to doubt myself that maybe she doesn't trust me. She never told me she got a tattoo.

"It's a rune," she goes on to say. "It just recently showed up on my skin along with two others. Supposedly, it has to do with me being Elarian. I was told around the age of nineteen, Elarians can get one or two runes that indicate a power or exceptional skill they can access when needed," she says looking at my awed face. "This one on my wrist is for nature and animals. I have an affinity for them."

I take her right wrist in my hand and run my other fingers over it, memorizing it. She looks amazing with a dark tattoo on her golden skin. I didn't think she could get more attractive, but I guess I was wrong. Suddenly sitting still is difficult with my slowly tightening pants. "It's exceptional just like you. I was going to ask who your tattoo artist was …" I say with a soft chuckle. "Can I see the others?"

She nods hesitantly then turns her back to me and reaches with both hands to lift her shirt. *Dear Goddess have mercy on me!* I quickly adjust my aroused cock in my pants while her back is turned and she can't see. There's a large rune in the center of her upper back extending from her neck base to her shoulder blades. I run my hand over it, unable to prevent myself from touching her soft golden skin, causing her to shiver. She looks over her shoulder at me and for the first time tonight I see something other than despair in them. Heat is burning my sunshine's eyes while I rub her back with my hands. I then reach up and help her remove her shirt all the way. "And this one, what does it mean?" I ask with a slight rasp in my voice realizing she's naked from the waist up.

"Healing rune," she replies covering up her breasts. I slide off the edge of the bed and kneel in front of her. I'm a big man, in more ways than one, so kneeling in front of her still puts me at nearly eye level but I look down to her hand-covered chest and groan. I scoot forward so I'm between her legs. Then looking in her eyes for consent, to which she nods nervously, I reach forward and pull her trembling hands away.

Praise Yasmil, goddess of beauty! She's stunning. I can't help but stare at her luscious chest. She has perky, moderate-sized but full breasts with dusky nipples that start to harden under my gaze. I reach forward and palm them in my hands eliciting a loud moan from Sol and causing me to smile. Then rubbing my fingers over her nipples, I lean forward and roughly plunder her lips in a soul-searing kiss. She falls backwards onto my bed while we nip and lick at each other roughly, each of us trying to gain dominance in the kiss over one another. But when I twist and pluck her right nipple, I feel her moan into the kiss and submit to me and my kisses fully. *My fierce little tiger likes that,* I think to myself cataloging in my head all the small things she seems to enjoy. I run my left hand up into her hair which I loose from her braid, splaying her hair across my blankets, and continue to roughly palm her full right breast.

I start to move down her neck kissing her and sucking on the skin above her right collar bone in a possessive manner. *Mine. Always mine.* I think, hoping my neck kisses will leave a mark in the morning. Then I take her left breast and nipple in my mouth and suck forcefully causing her back to arch off the bed with a mewling sound. *So responsive.* I think groaning and rubbing my hard cock, that's still in my tight pants, over her center.

"I have one more rune," she gasps out when I tweak her nipple again.

"Where?" I ask with a more forceful voice than I meant and looking her in the eye, hoping it's close to a *specific* location on her body. I then suckle her left nipple making her grab my hair.

Instead of answering, she reaches down with her other hand trying to unbutton her pants. I quickly shove her hands away. Releasing her nipple from my mouth with a pop, I then lick a trail down her abdomen and un-button her pants with my teeth. She props on her elbows and watches me with panting breaths.

I slowly pull her boots and pants off then return to my favorite posi-tion between her legs. *Oh God!* Her golden thighs slowly spread under my perusal. I look over her nearly naked body splayed out on *my* bed with amazement. The only thing covering her now is a thin pair of lacy black underwear. Running my gaze over her last rune on her right upper thigh, I ask, "And this one, sunshine?"

"Agility, speed and *flexibility*," she says stressing the last word making me imagine all sorts of possibilities for our time together.

I run my hand over the rune again making her shiver then say, "I think this one is my favorite then." Smirking at her with wink, I then drag her more towards the end of the bed and push her thighs apart forcefully spreading them until her knees touch the bed. I push all the way flexing her at the hips until she's fully exposed with my hands on the back of her thighs and testing her supposed *flexibility*, which is good, really good. Then I say, "Don't move."

I slowly kiss and lick and nip my way down her inner thigh to her lace covered slit. Then I lick all the way up from her slit using the flat of my tongue causing her to quiver and gasp out loud.

"More, please, Vi," I hear her beg softly. Best words I've ever heard her say. I then take a finger and pull aside the lace. I breathe onto her exposed clit and plunge a finger into her soaking wet cunt. She flinches and stills for a second making me worry I hurt her. Then she starts to moan and whimper. *Damn, she's so tight!*

"So responsive, sweetheart. So wet. Going to be hard to stop, sunshine," I say finding difficulty in making full sentences with my panting breaths.

Plunging a second finger into her tight wet channel, I start pumping while she moans and writhes on the bed. She's gripping the blankets and arching her back so beautifully that I can tell she's close. Her breasts are heaving with each deep breath she takes. You'd almost think she's never had an orgasm before the way she responds to each little touch.

I lean in and lick up her slit while pumping my fingers before I suck hard on her engorged clit. She screams out her pleasure, possibly waking my elderly neighbors but I find I don't care, and then collapses back letting her legs drop down.

I still have my fingers in her wet cunt and say, "I told you not to move, sunshine." Then I take my fingers out of her and suck them clean. *Mmm. Honey sweetness.* "Damn, Solveig. You're going to kill me." I look her in the eye and then push on the back of both her thighs making her hips flex until she's contorted in a manner most women couldn't accomplish. I then tell her, "Grab the back of your thighs, we aren't done yet."

She hesitantly reaches forward and grabs both her thighs holding them fully flexed against the sides of her chest. I reach down and rip her lacy underwear away and stuff it into my pocket then look down at her pink dripping wet opening. I slide two fingers into her cunt again causing her to whimper and ask seriously, "Have you been with a man before, Sol?" I pump my fingers twice then try to add a third finger but meet some resistance. "You're so tight."

"I—I haven't ever had sex before. I'm a virgin but ..." Then she chokes up and I see tears in her eyes. "That's part of the issue. I have had a man touch me before. I wanted to tell you—" she says then closes her eyes like she's ashamed. I instantly pull her legs down and take my fingers out of her.

With sudden clarity, I realize then how she got that look in her eye. It was shame! *Some fucking cock-sucker touched my girl!* And I realize it doesn't seem to have been with her consent if her tear-filled eyes are anything to go by. I get up quickly and start to pace in my anger. "Tell me, Sol!" I shout causing her to flinch. She sits up and covers her chest with an arm.

"There's a man, a powerful man, in my father's inner circle that—" She starts to say and then hesitates. I realize how hard this is for her and try to calm down. So I walk over and sit next to her putting a throw around her shoulders. She shoots me a grateful smile and then taking a deep breath continues: "He and sometimes my father would give me *lessons*. Lessons for my poor behavior, for talking back, for speaking when I should be silent, for being too wild, for my unusual looks, for—well really anything. It started after my mother died, when I was thirteen, nearly fourteen. My father was angry and told this man that he can punish me to teach me a lesson." She takes a shuddering breath with a far off look in her eyes. "He always creeped me out and was leering at me. He mostly just hurt me and sometimes father would participate or watch him dole out punishments. Then they would lock me away in a cold dark room in the dungeon to let me think over my mistakes. It wasn't *too* bad back then when I think about it. I could handle the pain after a while."

She keeps talking but I have to get back up and pace. I'm so angry I feel like I'm going to break out of my skin knowing that she had to endure that as a child. That she felt it "wasn't too bad" makes me sick to my stomach. I can tell she's leaving out some of the gory details to not anger me.

"It was only this past year that things have started to change," she says looking down twisting her hands in her lap nervously.

"Wait—wait one second." I turn and look at her in shock. "You mean this is still going on? Sol! Sunshine! Why didn't you say anything?" I demand.

She holds up her hand and looks at me with her lip trembling. "Let me finish or I never will. I need you to know. Since no one else knows this part." She pauses then says, "He started to get mo—more … sexual over the past year. He's been touching me inappropriately down there and threatening to do more. I'm worried it's only a matter of time. He touched me—with his hand—causing me to feel humiliated and embarrassed. And … shameful. That's why I looked the way I did when you saw me tonight. I'm worried about what's going to happen," she finishes and blows out a big breath like she feels a big release just telling someone this burden.

"He touched you! Like *touched* you without consent? *Fuck*!" I get up and punch repeatedly into the wall next to the bed making the plaster crumble and my knuckles a bloody mess but I can't help it. I need to do something. That sick disturbed man touched my sunshine! While I'm lost in my thoughts, Solveig had gotten up and put a hand on my shoulder. I turn around and pull her to me engulfing her in my embrace and squeezing her. I'm scared that if I let her go someone will hurt her again. "What can I do? Please tell me I can kill him? Will people notice if he disappears suddenly?" I ask.

She shakes her head against my chest and squiggles a bit in my tight embrace making me aware of her nakedness again.

"I have a request for you, Vi," she softly asks looking up at me.

"Anything! Please, Sol! I'll give you anything just tell me how I can make this better." I plead and wait for her to tell me.

"I want you to be with me," she whispers and then bites her lower lip. *Damn. I need to kiss those full lips again.* I think to myself.

"I am with you, sunshine. Anytime you need me, I'll be there with you."

She shakes her head no as if I'm not understanding then says, "No, I mean—I want you to *be* with me like, you know … intimately." Her face turns a bright shade of red in a cute blush. "I turn nineteen tomorrow night and, well, the one thing I want is to not have to worry about my first time being with a man as a bad thing. I want it to be with you," she quickly says nervously.

I'm floored with shock at her request and then realize the kind of trust she must have for me in order to ask such a thing. I feel sort of…honored that she would pick me, want me. Then understanding what this means, I'm instantly aroused again.

"You turn nineteen tomorrow night?" I confirm. I forgot her birthday was coming up with all the crazy rebellion dealings I've been distracted by. She nods her head waiting for my reply. "Well then, how could I refuse you such a birthday gift?" I say with a wink and a devilish smile trying to alleviate some of the tension in the room. "And what a *big* birthday *present* it is! Just you wait and see, sunshine!"

She smiles and chuckles then swats me on the chest causing the throw blanket to fall from her shoulders.

As the blanket falls from my shoulders, I'm instantly aware of my nakedness again.

How embarrassing that was to ask a grown man to take my virginity! I swear he was being dense just to make me say it out loud. Ugh, he has to think I'm so naive! Hopefully, he is truly attracted to me and not just going to have sex with me because I asked him to! Oh no … why did I ask him?

I have all these thoughts running through my head making me distracted when he suddenly grabs me under the ass and picks me up. My legs automatically go around his waist and I arch my back a bit to rub my breasts on his now naked chest. *Wait! When did his shirt come off?*

He leans forward and grabs my lower lip with his teeth starting to kiss me with such dominance that I'm instantly wet again. Meanwhile, his hands on my ass are kneading it roughly making it spread open to the air and adding more sensitivity to areas I've never had explored.

I'm air bound for a second as he throws me on the bed and I bounce making my hair fly into my face. He then unbuckles his belt and pants, sliding them down over his V-shaped pelvis—yes Vidarr has a V-shaped pelvis, the irony isn't lost on me. *Goodness! The man is all sin and rebellion,* I think before my mind explodes with the perfection that is Vidarr's tattooed body. I barely spare a thought for the fact he wasn't wearing any underwear under those tight leather pants before I look down at his fully erect cock.

All I can think of is … too big to fit. Its huge but beautiful in a way like a carved statue with veins running along it and a slight upward curve at the end. With my gaze intent and concerned I ask, "Maybe this isn't such a good idea, I mean, don't get me wrong, I want to its just—" I ramble on while he interrupts.

Smiling he says, "Too big?" Then when I nod, he says, "Trust me it will fit perfectly, sunshine. Like it's meant to be there. Now close that gaping mouth or I'm going to put my cock there before we begin." He chuckles and I snap my mouth closed quickly. He fists his cock and slowly pumps it while he walks up between my legs on the end of the bed all while staring at my slit. I then squint and notice he has a scrolling tattoo on the base of his cock that connects up to his pelvis. There are words within the scrolling design but I can't make them out in my position. Whispering, he says, "Tell me if anything I do hurts you and I will stop, love."

I snap my gaze up to his at that last word and nod but he's already moved on reaching out for my chest. He leans in kissing me hungrily and grabbing my breasts roughly pushes them together. He then pinches and rubs my nipples with my breasts pushed together and stares down at them. I can't help the moan that escapes me at him touching me that way, with such dominance and possession. Kneeling and crawling up my body he straddles my waist all while holding my breasts, then he pushes his erect cock forward between my heavy and now heaving breasts. I look at him in fascination then back down at his cock while he pumps it between my breasts.

He closes his eyes and leans his head forward causing his dirty blonde hair to fall forward into his eyes while he thrusts towards my face rocking his hips. He groans loudly with pleasure and I reach a tentative hand toward his cock causing his eyes to snap open. His cock feels soft and yet oh so hard, unforgiving in its firmness, but silky as I run my hand down towards his sack as he starts to pump again. I cup his balls and marvel at their feel of heaviness, getting distracted in exploring his body. I feel a tweak of pain in my nipples when he twists them to get my attention, but somehow it just arouses me more causing wetness to pool down my legs and onto the blanket.

He groans and suddenly slides down grabbing my legs and putting them over his shoulders. "Too close, sunshine … it's your turn now. Let me see that pretty golden pussy," he says leaning down and staring at my wetness in adoration. He then starts licking my slit up to my clit and eating me out like it's his last meal.

I struggle and writhe on the bed since the sensations are too much. Then finding a good hand-hold in his hair I hold onto his head firmly keeping him there while he lathers up my wetness. He slides two fingers into me and then gently runs his tongue over my clit shooting me off into pure bliss. I think I almost lose consciousness but before I can fully become aware again I realize he hasn't stopped.

He sits up some and then taking his cock in his hand he shifts forward. I feel a firm pressure at my entrance making me stiffen up. But he then leans down kissing me and starts to knead my breasts pulling at the nipples until I'm begging for more. Then he thrusts his hips forward spearing me with his hard cock in one deep thrust. I cry out from the pinch of pain and pressure. Then I bite down on his lip in retaliation to the pain while he holds still.

He tries to shift slightly so he can lean on one of his elbows and the subtle motion of his cock in my tight channel gives me flush of pleasure all the way to my toes. I start to moan and tilt my hips up giving him the signal to move. I hear a whispered "Oh, oh, good god, sunshine," before he starts to thrust more. Then he says, "So tight. Fuck! You're going to take me all the way to the hilt, aren't you? Yes, just like that … this cock was made for your cunt. You can take it all, Sol. Fuck!"

His hips are pumping hard pushing his cock all the way into me in a repetitive motion while he holds onto my left breast with a hand and the other at my hip. I arch my back and then start to shift my hips trying to tip over the edge into an orgasm but missing something.

Vidarr seems to notice this too and with a smirk quickly pulls out of me. He grabs my waist and flips me over onto my hands and knees. Then he says, "You're doing so good, sunshine. Just like that, push your ass into the air a bit more and arch your back. Here like this—" He takes one hand tugging my hips back and the other putting pressure on my upper back. He shifts his legs between mine pushing my knees apart then uses one hand to push my chest and face into the bed holding me there dominantly. I have to turn my head to the side to breathe when he suddenly impales me again with his hard, tattooed cock. My wet cunt almost seems to suck him in with this position.

And … *Oh! Oh! Yes! That right there! That spot!* This position seems to hit some magic spot inside me that I was missing.

I'm so close to coming and I must say that out loud because I hear Vidarr say, "I'm close too, love, just a little more."

Then while continuing to thrust into me he grabs my long hair and, twisting it around his right fist, pulls back firmly on my head, causing just enough pressure to border on pain. It somehow turns me on more to feel someone so dominant and in control of my body. His roughness feels good, it feels different to any prior touches I had, because I trust him. I know he would never truly hurt me, at least not in a way I wouldn't enjoy.

He continues to firmly hold my hair making my back arch further while he thrusts hard into my pelvis. Reaching down under us he then pinches my clit causing me to lose all control and spiral into a screaming orgasm that doesn't stop for several minutes. He shouts his own release loudly and then moans, "Solveig, my sunshine. Mine." All while he's still softly pumping into my wetness and bent over my back now. We both collapse onto the bed and he holds my back to his chest while he's still inside me.

Once we both catch our breaths, he says, "Are you okay? Was I too rough? God Damn Solveig! You nearly killed me." I can't help but chuckle then twist over my shoulder and gently kiss him on the lips.

"It was—hot … wet … dirty … but somehow it was—" I pause for effect. "Perfect. And by the way I like the roughness but only with you." I then hear his relieved release of breath that he was holding awaiting my answer. He starts to comb my hair back behind my pointed ears with his fingers. "Do they bother you? My deformity—" I ask him, referring to my ears.

He gets this confused and slightly insulted look on his face then pulls out of me and turns me so I'm facing him all the way. We're almost nose to nose we are cuddled up so close. His gaze shifts to my ears and he traces them with a finger, then looks back at me in the eye.

"Don't ever talk about yourself that way. I can only assume you learned that from that disgusting piece of trash, whom I need a name, but you need to know how wrong you are. I—I love everything about you, Sol. Always have since that day I looked into your pretty, blue eyes. Your spunk and fierceness. Your recklessness. Your wildness in the outdoors. Your compassion for others, being around you makes me act like I'm a better person. You give me hope that this kingdom could have a future someday, free of suppression, based on compassion. Your ears are different, yes, but they are exotic and beautiful in a way that only adds to your allure."

I can't help but tear up in a happy way and smile at him. He smiles back taking my hand and kisses the back of it. Then he gets up and grabs a wet cloth gently cleaning me between my legs. He walks to his kitchen and grabs some water bringing it to me.

I take a sip of the water while he says, "Now. Drink up because round two is about to begin." That characteristic devilish smirk of his makes an appearance while I look up into his eyes with surprise. "What? You thought I was done? Oh no, no, sunshine! You got into bed with a rebel and I'm going to show you all the ways we can be free," he says while crawling up the bed like a predator towards me. I can't help the smile that comes over me and the thought of how deliciously sore I'm going to be in the morning.

CHAPTER
Twenty-Two

SOLVEIG

I make it back to my room in the castle just before the sun rises into dawn. Yawning loudly, I decide to take a quick bath to ease some of the soreness between my legs.

I can't help the big girlish smile that overtakes my face at thinking about all the ways Vidarr showed me his prowess as a rebel leader in the bedroom. My face heats thinking about it and I quickly finish up the bath, getting into a sleeping gown. I'm hoping to get a few hours of sleep before I have lunch with some noblewomen set on discussing my upcoming marriage to Counselor Malphas. *As if that's going to happen!* I really need to come up with a plan for that one, but unfortunately it's lower on my list right now because it's my birthday and tomorrow I'm heading a mission to those work camps.

I must sleep for only a few hours before I hear someone opening my door. My hand instantly reaches for a dagger I keep under my pillow while I pretend to still be sleeping. I slowly release my hold on the dagger when I hear Marion's humming and her rustling around in the room.

She walks over and sits on the bed then places a hand on my forehead saying, "Solveig, dear, are you feeling ill? You've never been a morning person, but you've slept in past breakfast, and I came up looking for you."

Clearing my throat since I definitely need some water after all the activities last night, I reply, "I'm fine, Marion. No need to fret. I feel fine. I couldn't sleep last night and was up late." I hate lying to her but I feel that even Marion would frown upon my involvement with the rebellion and sleeping with their leader. Not that she wouldn't support me but she wouldn't want me to place myself in any dangerous situations.

"Well then. Up with you, dear. You have a lunch with those noble ladies in just over an hour. I'll send up Isa to help you get ready. I need to set up for the lunch and make sure all the laundry gets done this morning," she says while scurrying over to the door and leaving without my response.

I slowly get out of bed with a stretch and go about my morning ablutions to get ready. No need to bathe since I did it when I got back earlier. I just leave the bathroom when Isa wanders in.

"Morning Prin—Solvieg! Here let's get this on you," she says with a hurry holding out a pale yellow dress with off the shoulder sleeves. "It's such a sunny day, this dress is perfect for your lunch. I believe the ladies are setting up outdoors in the garden."

Isa chatters on and updates me on any gossip around the castle. Once I'm done dressing, I mosey on down to the garden. Humming to myself in a good mood. *At least I get to be outside while I have to hear them complain about things.*

There's about six other women at the table setting with the head seat open for me. I step up and all the women stop conversation until I sit down. Then they greet me with fake expressions and offer their congratulations on my engagement. Remembering my mother's advice, I start to chant it in my head, *Grin and bear it but don't share it.* Keeping a cold blank princess expression on my face I ask them about their own relationships and we make it through lunch without me stabbing anyone. I did notice a few of the women glancing at my neck giggling then shifting their gazes away quickly. *Weird. Maybe I dropped a crumb?*

I go back to my room and look in the mirror seeing a noticeable marking above my collar bone, probably from Vidarr and his dangerous sexy mouth. *Oh shit!* Now those women must really think I'm a whore. No wonder they kept looking down and giggling like idiots. I find it hard to care though since I'm almost proud to have a mark from Vidarr on my skin. Smiling I change into more comfortable clothing donning a white tunic and soft maroon pants. I have some time before dinner tonight with my father so I head down to the library looking for Jorah.

He's right where he usually is, however, he seems to have fallen asleep with his face in a book. It's cute, I think, as a I chuckle to myself. I lean over and close a book loudly that was on the table startling him awake and shooting him upright in his chair. He has a few ink marks and impressions of the book on the side of his face making me chuckle again and reach over to wipe off a few. He rewards me with a blinding smile and then reaches out to hold my hand. "Morning—or should I say afternoon?" I ask.

"Yes, yes, afternoon, Solveig. I was up late studying a new scroll, then I found this other reference in a book which led to another book … and well you get the idea. Sorry. Happy birthday by the way!" Then he shifts around some of his papers and books on the table and pulls out a small package.

"For me?" I ask surprisingly pleased that he remembered my birthday then I open the package. Inside the package is a small older book no bigger than the size of my hand. Curiously I open the book and see that it contains pictures and notes about various plants.

"It's a small book I purchased from a scholar I met containing various plants and trees in the Elaritian Forest. It has notes about medicinal purposes for some of them and some more practical uses for the plants! I thought you would like it," he says excitedly than in a softer shy voice says, "I always think about you." He reaches with his hand and places it over mine which is on the small book.

I smile back at him and close the book. "Thanks, Jorah. It's amazing! I can't wait to bring it out in the forest and use it. What's this other book?" I ask curiously. It's another small hand sized book that looks slightly newer and when I open it all I see are blank pages.

"Well …" he says rubbing the back of his neck. "It's a small notebook for you to write in. I thought maybe you could write your own notes about the Elaritian Forest. Like notes about animals or the location of rivers or caves. There's so much we don't know anymore about the forest … I know it may be stupid …"

"No! I love it! It's so thoughtful, Jorah. I think it's good we will bring back awareness of Elarians. Thanks," I say before leaning forward over the table between us to give him a hug. He relaxes into the hug and turns his face into my hair taking a deep breath. When we pull apart, he looks at my neck near where the collar of my shirt has pulled away. He brushes a hand over my neck and has a hurt and intense look in his eyes confusing me. Suddenly, I remember the mark from my late-night activities with Vidarr and try to pull my shirt back over it flushing with embarrassment.

"Maybe some time I can go with you into the forest? Spend more time with you? I've been training some with my father and won't be totally useless anymore like I was as a boy. You might be surprised! I'm not too bad with a sword and can move more stealthily."

"I'll look forward to it. Unfortunately, I have to make it through dinner tonight though." I say rolling my eyes and taking a deep breath. "For now, show me what you've learned. I need to know about those work camps and their locations better."

We spend the next few hours poring over everything he's learned. I have a good idea on the route we will take tomorrow and more knowledge on the forest since we started. But I feel like we are lacking so much knowledge about Elarians and their genocide. If only there was more history in these books, but it seems it was all hidden or destroyed. Let's just hope I'm prepared enough for tomorrow. I have a bad feeling that no matter what I do, I'll never be ready. Unfortunately, we can't go back in time and change the past. But we can start tomorrow on changing the future.

CHAPTER
Twenty-Three

SOLVEIG

I spend some time sharpening my katanas and daggers, then cleaning all my weapons, so that I am ready for tomorrow. There's no room for mistakes tomorrow. I will succeed. *What if my real father is in that camp tomorrow? What if he's not actually dead?* I think to myself.

A knock on my door makes me pause in my thoughts and I call to whoever to enter. Isa sticks her head in the room and then seeing me with my large katanas out pales slightly. She closes the door and shifts a little asking, "Can I assist you in getting ready for dinner Princess Solveig?"

"Isa! I told you to call me Sol in private." I finish wiping down my blades and then gently place them back in my trunk at the end of my bed. "Alright let's get this over with." I then walk towards the bathing room.

We run through a quick routine of getting ready. She leaves most of my hair down and curled with a few strands tied back. Then, she pulls out a silky pale pink dress if you could call it that. There's hardly any material!

"I'm guessing Counselor Malphas sent this?" I ask Isa with an irritated look. She fidgets in place and nods her head. She seems more nervous than usual tonight. "Are you okay?"

"I'm fine, Prin— Sol. It's just I was strongly encouraged to prepare you properly for your dinner tonight. Counselor Malphas spoke with me at length." She looks at me and starts to rub her arms. "I'm sorry, Sol. That man … he feels wrong. The way he looked at me … sorry. Let's just get you ready." She then shakes her head and holds the dress out.

The dress is short coming only to mid thighs and luckily doesn't have a slit at the hips. It is a very thin silky material and plunges into a deep V nearly to my navel with straps getting thinner at my shoulder than criss-crossing over my open back. The straps look like pale pink rope twined with gold. It would be a very beautiful and sensual dress if I were wearing it for someone I wanted looking at my body. But not *him*. Unfortunately, the rune at my wrist and on my back are exposed. So I make sure my hair lays over my back and I have to think about what to cover my wrist with. *There!* I see a small pale pink ribbon that matches the dress on the table which was going to be tied into my hair. I grab it hastily and wrap it around my right wrist like a bracelet covering the rune. *Good enough.*

"I'm sorry you had to interact with Counselor Malphas. Stay away from him if you can. He's like that guard, Buck, just worse," I say to Isa with a serious look to impart my sincerity. She swallows and nods. Then grabbing a small box off the table opens it revealing more jewelry like last time. I roll my eyes at the display of wealth Malphas likes to show off.

The necklace is delicate looking with a thin gold chain and a few clear stones dangling that resemble diamonds if it weren't for the subtle tinge of green to them. I squint at the stones feeling like I've seen them before but unable to think of what type of gem they are. The largest stone sits in the center of my chest between my breasts. When she places it on my chest and latches it, I immediately get a burning pain where the necklace sits. It's mild enough to manage but it is painful and uncomfortable. I lift the necklace and look in the mirror. There's a small red mark where the largest stone was sitting but it's subtle. *Hmm, weird?*

She then places a bracelet on my right wrist over the wrapped ribbon which she looks at questioningly. The bracelet has several of the same stones on it but it's not painful. Maybe because of the ribbon underneath at my wrist?

"I don't know about this necklace," I say to Isa. "It feels uncomfort-able, maybe my skin reacts badly to it. Can't we choose another?" While

I'm talking, I get this overwhelming fatigue and feel like I'd rather just curl in front of the fire rather than go to a tedious dinner with my father.

"Counselor Malphas strongly said that you must wear this jewelry, that it's important to him. Maybe it's some sort of heirloom? Or gift?" She says nervously again. "He told me there would be a punishment to me if his instructions weren't followed correctly."

Nodding my head, I reach out and pat her shoulder. "It's okay Isa. I can deal with it. It's just a necklace." Then turning towards the door, I stumble a bit due to an abrupt weakness in my legs. I tell her thank you while fiddling with the necklace the whole way down the hall.

I enter the formal dining room and notice a large crowd of nobles starting to take their seats. I walk over to my usual place to the left of my father, but the steward intercepts me and whispers, "I'm sorry, Princess Solveig, but I was instructed that you no longer sit here. Your father the King wants you sitting with your future husband Counselor Malphas." He waves a hand toward the seat I was forced to sit in last dinner. The nice elderly steward gives me a pitying look before hurrying along to his other duties.

I meander over to my new position and think to myself, *this is your future now: some revolting older man's wife. Silent and pretty.*

Malphas walks in and runs a hand over my bare shoulder pushing some of my hair that I try to keep in place to cover my rune. He bends at the waist and kisses the back of my left hand and says formally, "Good evening, Princess Solveig, my dear betrothed, oh—and happiest of birthdays to you." Several nobles around us smile and sigh like he's sweet on me and not a monster. Then he says, "I hope you like the present I gave you to wear." He indicates the necklace and bracelet.

Before I can reply that he can take his dirty hand off me, my father King Batair walks in. He stumbles to his chair reeking of alcohol. His face is flushed red and he chuckles at something to himself then nods to the nobles before sitting. Everyone starts up conversation and sits. The servers start to pour drinks and bring out the first course.

King Batair then turns his cruel eyes on me with anger and says, "Solveig, *daughter*, I believe it is your birthday today? Well, I think now that you are nineteen you need to be more conscious of acting like a lady in public," he chuckles to himself and sips his wine, "but you can be a whore in the bedroom for your future husband as is appropriate. Malphas wants some alone time with you after dinner and you will acquiesce to this, being that he is marrying you in less than a month. I heard from some of my guards last week that you have been dalliancing in the barracks and training yard acting like a soldier and waving a sword around like you know how to use it." He snorts and then angrily says, "This behavior stops immediately, you are marrying one of the most important people in our kingdom and you will act as a lady. I informed Captain Mavin of my order and told him how disgusted I am that he allowed a woman to run around pretending to fight. He was punished as appropriate and is off duty tonight."

Fuck! Who told my father about my sparring? I've hurt one of the only people who helped me as a child. He'll probably never want to train with me again. I'm rapidly panting with anxiety and worry. Also, this stupid necklace is burning like hell! *What did my father mean I have to be alone with Malphas after dinner?!* My thoughts are spiraling, and I know I'm having a panic attack. Trying to keep my expressionless princess mask in place, I can barely hear Malphas talking.

"Don't worry your majesty. I will talk with Solveig and ensure she knows her place. She is growing into a beautiful woman regardless of her … small deformities. I'm glad you punished the Captain. Things have been getting rather lax in the guard and the army lately. We need to en-force rules more stringently. Perhaps it's time to put some new faces in charge of the guard." Then Malphas turns to me and runs a hand under the necklace, looking at my chest and then down to my nipples which are easily seen through the thin material. "I love this necklace on you, Solveig. It turns your skin a beautiful pink like your dress. I may decide to buy all your future jewelry with similar gems."

My anxiety still has a hold of me and as I start to focus on his words I wonder why he's so fixated on the jewelry. I feel my energy draining and suddenly can barely keep my head up I'm so tired. Maybe coming out of my panic attack is making me so tired? I turn my head to him and whisper, "Get your sick disgusting fucking hands off me. There will be no future with us. I'll make sure of it." Then I say louder for the nobles near us, "And I'm rather tired. I think I will seek my bed after dinner. I apologize."

Malphas looks down on me with anger that he quickly converts into a fake conniving smile for the surrounding nobles. He says, "No my dearest. You can't go to bed so early on your birthday! I need to get a birthday kiss from you! Everyone expects it!"

Everyone starts to clap and cheer at his words. Some even calling out to kiss! I see several noble ladies with the hands fluttering over the heart like it's some romance novel they are reading. *Honestly? Stupid fucking idiots!*

Then I cringe and try to withdraw when he grabs my face in both hands. I glance over Malphas's shoulder to see my father glaring daggers at me and an eyebrow raised. Realizing the horrible situation Malphas's put me in and the threatening gaze of the king, I sit still like a good princess.

Be calm and know yourself. I repeat in my head as a distraction from the humiliation that's occurring in front of everyone at dinner.

Malphas' cold wet lips meet mine in hard kiss making me swallow my revulsion while several nobles call out leers and cheer. He reaches with a hand down to my waist and using a bruising grip pulls me closer causing me to gasp in pain. He takes advantage of this by shoving his tongue down my throat and gripping the back of my neck to hold me still as I struggle to push back against him.

After several agonizing seconds, he withdraws and smiles down at me. Then nods his heads at the cheering noblemen nearest to us like he just won a battle and didn't just force a kiss on a woman.

I'm left gasping for air and feeling vulnerable with a tinge of worry. I need to get my mask back on my emotions, so I take a deep breath and center myself. Once I feel more myself, I say to King Batair, "Now that dinner is over, Father, I'd like to excuse myself back to my room since I'm feeling rather fatigued."

"You may be excused—" he says and I let out a sigh of relief starting to stand up quickly.

But then Counselor Malphas starts to stand and interrupts. "She wishes to rush off to be alone me with your majesty," he says laughing and with a leering expression. "My betrothed can't wait to spend time with me and I need to give her my other birthday present. If I may sire?"

My stomach drops when the king agrees and waves a hand at us spilling his wine over the table. I can tell he's drunk again and hardly aware of what's going on at this point. *Useless, that's what he is.*

Counselor Malphas grabs my arm and links it with his. I have to allow this for appearances as everyone is watching us with smiles. As soon as we walk out of the dining room, I pull my arm from him and he turns back-handing me.

"Enough! Stop your childish temper tantrums and act your age now, Solveig! You are nineteen and a woman. You will do your duty to me. I could tell you enjoy my attention and the kiss we shared. You don't have to fight your attraction to me anymore, Solveig, now that we are betrothed," he condescendingly says to me while I lean against the hallway wall and place a hand on my sore cheek. My other hand rubs my chest in an attempted to relieve some discomfort. *Fuck this necklace! It burns!*

I see some of the guards near the door to the dining room looking at each other then at me. One starts to step towards me, but I subtly shake my head and he gives me a sad pitying look stopping where he is. I recognize him, he's kind, a friend of Camaeron's whom I've had an ale or two with in the past.

Counselor Malphas notices my attention and shouts to the guard to attend his station. He then grabs my arm and starts to pull me gently down the hall. He signals to some other guards, that I don't know, to follow us as an escort. I think he's taking me back to my room when I see him turn directions and I cringe. I know this hallway, too well, unfortunately. It leads to the stairs going down to the dungeon. Two bulky guards trail behind us menacingly.

"I thought you were giving me a present? Not giving me a punishment! I sat still for your disgusting kiss. I haven't done anything wrong you pig!" I say to him trying to pull my arm.

We make it down the stairs and he pushes me into a familiar cold stone room in the dungeon. I see the guards standing at attention outside the door and one leers at me over his shoulder before the door shuts. The lock snicks with the door shutting and Malphas turns towards me.

"I do have another present for you, princess. I've been wanting to give it to you for a long time. Honestly ever since I met you. But you were hardly ready for it. Sometimes, princess, the best presents are in the form of a punishment. Now let's see what you learn." He smiles cruelly at me and walks towards me.

I instantly panic and pull a small dagger from a thigh sheath I keep on my right thigh which somehow he anticipates and grabbing my hand bends it backwards before I can stab him. I hear the snap of my bones in my wrist but he doesn't let go and keeps folding my hand back towards my forearm making me scream in pain and drop the dagger from a useless limp hand. I reach with my good hand for a sharp hair pin that can work like a tiny dagger and swiftly bring it across his face scratching his cheek and drawing blood before I swing it to stab his hand that's holding my dislocated and broken wrist.

He roars in pain and slams my head back against the stone wall with a thunk. Feeling dazed for a moment, I try to shake off my blurred vision and continue to push against him but I feel excessively weak. I'm extremely tired for some reason. He grabs me easily now and I can't clear the fog from my head quickly like I usually can. My healing should already be clearing the head injury and my wrist some but it's almost like it's delayed.

Malphas drags me over to the table he loves to punish me on and I whimper unconsciously. *Stop it Solveig! Be calm! Don't show any weakness!* I try to mentally prepare myself and stop the rising panic. Memories of being tortured and touched on this table play through my mind on an endless reel and I struggle to center myself. I can tell I'm shaking all over either from shock or panic or both.

He locks me to the table on my back with iron cuffs, then walks around and fits that stupid iron neck collar tightly around my neck cutting off some of my air.

"There we go. That should help stop that dirty mouth and make you more compliant," he says when he finishes putting the collar on me and patting my head like an unruly child. Then he runs his hand under the necklace on my chest that is still burning my skin and says, "I'm surprised you didn't recognize the gems on this jewelry you're wearing. That was part of my present to you … its avralite. You're not nearly as smart as you act, dear. Avralite is the gem that I found from Beamus if you recall. It seems to be the only harmful substance which can scar your beautiful skin and slow your special healing powers. You may find that since you've been wearing that jewelry all night, you might feel slightly … drained?"

Understanding dawns on me and I do, truly, feel stupid at his words. How did I not recognize the avralite. It was in that dagger he used on me before. I whisper to him, "You're sick."

"Now, let's see if those beautiful scars and my markings are still on your abdomen and hip where I left them," he says then pushes the short silky material of my dress up over my thighs and hips revealing the puckered pale scar on my right hip and the now healed puncture wound on my mid abdomen just right of midline. The scars are pale and slightly pink compared to my golden skin. They're still tender sometimes if tweaked the wrong way as if they didn't heal fully like my other wounds.

He gasps in outrage and confusion when he sees the rune on my right thigh. Then running his hand over my upper thigh asks, "When did you do this? This- this travesty! You look like a common street whore with tattoos on your perfect skin." Then he stares at it a bit in confusion. Abruptly he reaches up and rips off the rest of my dress and underwear fully exposing me to his perusal then asks, "Do you have any more? Where are they?" He looks angry and dare I say slightly panicked.

"Fuck you—you cock-sucking son of a pig!" I shout as loud as I can with this contraption on my neck. Drool starts to come out the corner of my mouth since I can't even fully swallow with it on.

He slaps me across the face and then notices the bracelet and beneath it the ribbon around my wrist. He rips the ribbon off revealing another of my runes and his eyes comically get wider. "It can't be ..." he says to himself. "I knew you were of mixed blood with your ears, but—this means you are more than half Elarian." Then he mutters, "We will have to hide these somehow. Suppress them."

He reaches out and runs his hands almost tenderly over my abdomen then up to my chest over the necklace and says, "You must wear this necklace at all times. It will help suppress any *urges* and special healing that you possess. It will help keep you *normal* which you must be as my future wife." He then grabs my breasts roughly while I tuck myself into the back of my consciousness and ride out the punishment like I usually do to protect myself. I think of Vidarr and how dominant but sweet he was with me for my first time. Then I think of Jorah my adorable book worm with his caring hands as he bathed me. Lastly, I strangely think of Cadoc with his powerful presence and protective but sweet attitude. Thinking of them helps

192

distract me fully. My wrist is still dislocated and throbbing in pain, my chest is burning and I have a headache but overall I'm ok. Just weak and tired. I can do this … I think.

The protective bubble in my mind is completely shattered when I feel Malphas climb on the table between my legs and notice he's naked. "Time for your other present, princess."

CHAPTER
Twenty-Four

CADOC

Fucking idiot! I think to myself.

I'm pacing my chamber with Eirik sitting with his arms resting over his knees watching me. I feel angry, restless and useless.

I finally met with King Batair yesterday and it went horribly. I knew he must be an utter asshole since he hit his only daughter in public but I didn't know he was a complete drunk. The only thing he was interested in at our meeting was obtaining more Gorvian wine! *Fucking idiot!*

He lets his people starve in the streets while he overindulges in expensive wine and liquor. And yes, I noticed the state of his people in the city and countryside as we traveled through Laevaris on our way here. Let's just say I was embarrassed and disgusted for him.

Eirik and I are trying to plan our next step and form this idiotic alliance which I am doubting will occur as the days pass. Each day brings to light more issues that the kingdom of Laevaris has. Who wants an alliance with a kingdom that can't even take care of its own people? Or simply doesn't care for its people?

I'm talking with King Batair that I would be willing to marry Solveig and form a strong alliance through marriage between the kingdoms of Gorva and Laevaris. I list all the reasons this is beneficial to him in a logical manner including our large and well-trained army, well-bred and battle trained horses, as well as several other reasons. He blankly stares back at me with a bored expression and belches noisily. It's difficult to keep the look of disgust off my face but I think I manage to accomplish it.

The disgusting man then asks about our Gorvian wine. I look over at Eirik with a concerned look who simply shrugs then returns to guarding me. I then try to promote our wine based on his interest and also our fish which we specialize in, which leads into the discussion of trade that will occur easily with this alliance.

King Batair then looks over at me with an amused expression. "My daughter Solveig is already betrothed to my well trusted Counselor Malphas. I'm sorry but I will have to decline a marriage alliance unless it's through a noble cousin related to the throne. You wouldn't want my daughter anyways, she's wild and unruly. Although she seems rather pretty from a distance, she is actually deformed from her distant mixed heritage on her mother's side." He says this with disgust and a tapping of his ears in reference. "The only person who can handle that girl is her current betrothed, he has been grooming and working on taming that girl for years and he is due his reward. I will not go back on my word to him."

"I see," I say seething in suppressed anger at his dismissal of my request and of his insult to his only daughter. "There must be some way we can reason with your Counselor to see the benefits of such an alliance. Perhaps he may wish to marry this noble cousin of yours and free himself from such an unruly betrothed? In my kingdom, the princess would settle in nicely and I feel we would make a good match," I attempt to reason with him and keep my temper at his slander against his only daughter, but it's hard.

"No, this is final. She will marry my counselor. Now … let us talk of trade and I will think about an alliance in the future. How many men did you say you have under your command?" King Batair asks looking at me shrewdly.

I shake off my memory of the meeting that didn't go well at all and think about what a disappointment I will be to my parents. No. I shouldn't think that. There are factors outside of my control here so I need to bide my time and find out more information before committing to any plan.

"What are you thinking, Cad?" asks Eirik while I pace.

"I think we need more information and to bide our time." I say my thoughts out loud to him.

"The King is a drunk and an ass. We would be better to stay away from him. Screw an alliance with him, I wouldn't trust the man with my horse! Where do you think we can get more information?" Eirik says with a raised eyebrow.

"Well we could always go back into the capital city. Also I'd like to talk more with Solveig. She doesn't seem to be happy with the betrothal and I'd like her thoughts on it. Perhaps she may be interested in asking her father to cancel it?" I say then shake my head. "Unlikely, but either way I want to see her again. There's something about her …"

"Other than the fact she's *stop you in your tracks and blind you* with her beauty? Or the fact that she's kind and intelligent? Or that she can probably kick my ass sparring or at least come close?" he says dreamily then leans back and runs his hand through his hair and making me look closer at him. I then realize Eirik may have a bit of an infatuation with the princess as well. "Honestly, Cad, she's one in a million. We don't have women like that back at home."

"I know Eirik! Goodness Valirr! I know!" I say swearing to the father of all gods and groaning. "She's an exotic beauty and different in a way that I can't get my mind off of. She consumes my thoughts, and I've only just met her." Then adjusting my pants which are slowly getting tighter in the groin thinking about Solveig, I say, "Come on let's go find her."

SOLVEIG

I WAKE UP TO SOFT HANDS SMOOTHING THE HAIR BACK FROM MY FACE AND someone whispering soothing words to me.

I slowly open my eyes and squint at the small amount of light from the lantern set next to me before looking into the eyes of my frequent healer (and good friend), Liv.

Then blinking rapidly, I try to focus through the fog in my head. I slowly start to piece together my memories. My eyes quickly tear up as I recall what exactly happened in that room for the first time.

Eventually, I'm able to focus in on Liv and what she's saying.

"Can you hear me, Sol? I'm so sorry! What did he do this time? Where are you hurt? They've never brought me down here before! Why are you naked?" She is asking rapidly with a shaky voice and tears running down her face.

I look around the cell and can see her supplies laid out around me and a blanket is quickly thrown over my naked body. I'm curled up on my side on the cold stone floor. Then looking past Liv, I flinch when I see a man standing in the open doorway of the cell, but I relax once I realize its only Healer Thaemon.

I flush with embarrassment at him and Liv seeing me this way. Then I start to cry unintentionally for one of the only times since I was thirteen when I realize what they must see. A dirty used up whore of a princess. I try to reach up and cover my face but realize my right hand is limp and still bent strangely. I then take stock of my body and feel all my injuries at once including a searing burning pain on my chest still.

Liv continues to try and soothe me rubbing my shoulder she asks, "Do you want Healer Thaemon to—to stay where he is?" I nod my head through my tears and she says, "Okay he's just here if I need his guidance but will stay back. Where does it hurt, Sol?"

"My wrist …" I start to say showing her then continue. "My face, my left ribs, my stomach, right thigh, and—and … down there," I stutter out at last. She gulps anxiously then flushes with anger at my last words.

"Let me see. Best to start with the worst, Sol," she says looking me in the eyes. Holding my cheeks in her hands she quietly asks, "Did he rape you?" She was always direct but that must be because of her healing training. Healers tend to be very clinical when they are focused. I nod my head and look away not wanting to vocalize everything that happened. Some of which I can't even remember since I lost consciousness at one point.

"Alright, I'm going to do an exam and Healer Thaemon will turn around but I may need to at least talk with him," she says then does a quick exam. I'm sore and bleeding down there but she says I should heal quickly. It reminds me that I'm still wearing that fucking necklace and bracelet.

I start to irrationally claw and scratch at my chest causing more injuries. I can't get the necklace off and then I start on my bracelet but it's stuck as my wrist is so swollen and deformed. Liv tries to calm me down and grabbing my wrists to hold me still says, "Stop! Just stop, Sol! What's wrong?"

"The necklace … get it off me! Get it off! It hurts and it stops me from healing fully. Makes me weak," I yell while crying and panting with breaths in a full-blown panic attack.

"Okay, I got this. There must be a clasp." She reaches around and then mutters angrily about useless jewelry as she struggles to get it off. She reaches into her bag and pulls out a scalpel putting the end into the latch and finally freeing it from me. I release a sigh of relief and start to calm some. She then tries to get the bracelet off me, but it won't budge and it won't pull apart with force. "Let's try to get this off later after I splint your wrist and get proper tools."

She then tends to my other injuries stitching up some superficial lacerations to my abdomen from a knife, wrapping my ribs and making a temporary splint for my wrist. She covers me again with the blanket and Healer Thaemon cautiously approaches me kneeling down.

"Princess Solveig. I feel the need as your healer to address an uncomfortable issue here. I heard you had relations with a man without consent." He swallows and awkwardly asks, "Are you on a form of contraception?" I pale at his concern and then shake my head no. "Don't worry dear." He pats my hand comfortingly. "We just mix up a stronger dose to prevent pregnancy this time and then continue it at a lower dose. Liv here knows how to make the mixture for the future and I brought the first dose myself. But … I should tell you that Counselor Malphas is your betrothed and ordered me not to provide you with contraception." He swallows roughly again. "However, I am an honorable man and I took an oath to care for my patients, therefore you have a choice. That man has no say over the treatments of my patients in my mind especially knowing what he did to you and has in the past. I just want to stress that you need to keep this hidden and confidential between us. Okay?"

I can't help but cry again as I sit up and hug the elderly man gently. Liv hands me the mixture which I slowly swallow. It has a floral taste to it but isn't too unpleasant. It's difficult to swallow since my neck is sore still from that neck cuff but I manage to finish it and say, "Thank you both. I'm sorry you had to witness this. You've done so much for me. You have my word no one will ever know."

They help me get up and put a clean sleeping gown over me before walking me upstairs to my room where Liv helps me bathe and get into bed. We managed to get the bracelet off by calling up Sigurd from the stables with a blacksmith tool to clamp the metal and break it. He was concerned but didn't hover or ask questions. I already start to feel myself healing with that wicked avralite removed from my body. Just before I pass out from exhaustion and slipping into a healing sleep, I ask Liv, "What day and time is it?"

"It's only the day after your birthday Sol, about noon. I'll have the girls send up something to eat that's light. Call me if you need anything and I'll send up that mixture every day in the morning, I'll tell Marion it's for a stomach condition or something and that you must take it. Sleep well."

"Thank you, Liv," I say as she closes the door. *Thank goodness I still have time. Just a few hours of sleep and I should be good.*

SOLVEIG

I wake up to someone rustling beside me in my bed and reach for my dagger under my pillow.

Thrusting the dagger towards whoever is trying to attack me in my sleep, I feel it just touch skin and hold it there before opening my eyes. I blink to clear the fog from sleep and realize I'm holding a dagger to Jorah's neck who is sitting rather still with wide eyes looking at me.

"Sorry, Jorah. What are you doing here? In my bed?" I ask while putting the dagger away and rolling towards him in the bed with an elbow holding me up.

"Goodness, Sol!" he says while wiping away a few drops of blood on his neck. Then he gets a sad almost tearful look in his eyes and asks, "Are you okay? My father told me you were injured in bed and you looked … well, not yourself. He used the word 'vulnerable' which freaked me out knowing you. He said you were crying—you never cry, Sol …"

He then runs a hand through his messy blonde hair and pins me with those emerald eyes of his, saying, "When I came in you were yelling out and screaming. I think you were having a nightmare, so I started to read to you which helped calm you down." He says this waving a hand at the discarded book on his lap. That's when I notice he's shirtless and all his golden skin and muscles are on display for my hungry eyes. I run my eyes over his chest and the scar that I know so well. I must've not been very subtle in my ogling his muscles because when I look up again, he has this self-satisfied smirk and reaches towards me to push some hair behind my ear.

"Thanks. About the reading part and helping me with my nightmare," I say blowing out a rough breath and sobering at recalling everything that happened in the past night. "I'll be fine. I'm already pretty much healed. See?" Showing him my splinted wrist, I notice it feels pretty much normal now. I attempt to smile at him in reassurance but it feels forced.

He looks at me as if he can see right through my mask and fake smile. Then he asks, "It was him, wasn't it? He did something to you... I've never seen him upset you like this except for that last time in the hallway."

"It doesn't matter. It's over. Father told him that he could have alone time with me since we are betrothed and it was my birthday," I tell him with my lip trembling. "I—I'm revolting. Dirty. I don't even think I can look at myself in the mirror. He did this—made me feel this way. And I hate him. If he marries me, Jorah ..." I say with a sob and struggle to look up at him.

If looks could murder someone, then Jorah has that look perfected right now. I've never seen him so angry. He suddenly rips the book in his lap apart in one impressive move then throws it across the room and rolls out of the bed. In shock I can't help but watch. Jorah—Jorah just tore a book! Wow! That man honors all literature and writing so to see him ruin a perfectly good book has me nervous.

He paces the room a bit while I watch. Then I see his shoulders lower a bit and walk back to the bed where I'm sitting up now. The sheet falls to my waist, and I realize I'm in nothing but a thin, white, nearly-sheer sleeping gown. My disheveled hair falls down around my face and shoulders.

Jorah kneels on the bed in front of me and taking my face in his hands leans forward slowly giving me plenty of time to pull away if I wished. Then he softly kisses me on the lips in a chaste sweet kiss that only lasts a second. He pulls back and leans his forehead against mine saying, "Listen, Sol. None of this is your fault. *None!* That man has a sick twisted mind and has been messing with your head and your body for far too long. I won't allow him to marry you. We will find a way … I'm so sorry, Sol." He whispers at the end and pulls back with tears in his eyes.

"Sometimes, my Sol, compassion is born in the darkest places of despair. You can only get stronger from here if you're willing to rise up from his darkness. You're my sun, my Sol, and I hate to see you so dark. I need to see you shining again," he says then kisses me gently again, only this time I open for him and our kiss turns more heated.

I wrap my arms around his neck and lean into the kiss pressing my chest against his. I can't believe this is happening! He kisses me back with a passion that I've never felt in him. Our tongues tangle and his sucks gently on mine making me moan again. He tastes like sweet berries and mint. I feel his hands side down from my back to my ass where he grabs both cheeks and softly squeezes. He continues to kiss me into a fervor. My tears and sadness long forgotten now as I give into him, my best friend.

He lays me back on the bed while continuing to kiss me. His hands come around from my ass and rest on my waist as he pulls back from our kiss looking down on me from above. His gaze is full of desire and heat making my core tighten. He looks down at my chest which reveals one breast nearly exposed through the loose collar of the gown and my nipples start to harden and poke through the thin material of the gown. He slowly runs his hands up to my breasts while looking me in the eye again for consent. His hands close over my breasts and he groans while cupping their fullness. I can't help but arch my back and close my eyes while he touches me.

I'm not sure how much physical experience Jorah has with women since he's never told me but I would guess it wasn't much. He tends to be more of an introvert and prefers the company of books than people. Right now though, he seems so entranced by me with his focused gaze on my nipples while he touches them and observes my responses like he's memorizing a book. He then pulls my sleeping gown down exposing my breasts to his vision and he leans forward to take one in his mouth. He sucks on my breast and licks it until I'm a panting mess then he moves up and kisses me with an ardor.

He starts to thrust his hips directly into my center and I can feel just how hard he is through his pants. I moan and arch my back further so he starts to reach down towards my core, cupping me there and realizing I have no underwear on. Fascinated, he leans back, gently pushes my gown up and looks at my slit. He runs his finger over it and then stops at my clit moving in a slow circle while gazing at me for my reaction. I can't help but thrust my hips up toward his hand and bite my lip however as soon as he starts to run a finger into my wet opening I tense up.

He notices immediately and withdraws the hand seeing my suddenly stiff posture. He sits back on his heels and runs a hand over his eyes nervously.

"Shit! I'm so sorry, Sol!" He's looking down at the bed angrily with his hands fisting at his sides. "I'm such an idiot! I don't know what I was thinking but you make me lose my mind with desire. Here you are telling me that man touched you without consent and I'm—I'm taking advantage of you in your vulnerable state! Fuck!" he shouts and jumps up from the bed.

I slowly sit up and pull my sleeping gown back in place. Looking down at the bed I say embarrassingly, "Stop, Jorah. It's not that—you did nothing wrong. You didn't do anything I didn't want you to do, trust me. It's just—I'm—sore … down there still. I'm sorry I stiffened up like that."

He practically runs back over to me and hugs me. "Damn, Sol! Still, I'm sorry. It was wrong of me. I just can't help myself around you now, knowing you're attracted to me. I've always wanted you. Maybe, you should soak in some warm water to help with the—the soreness," he stutters out. "I'd best get out of here before someone sees me. Let me know if you need me. I'm going to think of a solution for this betrothal you have, promise!" Then with a quick kiss to my forehead he slips out the door leaving me alone.

I get up and look out the window noticing the time. It's around dinner and I see some food already laid out on a table by the fireplace. I sit down and eat lightly. My appetite is a bit low and overall I feel better physically. It's mentally that I'm a mess. I can't believe I got into an impromptu make out session with Jorah! I need to sort myself out. I mean, I already had sex with Vidarr, so does that mean I'm in a relationship with him? Ugh. Then there's the matter of—last night.

My eyes tear up quickly and I try to suppress my emotions but memories of last night keep flashing through my mind making me feel dirty again. Maybe I am a whore as Malphas likes to call me. *No!* None of that was my doing! I push thoughts of men from my mind and clean myself up in the bathroom.

CHAPTER
Twenty-Six

SOLVEIG

I quickly dress and after some time make myself more presentable. Then putting my weapons in place on my body, I sneak out through a servant entrance. Running to the stables, I let Sin out of his stall. Luckily, I see no one as they are probably eating dinner still or nearly finished.

You seem different today, Sol, Sindari projects into my mind.

I am different. I'm trying to rise—rise up from my past. And today will be the start of it. Will you help me, friend? I ask him thinking about what Jorah said to me. Sindari responds back, *Yes! We will live in today as horses tend to do. Accept the past and run free.*

We ride through the city gates and towards a house near the Broken Forest; the house belongs to a longtime friend of Vidarr's and is our meeting place for our trip. He told me that the woman who lives there was best friends with his parents before they died and she gave him a roof over his head when his sister and him were homeless on the streets.

I get to the house quickly. There's about an hour before sunset and I see nearly everyone's here already. Supposedly, Sandy, the owner of the house is a big Rebellion supporter. Her house made the perfect location to meet up since it was near the southern edge of the Broken Forest.

Dismounting from Sindari, I pat him on the neck and let him know I'll call him when we are ready to leave. Not seeing anyone outside the house I make my way inside. There's a large group gathered around the kitchen table drinking karaf to help keep everyone sharp and awake. I count five men and one woman, Kira, in the kitchen and Sandy standing filling mugs. Walking over to her, I give her a big hug which she returns and smiles at me.

"Well met, Sandy. It's been too long since I had your karaf and pastries. I need to come more often for a visit!"

"Sol! I missed ya, girl! You don't look well. Too pale. Are you not getting enough sleep, dear? Let me get you a mug of karaf before you all are on your way," she says then hustles back for a fresh mug in the kitchen.

I look around for Vidarr and just as Sandy hands me a steaming mug, I see him walk in the back door. He stops in the dining room and looks at me in a concerned way. Ignoring his strange behavior, I walk over and greet the rest of our group for this journey. Vidarr eventually walks over and puts a hand around my waist squeezing me gently in greeting.

He leans over and whispers in my ear, "What happened, sunshine? Don't lie to me. You're lacking your usual glow and confidence."

Trying to put on a confident smile which he knows is false I say, "Let's not worry about it right now. We have bigger issues. I'm healing and will be fine." Then I look up at him shyly saying, "I missed you."

He huffs a breath of annoyance out and then leans in kissing me softly on the lips. "Missed you too, sunshine," he says, then like the child he is he reaches behind me and tugs on my braid making me softly growl at him. Darritt and several other guys chuckle at our antics before Vi clears his throat.

"Alright, let's go over the plan and review the map," Vidarr says while unrolling the map we have on the table (the one I stole from my father's office). He points at several locations. "Solveig will lead us through the Elaritian or Broken Forest as we know. I'm guessing we will meet up with your Elarian contact somewhere?" I nod in response to him and cross my arms. "Okay, they can update us on the location of the camp and then we will scout the area before deciding on a best course of action. Here is the suspected area of the camp near the base of this mountain. Any questions?" Everyone shakes their head no then he says, "Let's go then. Mount up people."

We all ride through the forest silently with me in the lead. About twenty minutes into our ride, I hear a *kek-kek kek-kek* to warn me of Tyr's arrival. He swoops down and lands on my shoulder then nuzzles his face into my neck. I reach up and scratch his underbelly feathers.

The Elder of the forest is up ahead awaiting your arrival. The sneaky one is trailing you to your left and the clingy one is just ahead in the branches to your right. They cannot hide from a goshawk like myself, Tyr projects proudly and a bit smugly.

I chuckle while petting his belly then respond, *Thank you, Tyr. You are truly skilled and will be a huge asset for this mission. You must miss your mate. I would like to meet her when we travel closer if she's able. Now, let's have some fun …*

I slow Sindari down to a trot and pull out a dagger in a flash of movement, throwing it to my left just at the height of where I would suspect a tall sneaky camouflaged male's head would be. Then I glance up and hear a subtle shift in the leaves in the canopy as the branches slightly part for me just ahead and to the right so I throw a second dagger swiftly in that direction.

The group I'm with immediately pull their swords and weapons thinking an attack if occurring when Zxian steps out of thin air holding the blade of my dagger between two fingers and grinning like a fool. Then Yaeril drops quietly from above directly in our path and flicks my other dagger up at me on Sindari which I easily catch and put away. Yaeril is shaking his head with a smile and walking towards me.

Vidarr gallops up from the back of our group on his grey gelding with his own short sword out and a threatening angry look on his face. He pulls in front of me and says, "What's this? Sunshine, I didn't see or hear anyone! What the fuck?"

"Calm down, Vi! These are the Elarians I told you about: Zxian, the sneaky one," I chuckle and then say, "and Yaeril, the clingy one!" Both Elarians look affronted at their nicknames and cross their arms over their big chests.

"How did you know where I was, Princess?" asks Zxian with a confused look and a head tilt.

"I mustn't give away my secrets, Zxian, or else I can never sneak up on you!" I smile at him which he returns. Then I turn to Yaeril and nod my head, "Well met, Yaeril." He places a hand over his heart and bows his head.

"Elder Aren is just ahead. Follow me," Yaeril says.

We all walk the horses forward less than half a mile and then see three horses and Elder Aren resting on a boulder. He smiles while I dismount and then hugs me saying, "Glad to see you again, Granddaughter. I was worried." Then his smile fades and he looks over my face intensely. "You seem drained and your energy isn't bright. What happened, child?" he asks me concerned which catches the attention of the other two Elarians who lean in and look me over more.

I look down at the ground and push dirt with the toe of my boot saying, "Can we just focus on the current mission. I'm healing and will be fine with more time. I had an encounter with a gem called Avralite, ever heard of it?" I ask then look up at his continued silence. All the Elarians are stiff and pale. Yaeril and Zxian glance at each other imparting silent words as if I'm missing something.

Vidarr walks up and puts a hand around my waist to listen which both Elarians notice flaring their nostrils in an annoyed way and makes Zxian growl softly.

"Oh no, no ... it can't have been found again," Elder Aren softly says, then he appears lost in thought. Taking a deep breath, he continues saying, "Avralite is supposed to have been hidden after our people fought a war many generations ago. It's the one thing in nature that is truly harmful to us and has the potential for killing us. Of course we can die from a mortal wound if not healed quickly or without nature to do so but we tend to live longer than normal life spans, dear. Avralite drains our energy and our life force away when in contact with us. It shortens our lifespan and can suppress our unique powers, such as you have in your runes. Our ancestors collected any known avralite and hid it away along the coast supposedly in a secluded location. I'm deeply concerned if this is making an appearance again." He then looks at me with a shrewd and dare I say an angry expression on his face. "I need to know who would *dare* harm my granddaughter with such! No wonder you look like you just survived a serious injury!

Avralite can stay in your system for a time depending on the amount of exposure you had to it. When was it last in contact with you?"

"Oh, um—perhaps ten hours ago. It was part of a necklace and bracelet that was forced upon me. I didn't know the crystals were avralite or what they could do to me. They did burn on contact with my skin and made me excessively tired," I say contemplating. "I am feeling better now and my energy is slowly improving."

Elder Aren looks like he's about to explode with anger. I've never seen him like this, although I haven't known him long. I don't think he's the type to anger easily. Zxian and Yaeril both look angry and are fidgeting with their weapons.

"You must be more careful, Solveig," Zxian says with a hand to my shoulder and looking me in the eye. "You tell me and Yaeril the name of the person who gave you these jewels yes? We will take care of him," he says with a glint of aggression and murderous intent in his eye while rubbing his thumb over the blade of an axe he carries.

Vidarr looks concerned and then asks Aren, "How do we restore her energy and power then? I'm Vidarr, the Rebellion leader and Solveig's … friend, by the way." He says this awkwardly holding his hand out to shake and looking at me out of the corner of his eye as if I will bolt away. Elder Aren just stares at his hand then places a fist over his heart as greeting.

"Well met … friend. In Elaria, we greet with a fist over our heart. And, as to Sol's energy, this will return with time and being out in nature under the sun. She needs to avoid any more exposure to the crystal."

"Why do you place your palm over your heart when you greet Solveig then?" Vidarr asks.

It's Yaeril who answers: "Because—Solveig is our heart and our hope for Elaria to be reborn. She is our queen." He smiles proudly at Vidarr who gapes in shock then looks to me with an eyebrow raised.

I pull my braid over my shoulder and play with it nervously. Then say, "Well, it's complicated, Vi. You see—" I look around at all the rebels paying attention to our discussion and say, "Let's talk about his later? Okay?"

"Yes, well we should get going. You have that map you told me about, Granddaughter?" Elder Aren asks.

Vidarr pulls the map out and lays it over the boulder Aren was sitting on before. Everyone crowds around and we go over the route to get there.

Aren points out the location of the work or should I say slave camp. It's at the base of one of the largest more eastward mountains at the edge of the Elarian Forest.

Elder Aren says, pointing at the map, "It's about a two-hour journey there. We should go quickly. Also be careful—the Catchki are out tonight. I heard them prowling before you came upon us."

"Wait, what's a catchki?" one of the rebels in the group asks.

My grandfather goes to answer, but Yaeril replies first with a thoughtful expression. He says, "Catchki's are large predator type cats who live in our forest and are very good climbers. I would know." He smirks at the pale rebel who asked. "They love to hide in the branches of the ancient oak trees and pines. Their only weakness when hunting their prey is that they have very poor vision so stay quiet or you'll be catchki dinner."

Several rebels with us look at each other nervously and then, seeing us mount our horses, quickly follow our lead.

CHAPTER
Twenty-Seven

SOLVEIG

O ur group of ten plus Elder Aren make good time and are half-way there when I hear a soft rasping sound.

Skkriiiipp. Skkkkrrriiip. The soft, but yet harsh, crackles sound through the silent forest.

I pull a halt to our horses with Elder Aren mounted beside me. We look at each other and he nods before dismounting. I look back towards the end of our group and nod to Zxian and Yaeril who begin dismounting.

Skkrrrrrriiip. The sound is closer and just ahead. Another one sounds to the right.

I dismount my own horse and motion to the rebels to dismount as well. Vidarr looks pale and dismounts as well. He's nervous since he knows what that sound means. The Catchki's are here and must have heard us.

I see a flash of stripes and a long lithe body move between the trees ahead. One of the rebels in our group unsheathes his long sword making an echoing loud, metallic noise through the forest. I quickly glance over my shoulder at him with a harsh glare but it's too late.

The Catchki female prowls forward confidently, I know it's a female because they tend to be larger than the males, more dominant. This one must be alpha given its approach for first kill. It has a large body with its head coming up to my chest and a long sleek body of intermixing stripes with brown, blue-grey and black. Its long razor sharpe teeth are exposed and it's making its signature rasping crackle sounds. Long talons protrude from its front paws.

I walk forward slowly sliding my feet in a soft sound to let it know of my approach. Stopping about seven feet away I project my thoughts towards her.

Forgive us for encroaching on your territory, alpha. I then lower my eyes and crouch down making the rebels gasp behind me. *We are traveling through on a dangerous journey to rescue some of my people.*

You are alpha? You smell and sound different than the others, she projects back into my mind with a raspy quality.

Yes. I am leader of the group through the forest with an elder of my people. My name is Solveig. I'm sorry, I am unsure why I smell or sound different.

You can communicate with us. You are more intelligent than other two-legged creatures and you smell pleasant like the warm sun on our backs while laying near a creek. Your sounds are quiet and fit with the forest. I like you, Solveig, leader to your people. I am Vabira. This man next to you is your elder? He smells like a relation to you and is pleasant.

She starts to walk forward confidently and then nudges her face into my stomach when I stand. The others back away behind me making nervous whispers. *Well met, Vabira,* I say to her before running a hesitant hand over her head. She makes a raspy sort of purr sound and leans into my touch so I continue to run my hand down her back. Two other catchki's approach from the sides walking up to me and watching Vabira intently.

"Everything okay here, sunshine?" I hear Vi whisper and shuffle his feet a bit closer. He has an unnatural fear of the Catchki every time we would travel through the forest. Granted, they are rather big cats with large teeth.

Vabira stops her purring and looks up at me with his words. *This one is your mate, no? He is attractive for a two-legged. He has nice stripes on his skin too,* she projects then walks closer to Vidarr who looks like he's about to wet his pants. She must be referring to his tattoos that I guess could look like stripes in a sense. At her approach, Vidarr looks up to me with wide eyes and for reassurance, so I smile at him and nod my head to the large catchki.

Mate? I ask Vabira not quite understanding.

Yes. I can smell him on you. You share energies too. I can tell you would make many cubs well together, she projects back to me, making me blush in embarrassment then she says, *those two are my mates- Tiguar and Euri. My third mate is guarding our cubs.* She says proudly looking at the two other catchki's that approached me and are sniffing my hands.

They are very strong and attractive. You must be proud and very busy … three mates? I project with the thought of amusement to her.

She makes a chuckling sound in my head and projects back, *Yes. Alpha females tend to mate several males. This is true for your people too. I can tell you will be busy like me.*

"Solveig, ugh—is this okay?" Vidarr asks while Vabira rubs her face into his chest then leans up on her back legs with her paws on his chest. She then leans in and her mouth opens with the longest tongue I've ever seen that licks up Vidarr's neck over his face. I can't help but laugh loudly at his look of shock and disgust. The Elarians and my grandfather also start to laugh loudly making the rebels chuckle softly and release a breath of relief that they aren't going to be eaten today.

"She says you're attractive, Vi. However, you may want to stop making out with Vabira or her mates may decide to eat you," I say while pointing at the two male catchkis near me who are making a raspy crackle noise. I'm assuming it's the equivalent to a growl.

I run my hands over the male catchkis' heads and project, *Easy boys. He's mine.* They start to purr into my hands and stop their growling. Then I project to Vabira, *Alright, friend, get your paws off Vidarr before he passes out. We need to be on our way if this is okay with you?*

Yes, sorry, I was curious as to his taste and if his stripes tasted different. He is delicious, Solveig. Please pass through our territory anytime and safe travels. I will protect your backs when you return through here. I have seen disgusting things just north of here near the mountain. Trees cut and burnt down. Bodies of two-leggeds put into the soil. There is a scent of death and sorrow in the air up there which we avoid. Best of luck.

Thank you, Vabira. We appreciate it. Glad I am that I was able to meet you and your mates.

"Alright, we have safe passage through their territory. Mount up and let's make haste." Everyone makes a loud sigh of relief and practically race to their horses jumping up.

Aren is smiling at me fondly and … is that pride?

He says, "You are truly talented, Granddaughter. I've never seen anyone befriend and talk to the Catchki. There were scrolls that talked of an ancestor who was once allies with them in the forest but that was many generations ago. You will do great things and I can tell it's your compassion for life and nature that will make the biggest impact on our people. "

"Thank you, Grandfather. Honestly, she was a rather sassy and randy cat. I was worried she would steal Vidarr's virtue!" We share a chuckle while Vidarr scoffs behind us, but I can tell he's amused as well.

The rest of the journey there goes quickly. It's close to an hour before midnight or so. Tyr flies down from the branches with a quick *cak-cak* and lands on my raised arm.

Just ahead, the forest clears and there's an entrance at the base of the mountain. My mate is resting but should wake soon, Tyr lets me know.

"Let's dismount and scout the area. The camp is just ahead. Zxian, do you want to use your skill and get us more information on numbers of guards? Don't go in yet though before we have a plan."

"This is where we saw the camp before. Its entrance is at the base of that larger mountain and should be facing the forest," Elder Aren states. We leave the horses under Sindari's watch and silently crawl up towards the edge of the forest. Yaeril climbs up a tall pine near the edge of the forest to get a clearer view while the rest of us crouch in the brush and behind trees observing. Zxian must have left using his powers to go unnoticed since I cannot see him anymore among our group.

I can see several torches lighting up the area around the mountain base. Only one entrance is seen with several guards entering and exiting. There's a sort of clearing to the left of the entrance with a large stone post, a well, a larger campfire and some tents set up. To the right of the entrance, I can see stacked large stones, crates of iron and several wagons. There's also some covered supplies and stacked wood noted. There are a few horses tied near the wagons on the right.

Suddenly getting an idea, I attempt to project my thoughts towards the horses and receive several responses. A few are sleeping and ignore me but I can see several ears perk up in my direction and standing at attention.

Hello, friends. I need your help would you be willing to assist? I send to them.

Too many thoughts are sent at once, so I pick the strongest and most dominant. He's a stallion, whom he names himself as Ciru. *Elarian, what may we help you with. Your people are being hunted.* He projects to me.

Yes, Ciru, this is why I'm here with other warriors. I need to get inside to help my people and the others. Do you know how many soldiers are guarding this mountain?

This is hard for me to answer. I don't see in mountain. There are twelve horses here including me but they pair us up with wagons. There are three large wagons that periodically leave. I am the strongest here so I usually assist, he says proudly then his thoughts sour. *I do not like the men though. They use whips not just on us but on the Elarians and people they call slaves. Usually each wagon has two men with it when it leaves and I see two men stationed at the mountain entrance. I know there are more soldiers inside.*

Thank you, Ciru. Please tell the other horses to not startle or make noise when we sneak up. I may need your help when we free the prisoners, I say to him.

My attention is quickly pulled towards the entrance when I see a large man being dragged between two guards. His wrists are tied and his legs have iron manacles on them. Even though he looks thin, likely from poor treatment there, he's still a large man in size. He must be similar in height to Zxian. I look him over and see he has long overgrown dark brown hair that hangs in clumps down to his lower back. Something about him draws me in, makes me internally stand at attention, and it's not just the fact that he's being dragged in front of me.

The guards drag him forward towards that stone post in the open camp area. They start to say something to him and laugh loudly but he doesn't respond and his head falls forward. One of the guards roughly yanks his long hair back and that's when I see he has pointed ears and is clearly Elarian in his facial features even though it's hard to decipher everything. The Elarian abruptly surges forward in a burst of energy and slams his head into the laughing guard making the guard fall back with a yell. The other guard pulls his sword but the Elarian is already starting to run towards our position in the forest. I can hear the other people in my group start to softly pull their own weapons to help this man, but I see

Elder Aren shake his head stilling our hands. We all clearly feel for the man but we can't let it interfere with our overall plan. It's a good thing we don't reveal ourselves too because after only a few steps, five guards come running from the campfire. They overtake the weakened Elarian quickly due to the restricting iron manacles on his ankles.

The guards start to kick and punch the poor man while he's down. He gets in a few of his own punches but he's definitely at a disadvantage due to his tied hands and restricted ankles. I feel a flush of anger so hot at their treatment of him my hands start to shake. I must be breathing loudly in my irritation because Vidarr silently places a hand on my shoulder and gives me a look asking if I'm ok. I shake my head no and grit my teeth.

Looking back to the clearing, I see they dragged the man back to that stone post and tied his hands above his head to metal ring. One of the guards grabs a long scourge cat-o-nine tail whip and yells something then laughs. The other guards start exchanging money betting on something he said. The guard then starts to whip the Elarian several times making me flinch.

I stare at him as blood starts to pour from several lacerations on his back. He doesn't shout out or move a muscle. He takes the beating like a warrior, or like someone who's had this several times before, all the while staring off into the trees and closing his eyes.

Shweesh. Crack. Shweesh. Crack. Over and over … it's a sound I've heard many times before.

"Shut your foul disrespectful mouth, child! You never learn a lesson. I told you to be quiet and sit pretty. Yet you interrupted the Duke in the middle of a conversation," my father yells at me angrily.

Shweesh. Crack. Swish. Crack. He continues his "punishment" that he started over a half hour ago. The whip is cutting deeply into my back at this point but I'm past crying and screaming now. I only let out a few whimpers but even those are barely heard. I wet my underwear embarrassingly after the first three cracks. I tried to hold in the yells initially but I'm just not strong enough, I guess. My eyes fill with tears that I thought were all dried up. Who knew at fifteen years old I would need to learn a tolerance for the whip?

The only reason I'm not screaming now is because I can hardly feel anything anymore. My back is almost completely numb. A macerated piece of meat. There's so much blood on the floor beneath me, it's hard to understand that all came from me. Good thing

I've been healing quicker. I know from experience that it takes a lot to get me to the brink of death. Not that I haven't thought or even wished for it before.

Shweesh. Crack. Shweesh. Crack.

I startle awake when someone unlocks my wrists from the chains holding them above my head in the center of the room. I must have fallen unconscious during my punishment. Sorry, not sorry. I turn my head slightly but I'm so weak that it just flails to the side and I see my father is panting with the whip in his hand staring at me.

"You can take over the girl's punishment now, Malphas. I can't stand to look at her—or smell her for that matter," King Batair says raising a hand to his nose. "Pitiful child. Can't even take a full punishment from your father without pissing your pants. You embarrass me with your disgusting deformities and unruly behavior. Next time I see you, you will be silent, compliant, cover those damn disgusting ears in public."

His talking makes me stiffen up realizing it's Counselor Malphas that released me from the chains and is now holding me. He's running a hand over my hair like I'm some sort of pet to him.

"She will learn. I'll make sure of it. Won't you, princess?" Counselor Malphas says. He stands up and carries me to the table, laying me on my stomach.

Honestly, I never want to be with a man if they are anything like the counselor or my father. Why do I need to be punished for simply speaking? Why are men's voices so much more important than a woman's? My father and Duke Chavril, a noble from the southern aspect of Laevaris, were talking at dinner about the Duke's daughter being betrothed. He said he happily signed her over to some other nobleman who's nearly triple her age! Says she was starting to question his authority and was showing interest in a stable hand. Regrettably, I asked him why he thinks betrothing his daughter who's only fifteen years old to a repulsive forty something year old man is acceptable. Everyone at the table got quiet, staring at me, and my father stood up.

He said, "Because women are possessions, Solveig, just as you are, as you will always be. You exist simply for three reasons—alliances or trade, birthing an heir and fucking. Then he dragged me with a fist in my hair to my current situation in the dungeon.

Shweesh. Crack. Shweesh. Crack.

I open my eyes and feel a deep pain in my chest shaking off the dark memory. When I look back at the Elarian man, he's staring right at me while the whip mangles his back. *Strange.*

He's looking directly at me as if he can see me in the shadows. Not just the shadows of the forest I'm hiding in but the shadows and darkness of my soul. *It's like he's acknowledging me and my own darkness,* I think, but how?

I can't take one more second of this! I look over a Vidarr with tears in my eyes and go to say something but realize the whip stopped.

The man is being dragged back into the mountain now and is still staring right in my direction the whole way. Its disconcerting.

I back up silently and touch Vi's shoulder nodding my head back towards where the horses are. Everyone softly retreats back to where we can talk.

I sit down on a stump near the horses and put my head in my hands. I can't help but feel dread on what we will find in that mountain. Clearly these people need help and are likely to be injured which could make our escape harder. Vidarr rubs a hand over my shoulder and squeezes it.

"We got this, sunshine. You are strong. We just need a plan," Vi says to me.

Once everyone is gathered, I kneel in the dirt and clear some sticks to make a makeshift map on the ground. Zxian joins us suddenly coming out of the forest and startling several people who quickly grab weapons.

"Alright, first let's hear what Zxian discovered," I say quietly.

"There's an outdoor quarry around the mountain's left side past your field of view. There are at least twenty slaves sleeping down there with five guards standing fully armed above with crossbows. Several more guards are pacing the bottom of the quarry with the slaves. It seems like they are resting right now and some of the guards are distracted playing cards," Zxian reports then continues and draws out the layout of the quarry with several stick guards drawn in the dirt. "You obviously saw the seven guards outside the mountain entrance," He says angrily making a fist. "I snuck inside the entrance during the distraction but only made it so far as I wanted to make it out before they finished …" He trails off staring at the ground.

Zxian continues saying: "His name is Kaeden. He was—is—a friend that was with us when they took your father Lochlann, Solveig. He is a good fighter and would be useful in our fight but given his recent injuries, he will probably not be of much use. It gives me hope your father could be here or in another camp. I didn't see him though. I made it down one level in the mountain. There is a carved-out guard room initially with guards watching, then stairs leading down to a large cavern. I saw some stone and iron cells to the right and on the left a larger quarry in the mountain. I could smell water in there too so I wonder if there's another exit point as the water must leave the mountain somehow. Inside I counted four more guards mostly near the entrance and looked like seven more in the main cavern. Some of the slaves were in their cells but there was a lot of empty cells so I'm sure where the rest of them are."

Doing some quick math in my head I say, "So we have at least thirty guards and an unknown number of prisoners?" I get a nod from Zxian. "I say our best plan to get in is to distract them with more prisoners."

I see Vidarr shaking his head. "It's too risky, Sol," he says. "You could get trapped in there and have no way out. There's a lot of guards."

But I look over to Zxian and Yaeril who are whispering to each other. Elder Aren has an anxious look on his face so I ask, "Well? Any other ideas?"

"It's the only way, I've seen it with my foresight. But I can't risk you, Granddaughter," Elder Aren says. "You are too important to our people. You need to stay behind with me and can help heal the injured. I will help you."

"No, I'm going. I need to do this for myself and for my people, they're my responsibility. Plus … I can heal that warrior and he can help us free the prisoners if I go in," I say arguing with them. Aren is shaking his head.

"You don't have enough control of your power to be able to heal such a serious injury. You could overdo it and then be just as injured as him," Aren says.

"She's right though …" Yaeril starts to say. "It's a good plan. Use fake prisoners to be escorted in, getting us people on the inside while the rest of us fight on the outside. Plus, if half of us stay outside then there's less chance of the ones inside getting trapped."

Vidarr runs a hand through his hair with a frustrated look on his face and says, "Fine. We don't have much time or a better plan for that matter. Now me, Yaeril—" Vidarr breaks off his orders and we all fall silent when we all hear a stick break in the forest nearby.

I turn my head to look at the horses when Sindari projects to me, *There are two new horses approaching with two men.*

Swearing in my head I thank Sindari for the warning. Then I pull my twin katanas from over my shoulders quietly and say, "Two men approaching." Vidarr and all the rebels pull their weapons at my words while Zxian and Yaeril disappear likely to come up behind our mystery guests.

Vidarr and I step forward towards the direction of the sound and wait.

I'm completely shocked when Cadoc followed by his friend Eirik walk out of the forest into our small clearing. They're leading two horses and looking suspicious of us.

"Well, well, well … what is Prince Cadoc and his trusted guard doing way out here in the Broken Forest in the middle of night, hmm?" Vidarr says putting his short sword away and crossing his arms. He obviously doesn't think they are a threat and must have seen them at the ball to know their faces. Vidarr has spies everywhere in the city and in the castle. *Wait … did he say Prince—Cadoc?* I mentally try to process that. Cadoc never told me he was a prince. He only told me he was some noble from Gorva. I can see him hesitating to answer while he grits his teeth.

I slowly put my katanas away as I school my expression into boredom. Then I say, "Well? Answer the question, *Prince* Cadoc … we have important things we are doing which you are interrupting."

"I'm sorry for the deception I may have led you to believe about my identity, *Princess*, but I think the better question is: what are you doing out here traipsing around in the middle of the night spying with … eight other rebels?" Prince Cadoc says with an annoyed look raising an eyebrow. "Very unseemly for a *lady*. I thought you would keep better company than this after our last discussion."

Just as he finishes, Yaeril and Zxian walk up from behind them and stand menacingly over them.

"Watch your words, prince, no one speaks with disrespect to my queen that way," Zxian says holding a wicked curved dagger in one hand and an axe in the other. Cadoc and Eirik startle, hold their ground; they must not have seen him appear from the trees. I can see them look over Zxian and Yaeril with curiosity noting their distinct features and then Cadoc glances back at me.

"Who are you? You look similar to Solveig. I've never seen a people like you before Solveig and what do you mean by *queen?*" Eirik asks Zxian directly.

Cadoc is staring right at me and running his gaze over my features including my ears cataloging each similarity to the two men near them.

"They—I mean—*we* are Elarians. We are here *traipsing* around to free some of my imprisoned people and the stolen people of Laevaris. People have gone missing over the years from all over Laevaris but mostly from the city and we found out that they were being shoved into slavery disguised as work camps," I say angrily at him stalking forward until my chest is almost brushing his. "Now, if you don't mind. We'd like to get on with saving them before another is beaten nearly to death." I'm practically panting with annoyance by the end of my speech but when I look at Cadoc all I see is a very intense look in his eyes. Hunger. Desire.

Cadoc leans forward and my nipples brush against his chest through my shirt. He reaches up and tucks a stray piece of hair that fell in my face behind my ear asking softly, "And the queen part?"

Thrown off by his change in attitude I hesitantly say, "Well supposedly, I am the last living heir for the lost kingdom of Elaria." I bite my lip nervously and look at Elder Aren. He steps forward pulling me back a step and looks Cadoc over shrewdly.

"My granddaughter will be the rebirth of our people. We will rise again with her leadership and my support. Now, are you going to assist us or not?" Aren says directly to Cadoc.

Cadoc straightens up and stares directly into my grandfather's eyes. I feel like I'm missing something here almost as if their staring contest is relaying something else without words.

"I will gladly help Solveig and support her in any way I can. I just hope I can somehow gain her trust and yours," Cadoc says with a nod deferring to my grandfather.

"Very well. I am Elder Aren. These two Elarian warriors are Yaeril and Zxian." Aren says with nods to each warrior. "And the remaining members of our group are part of a Rebellion movement in Falal."

"Enough! Time's wasting …" Vidarr says in irritation looking at where Cadoc pushed my hair back and then crouching down points to the dirt map we were drawing. "Elder Aren, you keep watch on the forest protecting our escape route. Yaeril, myself, Cadoc and his friend, and you three will be freeing the prisoners in the quarry—" Vi orders, pointing to three rebels in our group.

He's interrupted by Cadoc who says, "Excuse me but I'm going with Solveig. Nonnegotiable." Then he crosses his arms and stares Vidarr down.

"You will do what you're told if you want to be a part of this mission." Vidarr stands up and puffs his tattooed chest out. *Let the testosterone contest begin!* I chuckle to myself.

"Boys. Let's get through this... Vi, let the *prince* do what he wants. I'm sure he will find a way to be useful somehow," I say mockingly at Cadoc making him flush angrily.

"Fine," Vi says with a smug smile backing up and putting a hand on my low back possessively. Cadoc looks irritated staring at Vidarr and makes a slight growl sound showing his displeasure. Something about the two of them getting all growly and jealous turns me on and makes heat pool in my core. Does that make me a bad person? I think about all the big handsome men that are suddenly showing me some interest. *Not the time, Solveig! Focus!*

"*Prince* Cadoc, his friend, Darritt and Jarel are going to pretend to be guards leading in new prisoners. You need to silently take down the guards near the entrance and use their uniforms for a disguise. You will then escort Zxian, Solveig and Kira as prisoners into the mountain gaining access through the internal guards which are just inside the door per Zxian. Once inside, you can assess for any exits and cause the slaves to revolt while we secure the outside. Basically, stall for time until we can meet you at the entrance," Vidarr says while looking at everyone for questions.

"Everyone good? Alright. I'll have the horses draw some of the guards over there and you guys handle them so we can get their uniforms. The first group needs to move into place near the quarry. Wait to attack until we 'the prisoners' get inside the mountain," I say while everyone nods their heads.

Then I project thoughts to those horses including Ciru who are over by the wagons. *Can you cause a ruckus and get some of those guards to come check on you guys? We need to get their uniforms.*

He responds immediately flicking his head up. *Of course, Solveig!*

No sooner than I sent that thought and responded, I hear loud yinnying and hooves stomping. The I see the horses starting to kick over at several containers of iron trying to knock them over. At all the noise, four guards run over to see what's making the horses upset. *Yes!* I nod my head to our group to handle them and then send look to Zxian to sneak over and take some of the remaining guards. I whisper to Yaeril who nods and climbs up a tree with his bow ready to take out some of the three guards that didn't go to investigate the noise.

I hear a slight scuffle then silence and back walks Cadoc, Darritt, Eirik, and Jarel in the guards' uniforms.

Zxian takes another minute but returns and Yaeril drops from the tree looking irritated.

"Next time, let me get one, Z! You're always such a selfish prick when it comes to battle," Yaeril says in a frustrated voice to Zxian who chuckles.

"You're too slow, Yaeril. Best practice more. I'm up three to your zero," Zxian says with an eager grin while Yaeril shakes his head and walks over to his group that will be handling the quarry guards. Zxian pulls out some hand manacles and chains holding them out for me.

I let him slip them on me and then Cadoc walks over holding the other end looking down at me. I see Darritt putting chains on Kira and Eirik slipping some on Zxian.

"Let's go., I whisper to our group.

We start to walk out into the open nearing the entrance to the mountain. One of the guards from the quarry walks over to the well for a drink and does a double take watching us. He's a bit away from the entrance but yells over, "Fresh meat?"

Cadoc yanks on my chain and pulls my braid yelling back, "Yup! Going to take these ones inside per orders!" The quarry guard nods, staring for a minute with an inquisitive look and then walks back the way he came. I start to feel some sweat dripping down my back from nervousness. At the continued pressure on my braid, I look down to see Cadoc's hand is still on my braid giving a slight pull. He has a look in his eyes that I recognize now from being with Vidarr. *Desire.*

He has the firm but yet controlled hold on my hair that indicates a man who would know just how to control my body, staying on the precipice between pleasure and pain. I look back up at him and instantly have dirty thoughts of him pulling my hair while he thrusts into me from behind. *Bad Solveig, no!* I reach up and run my fingers along his hand on my braid and gently remove it causing a clinking of chains.

"I like this braid. Makes me think of all the things I can do with it," Cadoc whispers in my ear making me blush and look forward as we continue walking.

This man is going to kill me, but only in the best of ways, I think to myself.

CHAPTER
Twenty-Eight

SOLVEIG

We make it to the entrance without any more issues.

There's an iron gate with a lock, which I just now notice and start to panic, but luckily Zxian's smart and pulls out a key from a pocket, unlocking the door, and putting the key back away in his pocket.

I breathe a sigh of relief grateful someone thought to take that off one of the guards, but it's quickly suppressed when we walk into the dark mountain tunnel.

I'm flooded with a sensation of suffocation. I feel cut off from the world, or more likely nature. When that iron gate closes behind us, all I can focus on are my deep panting breaths and rising anxiety. It's almost worse than the dungeon cells I've been in. I look over at Zxian and can see he must be feeling a similar emotion as myself. We share a look while staying silent. Something about the mountain stone and metal feels worse. It's like my powers and energy are instantly muted and it's only getting worse the farther we walk down through the tunnel. No wonder they keep Elarians prisoner in here, they probably feel this as well and are weaker for it. This could put a snag in our plans that we didn't think about.

Four guards see us up ahead and step out of a small room carved into the side of the tunnel. They are all armed fully. Two more guards are still sitting at a table there drinking ale and shuffling cards.

The guards look us over and the one who appears in charge squints his beady eyes at us suspiciously saying, "I didn't hear of any new slaves being brought over. We have orders to decrease their numbers not increase them." He crosses his arms. "I don't recognize any of you."

Cadoc takes the lead again thankfully. He yanks on my chain and pushes me to the ground. I make a whimper of protest when my knees hit the stone floor trying to make this more believable. One of the guards must since he smiles and watches eagerly like he enjoys seeing people suffer.

"You're right. These slaves were just found in the forest a few days ago and we apprehended them. We are just guards traveling with a shipment of iron from another camp when we caught sight of them." He starts to lie, and surprisingly is good at it. "We were too far from our own slave camp to take them there so our superior told us to bring them here. I'm just following orders." Cadoc says angrily at the end. "I just want to rest for a bit and have an ale before we head out again. I'm beat from dragging this bitch around the past couple days."

I see the moment the guard relaxes some and then he smiles. "Which camp you come from, Mortgaard to the North?" he asks while two of the guards go to sit with the others at the table. Now only the leader and the leering guard are blocking our way.

"Yah, that's the one. Ever been there? It's cold as fuck in the winter months," Cadoc replies calmly but I can see the tenseness of his shoulders. Internally I'm thanking Cadoc for his quick thinking! I mean he got a name and possible location out of the guard for another camp!

"No, never been. You see one of these cesspools, you've seen them all. One is more than enough for me. I have to smell these slaves all day, sticks in the nose you know?" he says with a chuckle then looking down at me the leader takes a second to really peruse my body and I start to shift with discomfort. His eyes rake my body almost as if I'm naked. "This one however still smells nice. You ever dip your wick in this one? She's not too half bad if you ignore the ears."

I see Cadoc tense up further and yank on the chain pulling me closer to his legs. His chuckle is a bit forced but he manages to grit out in a calm voice, "Nah, I prefer my women wet and willing. Can we get them put away? You guys take it easy then maybe we'll join you for a drink ya?" Cadoc starts to try to shift us down the tunnel but the guard still blocks our way.

"Well, if you don't want her. We want a turn with her before she gets passed around by the slaves. They all fornicate like animals down there. We always looked forward to fresh meat. It's the only benefit of being a guard in these camps, well other than the money. Me and Wevel here will take good care of her," he says taking a step forward and reaching for the chain. I can tell Cadoc doesn't know how to respond at this point but luckily he doesn't have to.

Zxian starts to yell and act like he's trying to escape by pulling on the chains and struggling with Eirik and Darritt. Zxian gets in a punch to Eirik and then Darritt tackles Zxian subduing him without much injury. All the guards are standing now watching.

"Alright, fuck, let's get these slaves into their cells then have a drink. We can always come back for the slave women tonight and give them a good ride," the guard says while grabbing my hair and pulling me up off my feet. He leers into my face and then sniffs along my neck.

Eww! He smells of stinky cheese and ale making me cringe away from him. Unfortunately, he has me held up by my hair which is pulling painfully on my scalp. Then he grabs the chain from Cadoc and leads the way with me stumbling next to him. We walk down a maze of tunnels … left turn, right, right, left … then a large, cavernous opening appears. To the right of the cavern, I see several cells built into the wall with iron gates over them and a series of walkways between them going up and down. On the left side, I see a large tunnel and mining excavation site. I only see a few slaves cleaning up some tools near the mining excavation site. This place is huge and I'm instantly anxious about our plan. *Where are the others?*

"Come on, most of the slaves are either bathing or eating their scraps of food before getting in their cells. We can take these ones on a short tour and get them changed into their standards," he says. He quickly grabs a few scraps of cloth from a storage room then leads us across the cavern to a smaller one with several tables.

At our entrance into the small dining cavern, everyone ceases their talking and all eyes turn to us. I see a few slaves slump down trying to avoid notice of the guards. There must be around forty slaves in here but it's a quick estimate and definitely larger than we expected. Everyone in here appears to be eating some sort of dinner even though it's well past time for it being the middle of the night. I guess when you live underground in a mountain time doesn't really matter. I can see they don't have much to eat. Looks like stale bread and few pieces of cheese and dried meat. Most of the slaves look severely malnourished with several sporting bruises or scars.

A rough yanking on the chain connected to my wrists catches me by surprise and causes me to stumble forward into a table in front of us banging my hip on it. The lead guard says loudly, "Get your clothes off now like a good little slave." He then unlocks my wrist manacles freeing me and allowing me to move easier. He must not think of me as much of a threat. *Idiot.* Then he stands back with his arms crossed waiting. I see the other guards gave similar orders to my friends.

I look around and notice mostly everyone's attention is on me and my friends, making me feel awkward. I then ask, "Change right now? Do you have a bathroom I can use?"

The lead guard throws his head back and laughs loudly then backhands me so fast I don't have a chance to brace myself. I see Cadoc behind the guard start to step forward with an angry face but I subtly shake my head no causing him to grit his teeth.

"Stupid bitch. You're a slave now. You do what you're told and don't talk to your betters. Now get changed, I'm losing patience. If you give us a show, then I'll give you your new dress."

I look down at my feet trying to calm my rising anger and to make it look like acceptance of his words, when all I really want to do is pull out a dagger hidden in my boot and shove it in his eye. I start to unbutton my shirt and remove it exposing my breasts and also the two runes on my upper body. I see several Elarians in the crowd start to sit up straighter noticing them.

The lead guard is staring with blatant lust at my generous breasts and licking his lips like a pig about to get his meal. I kick my boots off but put them within reach of me and then strip my pants off quickly. I look over my shoulder and see the other two "prisoners" in my group undressing but

Zxian is having a harder time since the guards are giving him trouble and haven't removed one of this wrist manacles.

Once I'm naked except for my underwear, I cross my arms over my chest to give myself some modesty while I wait. I need to stall a bit until hoping they will remove Zxian's other wrist manacle and chain. I hear several gasps in the crowd watching and then excited whispering which echoes through the space and making it louder in the area. I look around to see what is causing such excitement and see several Elarians standing up looking directly at me with their hands over their chests and a hopeful expression on their faces. One even points at the rune on my thigh.

The guards in the room notice the disturbance and start to walk away from the walls with long studded bats. They start to yell for quiet and threaten the Elarians to sit back down. They all look to me with questioning gazes. One guard gets eager and starts to hit an Elarian slave over the back with a bat causing him to yell out in pain and fall to the floor.

I'm brought back to my situation when I feel a hand on my breast and a scrap of fabric pushed into my chest. The lead guard is so close against me it's unlikely anyone can see him fondling my breast. *Sick narcissistic prick!*

"Get dressed in this and be a good girl. Then I'll show you your cell and visit you later," he says to me suggestively. I turn my head to avoid his nasty breath so close to my face and just in time to see Zxian get unlocked from his last manacle.

Just as the guard starts to step back, I pull a dagger from his belt and slice it across his neck in a smooth practiced motion showering me and my nakedness in his blood. It all happens so quickly as everyone leaps into motion. I reach for my other knife hidden in my boot and then duck as a guard swings a studded bat over my head. I twist and thrust up into his gut with the dagger knocking him away from me. Cadoc is already fighting three guards at once, so I come up behind one and slit his throat leaving Cadoc to the remaining two.

I can see Zxian fighting off a huge guard with a sword using only two knives like myself. Kira is holding her own against a guard further back.

Suddenly a guard wraps an arm around my waist pulling me back against a large chest, I stab back into his side hitting my mark and making him curse. He puts a knife at my throat tightly and says, "Drop the dagger and the knife and I might let you live servicing me on your back, slave."

I don't have time to answer him before I feel the pressure of the knife fall from my throat and his arm disappear. I turn around and see a large slightly malnourished Elarian male break the guard's neck and throw him to the ground limply.

The Elarian slave looks me in the eye and puts a hand over his chest then says, "My queen."

He starts to get on his knees and bow his head but I stop him quickly with a hand to his shoulder and say, "Now is not the time for that. Thank you—"

"Gavrael," he supplies.

I look at Gavrael about to respond and see another guard behind him with a short sword raised. Throwing my dagger swiftly and without thought over Gavrael's shoulder, it flies true directly into the guards left eye making him drop the sword with a scream and fall to the ground. Gavrael's eyes nearly pop out of his head in surprise or is that awe? Then he turns around and starts to bash the guards face in with his fists.

I take a second to look around and see that one of the rebels with our group is dead from a stab wound to his chest and several slaves are injured. All the guards are dead except one that Zxian is currently strangling with his bare hands. It almost looks like he's enjoying it. *Probably is.*

I turn and put a hand on Gavrael's shoulder making him flinch and say, "It's okay now, you can stop. He's dead." He was still pummeling that guard with my dagger in his eye, his head now looking like a smashed pumpkin with blood and gore splattered everywhere. Gavrael is breathing hard and has a wild look in his eyes that seems to calm with my words.

Just as a straighten up, Cadoc walks over with Eirik. "Well that was fun …" Eirik says in a strange voice and looking at the ceiling. Then he clears his throat and nudges Cadoc with his elbow.

I look at Cadoc then and see his gaze directed down at my naked breasts. *Shit! Forgot I was naked still! Looks like he doesn't mind.*

I look down and see I'm also completely covered in blood looking like some grotesque naked monster that came out of underworld. I must be quite a sight. But instead of covering my nakedness, I prop a fist on a hip and clear my throat making Cadoc pay attention and look me in the eye.

"Eyes up here, *prince…*" I say causing him to blush. "Like what you see?"

He almost starts to nod his head in response and then shakes it like he's trying to focus. I see Eirik has redirected his gaze from the ceiling to my chest too. Cadoc sees this and slaps a hand over his friend's eyes then thrusts my shirt at me. "Here put this on. You're too distracting. Are you injured anywhere?" he asks.

I slip on the shirt and look around for my pants and boots next saying, "Yeah I'm fine. Let's move quickly. There are still some prisoners in that big cavern on our way out of here." A sudden thought pops into my head making me look at the slaves scattered around the room. I then turn around once I'm dressed and ask Gavrael, the big Elarian I met briefly, "Do you know where they put a man named Kaeden? I don't see him in here."

Gavrael is sitting on a half-broken table staring at his blood soaked hands with a lost look in his eyes. He looks up at my question and then I see his gaze harden. "Yeah they threw him in his cell after they beat him just a bit ago. He was unable to get up and they wouldn't bring him food or water as part of a punishment."

"Take us to him," I say when I see the rest of our group ready to leave. We quietly leave once Zxian and Gavrael greet each other. I guess they knew of each other before he came here.

Zxian leads our group with Gavrael silently down the hall towards the cavern. The slaves from the dining room were told to wait there for now until they hear us finish up the guards. Most of them are in no shape to fight given their malnourished bodies so we decided to have them hide in the halls and the dining room until it's over.

Gavrael and Zxian walk slowly to the left of the cavern with me. We left Cadoc, Eirik, Kira, and Darritt at the entrance to the cavern guarding in the shadows until we locate Kaeden.

I see cell after cell along the walls as we walk. The area is somewhat hidden behind some walls and as long as we are quiet it shouldn't alert the guards in the cavern to us sneaking about.

Gavrael stops in front of a cell halfway down the row. He whispers some words into the cell and I hear a scuffle of feet shifting on stone inside.

"Shit. We need a key to open his door," Gavrael says. "There was one on that guard you killed, my Queen. I'll run back quickly and grab it." He takes off running silently back the way we came.

"Kaeden—it's me, Zxian! Shit! Oh no! I'm sorry, man," Zxian says quietly with sadness reaching a hand through the bars.

"Zxian ... I never thought ... what are you doing here? This place is death and shame for our people. You shouldn't be here," I hear a strong but quiet raspy voice say. I start to walk closer to get a look at this Kaeden and then kneel down next to Zxian making Kaeden's next words break off when he sees me, "Who—"

He looks up at me from the stone floor where he's laying on his stomach and I swear his eyes stab directly into my soul. It's so intense it's almost painful. I get s sharp burning pain in the center of my chest that travels deep inside me and makes me feel dizzy. Kaeden is panting deep breaths now and his mouth is hanging open in shock.

His eyes though, *Oh Valirr, Oh Goodness,* his eyes! They are this beautiful shining amber similar in color to the setting sun, I've never seen their like. I can't stop staring at him but I have to look down since my chest is burning so intensely it hurts. I look at my chest and rub with my hand. I can't see anything on it probably because it's covered in blood and gore. *Goodness, what he must think of me! I look a nightmare!*

I take a second to look at the rest of him and notice again how big he is. He's tall similar to Zxian or maybe bigger but he lacks some of the muscle Zxian has. Probably because they nearly starve everyone in here. He has that long dark brown hair that I saw before that I'm sure was once soft and beautiful but now is matted and clumped together down his back.

Oh no! His back ... I think cringing at how bad his back looks. It's a mess of flesh, blood and exposed tissues. I can see a few ribs through the lacerations from the whip. There's swelling and redness all around the wounds and I can tell he's struggling to heal himself with his malnourished body. He attempts to push himself up onto his elbows but winces and drops back down all the while still staring at me.

He starts to reach out and silently mouths one word ...

"What's going on? Kaeden? Are you okay? I mean ... that's a stupid question given your back, but you both are acting strangely," Zxian says looking between the two of us who won't break each other's stare. I think I could look at Kaeden all day. He's gorgeous even under all the dirt and blood. I feel this insane all-consuming need to be with him pulling me towards him. In fact, I start to shift until I'm up against the bars of his cell.

Mate. I softly hear projected into my head. It's slightly different than when I project thoughts with animals. This is like I could hear a voice and not just an image, maybe I'm finally losing my sanity from all my years of abuse.

"Well? What is it?" Zxian asks leaning in.

"Mate …?" I say to myself repeating what I heard in my head. I'm trying to understand what I just heard and not really conscious I said that out loud. "What does he mean?" Then when I only hear silence, I break Kaeden's stare and look at Zxian who has an incredulous look on his face.

"You—you're—what?" Zxian says to Kaeden then looks back and forth to me.

"Mate. I'm her mate. I feel it. I can't believe it. It's—like the most—intense feeling," Kaeden says then slowly starts to smile at me with a hopeful look.

"Wait—what are you two talking about?" I ask rubbing my chest for the fiftieth time. "Why did I hear a voice in my head?" Just as I say that I feel a burning sensation behind my left ear and shooting down my neck. *Ohh no, not again! I don't have time for this!* I could tell after undergoing it three other times that I just got my fourth rune and I'm assuming it has to do with the voice I heard in my head.

Just as Zxian and Kaeden open their mouths to answer, Gavrael comes running up out of breath and starts to unlock the cell door.

"What did I miss? Never mind, we have to hurry. I saw the guards starting to shuffle the other slaves towards their cells from the mining site," Gavrael says.

CHAPTER
Twenty-Nine

SOLVEIG

"Wait—what do you mean? Please tell me!! I'm losing it here!" I ask and point to my head. Then I start to rub my chest and behind my left ear. *Did he say mate ... like a mate an animal has? How could I be his mate! I've never even met the guy and I'm definitely not an animal, well I might look like one with how dirty I am right now.* I think to myself.

No one answers as we all shuffle inside Kaeden's cell. He's still laying on his stomach and we get our first up close look at his back. It's worse than I could see through the bars. I don't even know how he can tolerate breathing since just that small movement must hurt.

He's not going to be able to walk or help us fight our way out of here. He may not even live through the rest of the night if I don't do something. Suddenly I'm filled with irrational panic at that thought. *Fuck!*

"Alright, I'm going to have to try and heal you or we'll never make it out of here. Then you can sit down and explain why I feel like I'm going crazy later," I say to Kaeden who looks incredulous again. "What?" I ask him.

"You have a rune for healing?" he asks and then smiles so big like he's proud or something and reaches for my hand.

Our hands touch for the first time with a jolt through my system, almost like lightening shooting through my system, and I gasp for air. He looks just as affected and I pull my hand back quickly saying, "Don't! What did you just do? Don't hurt yourself anymore!"

He chuckles and looks at his hand like he is amazed. He looks up at me from the ground and says, "That is just the start of the bond. Don't be concerned, if anything I'm feeling better already with you near me, my mate." Then at my confused look he turns his head and looks at Zxian saying, "She is Elarian and yet she doesn't know about mate bonds?"

Zxian glances at me and then back at Kaeden and says, "She only just found out about us and her heritage, Kaeden. Please, let's discuss this later. Let her heal you."

Bond? I don't want to be bound to anyone! I'm panicking inside but trying to focus on the task at hand. I say to Kaeden, "I've never healed anyone else before, but Elder Aren says it should be possible. I'll try but tell me to stop if I hurt you?"

He tries to sit up and shakes his head no. But he's so weak he turns pale and falls back down. "You shouldn't risk yourself for me, mate."

"Shut up and don't call me that. Now lay still like a good little boy and let me do my magic." I order him confidently even though inside I'm scared and panicking since I have no idea what I'm doing.

I place my hands on his back gently and feel that zing at contact with his skin again. Luckily it's not as jarring as last time.

I then close my eyes and try to think of healing myself since that's something I know how to do. *Here we go.* I find my center and think about extending it outwards and finding any areas that light up almost like a beacon in my body indicating an injury. My power immediately surges to a few bruises I got from the earlier fight but I redirect the power out into my hands instead. *Wow! Nice job Sol!*

I think about Kaeden's back and the horrible, mangled mess of lacerations pushing my power out of my hands into him. He gasps out in discomfort and his hands fist but otherwise he lays still like I instructed.

"Well I'll be ... bless Valirr! I've never seen—" Zxian starts to say in awe watching Kaeden's back.

I open my eyes to see Kaeden's back slowly coming back together. *Oh Goodness! Its working!* Just as I get most of the tissue under the skin stitched back together I feel a resistance in my power almost like it's fluctuating and then I get a horrible cutting and sharp slitting pain across my back. It's so surprising I can't help crying out in pain. *Shit!* I immediately silence myself and grit my teeth together as more and more pain shoots across my back. I start to feel a slow drip of blood down my back under my shirt and I get woozy for a second. My hands fall way from Kaeden and I look up to see they are almost all closed but he does have some scars and a few are still red and swollen.

He starts to sit up when my hands fall away. The look on his face is complete awe and pride while he stares at me. I immediately put on my emotionless mask to try and hide the pain in my back and ask, "Well? Let's go!" I almost keel over from fatigue and weakness when I stand up but manage to hide it. Luckily years of abuse and torture are good for something. I can see Kaeden squint his eyes like he's about to question me. He's rubbing at his chest similar to how I was earlier. We hear a guard coming down the walkway yelling at a prisoner and it snaps us all into action.

Zxian reaches out as they pass the cell and slices the guard's throat shocking the prisoner. I place a finger over my mouth to silence the prisoner then tilt my head to indicate he follow us. We run down the walkway to the end hearing some yelling and see Cadoc and the others attacking all the guards in the open cavern. They must have gotten antsy waiting so long for us.

We make it to the cavern floor and join the fight, but when I lift my long dagger and thrust it into an opponent I almost lose it in the guard's abdomen. I got a sudden sharp pain in my back lifting my arm and I'm feeling pretty weak.

I'm assuming this is what Aren was warning me about. If I were able to look at my own back right now, I'm sure there would be several whip lacerations trying to heal. Usually, I can heal myself rather fast but Kaeden was injured pretty badly and also this damn mountain seems to suppress my power. Not a good combination of factors.

I cut down two more guards quickly but have to grimace through the pain and lean on my knees to catch my breath.

Watch out! I hear in my head abruptly causing me to look up. I'm slow to move this time due to my fatigue but I manage to dodge to the side before the guard can slice my head off my shoulders. Unfortunately, he does manage to slice across my upper chest making me fall to the ground gasping. I clutch a hand to the area feeling blood pour out and look up at the guard. He's turned around facing me on the ground and raises his sword to stab me when a blur of movement comes from behind me tackling the guard to the ground. His sword drops with a clang and I sigh in relief. Kaeden is on top of him pummeling his face and chest raining down blows with his fists until the guard takes his final breath.

I sit up and look around noticing all the guards are dead now and the slaves are all gathered in the center staring with a mix of emotions. Shock. Sadness. Anger. Hope. It's the last one which gives me enough strength to stand but I'm a bit wobbly. Kaeden sees me stand and runs over trying to support me but I push him away even though his touch makes me feel things I shouldn't. I don't have time for that strange feeling he invokes inside me. But I do say, "Thanks for the warning. You saved my life, I owe you a life debt."

He looks hurt at me pushing him away but then at my words he half smiles at me and responds, "No you don't, mate. You already saved me in more ways than one. Here, let me help you. You're bleeding." He stares at the cut across my chest and the torn shirt exposing a decent amount of my cleavage. He turns and says something to another prisoner nearby and they give him their shirt. Kaeden then walks closer to me and pushes the shirt against the wound on my chest making me grimace but immediately I put my expressionless mask back in place on my face. It's hard keeping up appearances in his presence since he makes me feel unsettled and exposed.

Out of the corner of my eye I see Cadoc stomp over with Eirik and Darritt a few paced behind him. "Get your hands off her!" Cadoc yells grabbing my shoulders and pulling my back into his chest. The sudden movement makes me stumble back and then gasp in pain when my lacerated back hits his chest. Kaeden's eyes fill with anger and I can feel a tension fill the air. Kaeden looks at Cadoc with his head tilted while Cadoc stares right back holding me tightly.

"You're hurting her more! I was trying to stop the bleeding! Let her go!" Kaeden says pulling me towards him and making more blood leak from the gash on my chest. *Damn it! Fucking men!*

"If you all are quite done pulling me around like a rag doll. I'd like to take care of myself. Let go Cadoc … Kaeden …" I say in a soft but low dangerous voice. I'm going to stab one of them in their abnormally handsome faces if they don't listen to me. Luckily, I don't have to as they both let go.

"You're hurt, Sol? I'm sorry! I didn't know—" Cadoc starts to panic and reaches for the tear in my shirt. He then looks down at the blood soaking his own shirt from where my back was in contact with his chest. He looks confused then turns me around and looks at my back. "When—you were whipped? How?!"

"It's complicated, Cadoc. I'll be fine. I'm already starting to heal some but I'll get better faster if we get out of this damn mountain. Vidarr likely needs our help out there," I say pulling away from all the men's grabby hands. Geesh! You'd think I was some weak female that's never been injured before. *If only they knew how often I've been injured and how much worse I've had it in the past.* I think to myself chuckling with my morbid thoughts.

"Fine. But put some pressure on your chest and stay back until you are more stable. You're not allowed to get injured anymore. Let us handle the guards near the door," Cadoc orders in a patronizing tone that usually would have angered me. I just don't have the energy right now to argue so I start to follow them out. As we walk, Kaeden is a solid presence following closely by my side. The slaves stare at me and all of them start to place a hand over their hearts as I pass making me feel uncomfortable.

We make it through the tunnels leading out without any sign of more guards. They must have all been killed in the fight down in the mountain. Zxian pushes his way to the front and whispers to Cadoc, Eirik and Darritt before disappearing out the front door. We wait a minute and I realize he must be using his camouflage rune to see what awaits us outside.

Zxian returns out of breath sneaking in through the cracked door. "We need to hurry, just like inside they have more guards than we counted. Must have come out of a tunnel into the quarry. Our guys are holding their own and the slaves are helping but—"

I'm filled with sudden panic for Vidarr, thinking the worst. I push through all the men in front of me before they can stop me, then I burst out the front door pulling on my agility power and leaping over rocks down the path. I can hear them running behind me.

What I see in the quarry fills me with dread.

Vi! I yell in my head panicking and see him look up confused right where I'm standing, almost like he heard me.

Vidarr is down in the center of the quarry with his short sword out fighting off three men. His left arm is holding his abdomen and he's covered head to toe in blood. I can see Yaeril by his side fighting off four men himself. Two rebels in our group are dead on the ground near them and the last rebel with us is fighting off two guards on the other side of the quarry. Most of the slaves are fighting as well using their picks and tools but I see quite a few dead on the ground from arrows or sword wounds. All the guards at the top of the quarry are dead so I quickly do a running leap and run swiftly down the side of the quarry into the central crater ignoring my own injuries.

I already start to feel better being outside the mountain, however it might also be the adrenaline pumping through my body in my urgency to kill whoever harmed Vidarr.

I make it to Vi leaping up and stabbing a dagger into the back of a guard's neck using it as leverage to kick out and knock over another guard. I pull my dagger as the guard slumps to the ground dead and then squat over the other guard slicing his neck. Vi finishes off the remaining guard he was fighting quickly then falls to his knees panting.

"About time sunshine. I was getting worried I'd have to save your pretty little ass," Vi says with a smirk but it falls flat when he grimaces in pain.

"Thank Valirr you didn't have to. Wouldn't want to inconvenience you. One second," I say and then, pulling out the smaller dagger I had in my boot, I throw it to the right of me into the eye of a guard Yaeril is fighting. He's now down to only two more guards after he dispatched one. Zxian just caught up to us though and is assisting Yaeril now. The other people in our group are running our way too. I must have really made good time getting here with my agility rune. I'm starting to think it's almost stronger than when I first got it.

Vidarr is kneeling in the dirt holding his side and gasping a bit. I crouch down next to him and rip his shirt away from a large wound that's leaking too much blood. He instantly pales when he sees the gaping wound likely from a sword to the gut. *Fuck!*

"It's nothing, just a scratch," I lie to him with a fake smile I don't feel. "Here sit down and let me help you. I swear I'm always stitching you up."

"I just like to keep your skills intact. Practice makes perfect, sunshine. Although maybe this time I went too far," Vidarr says grimacing and laying down in the dirt. "I don't see any wound kit and you don't look so good yourself."

"I'm fine. It's not the worst I've had and I'm already healing being outside," I say which is true. Although I'm still pretty weak and those lacerations on my back are still leaking blood. The gash on my chest has stopped and is trying to stitch close now with my healing abilities.

I reach towards his wound closing my eyes. My hands make contact and I focus on finding my healing power. It's centered mostly on my back and some on my chest so I pull it all away and towards my hands dispersing it out and into Vidarr's abdomen.

Oh shit! Oh no ... I think as I see in my mind a sword must have punctured his spleen making him bleed profusely into his abdomen. *Not good!* I struggle to push my healing power into him as I feel his life force draining from the loss of blood.

I get a hesitation in my power and then notice my hands are shaking as I push more power. More. I need more. Instead of focusing my power on containing the blood and the wound near the skin, I focus instead on the spleen and a small vessel that's pouring out blood. My healing power closes it off and then I back off healing any other injuries until I get to closing the wound in the abdomen wall.

"What's going on! She's using too much and she's already weak and injured! You idiots!" I hear distant yelling. *Is that my grandfather?* "Pull her off him now!"

Just as I hear that, I feel myself slipping into unconsciousness. *No! I'm not done yet! I need more ... his wound isn't closed. He's lost too much blood. I won't lose him!* I think frantically before I see nothing but blackness and peace.

CHAPTER

Thirty

KAEDEN

"...O ur guys are holding their own and the slaves are helping but..." I hear Zxian gasping out of breath as he races back to the entrance of the mountain after scouting. *I just want to get out of this mountain! Damn this place to hell!* I think before I realize what Zxian is actually saying. They must have attacked the outside quarry at the same time their group was freeing us inside the mountain.

Zxian and I go back a few years. We both served in the Elarian army under Lochlann and we developed a friendship after he took a knife to the back from an enemy for me. We obviously lost touch since we were attacked with Lochlann and I was put in this damn slave camp. I don't even really know how long I've been here honestly. Time blurs when you are essentially immortal. As Elarians we have extremely long lifespans. I feel like I'm older than my years given my recent captivity when in reality I'm rather young for our kind since I was only thirty when I was captured.

I look over at the woman next to me that has completely changed everything. My mate. *My* mate! I still can't believe it! And the fact she heard my voice in her head! It's happened before in our history but it's rare, very rare. Supposedly, you have to have the ability for mind-speak in order to communicate with each other back and forth. The chances of that happening is like one in a million. She must have a rune for mind-speak to be able to communicate with me and the mate bond developing allows me to speak into her mind like when I warned her about that guard. I can't help the smile that overtakes my face at the thought that she's mine ... *mine.*

I take a second to look her, like really look at her. She's gorgeous ... even covered in blood and pale from injuries with clothes torn up, you can't help but watch her. She graceful and strong. Long legs and a toned body with enough curves to draw the eye. Her features are delicate but there's an underlying strength in her eyes like she's been through just as much pain that I have.

Reaching a hand towards my mate to feel her and know she's not just a figment of my imagination, I grasp at air when she suddenly races off through the door at a speed that should be impossible. *What! No!*

I race after her as fast as I can. Pulling on my rune I smooth out my path to avoid stumbling but there's no way I can catch up to her. I carry a rune for earth that covers my whole left thigh as a sleeve and extends down to my knee and up to my hip. It allows me power in controlling the earth- soil, plants, trees, anything growing in the earth. Sometimes I can even move stone but it was difficult under a mountain. My power gave me more strength than the other Elarians down there, hence why the guards would periodically beat me into weakness.

I can hear the others running too but my mate is so far ahead racing into battle. I have no idea how she got the energy to do so given the injuries she carries. I can't feel her emotions or hear her thoughts yet since we haven't solidified the bond so I have no idea what's going through her head. *I have a brave and slightly reckless mate. I'm going to have to watch her closely,* I think.

I make it to the quarry and start to take the stairs down. When I look around frantically for my reckless mate, I spot her just in time to see her skewer a guard in the neck and do an insanely agile roundhouse kick knocking out another guard. She takes out two men so efficiently that I bet would have been effortless if it weren't for her injuries. *My mate is a warrior,* I think, wondering how she came to be who she is today. I will have to tread carefully in trying to protect her.

She crouches down and starts to hold another man on the ground making me instantly fill with anger. *Mine!* I growl in my head before realizing the man is injured. I race over with the others just behind me.

She's already healing him and I'm scared to pull her back. I don't know the repercussions of interrupting a healer. I see a guard running for her with a short sword and quickly kick his legs out then grab his head snapping his neck efficiently. The other men in the group finish off the remaining guards while the slaves in the quarry all cheer and look relieved.

Elder Aren walks calmly into the quarry then and looks around as if he's looking for someone. I didn't spend much time around him before my captivity but we had met in the past. He spots my mate and runs towards her. He's yelling now, "What's going on? She's using too much and she's already weak and injured! You idiots!" I realize he's talking about her and reaching to grab her. "Pull her off now."

When I grab her and pull her off the injured man, I swear I can softly hear her voice—*I won't lose him*—before she slumps forward in my arms unconscious and pale. I lay her down and Elder Aren flutters his hands over her inspecting every injury.

"Damn child! I warned her!" he mutters in a panicked voice. He puts his hand over a bloody wound in her abdomen that I didn't know she had. *Shit!* I think to myself. She's so small and fragile looking this way. Elder Aren looks up at me then and asks, "How many did she heal?"

"She healed me before coming out here and then healed this man. But she was injured in a fight as well on her chest. I'm unsure if she healed any others. I was gravely injured from a whip to my back," I say somberly and with respect to my Elder. He nods his head and grits his teeth.

"Stupid, stupid, child. I told her but I suppose you can't learn from mistakes until you make them. She's likely burnt out, used too much energy and has too many injuries," he says smoothing her hair back from her face and holding a hand over the wound in her abdomen. He then startles looking at something behind her left ear and gazes down her neck. "This is new…"

"Will she be okay? What can we do?" I ask pleading for some sort of instruction and grabbing her hand in mine. When I lean over to see what startled him, I see a scrolling detailed rune running from behind her left ear down her neck to her collar. *Interesting. I don't think that was there before.* I think while we both inspect it.

Elder Aren looks up sadly and says, "When a healer uses their power, they take on the pain and injury themselves then heal it using their own body." He shakes his head then squints at me confused. "Who are you? And why do you look so familiar soldier?"

Healers take on the injury and pain? I must have misunderstood him … but then I think of her grimacing in pain and stumbling weak on her feet. I roll her slightly and pull her shirt away from her back then pale instantly when I see several deep lacerations oozing blood on her back. I feel sick to my stomach and bow my head taking deep breaths. *Damiv, no! She took all my pain and the injuries! How could she handle such pain! It was unbearable!* I think cursing the God of Pain and Sadness.

"I don't know how she was able to withstand the pain! Why would she do such a thing!?" I say, then shaking my head I look at Elder Aren. "I am Kaeden Vailspire, previous Elarian Captain in the Army of Light for his majesty Lochlann Stonegaite. I served with Zxian and Yaeril over there until my capture here. And—I am this woman's mate," I say straightening up and giving the Elder a look daring him to contradict me. I brace for his refusal of my claim, but he just stares at me silently.

I hold his gaze until we are both interrupted by the man on the ground which my mate healed. He looks a little worse for wear but is moving around well now that he's healed. He grabs her hand and starts yelling for a wound kit from a man named Darritt.

"Get back and let me help her. Excuse me, elder," the man says gently moving Elder Aren aside and sitting beside my mate. "Who are you?" he asks me with an intense glare and looking at the hand I'm holding tightly around my mate's. A wound kit is dropped in front of him and he starts to rustle around pulling out some bandages and sutures. He cleans away the wound on my mate's abdomen and starts to run a suture with thread through it.

"I'm Kaeden, her mate," I say directly while protectively watching every move he makes on my mate. He seems to have a steady hand but he was just injured. Best to watch him closely and make sure he doesn't mess up or I will take over. I see his hand still so I look up and see him watching me with a confused expression.

"*What?*" he says. "I have no idea what that means but I can only guess. Whatever, Solveig is *mine,*" he says stressing the last word and continuing to suture her wounds. "Best get that mate shit or whatever you are thinking out of your head."

Solveig. I repeat her name in my head thinking how beautiful it is and appropriate for her. She seems like the sun radiating nothing but light and hope. I ignore the rest of what the man is saying and allowing him to finish tending my mate. I look down at the hand I'm holding and notice one of her runes on the inside of her right wrist.

I wonder how many runes my mate has … Solveig. I ponder running a finger over the rune and recognizing it as a rune for nature and animals. It has some similarities to mine being both are related in power to nature.

"Help me turn her over to look at her back. I heard you saying earlier she has some wounds there," the man who is caring for my mate asks me roughly. I grab her shoulders while he rotates her hips and we manage to turn her gently. She doesn't stir or make any sounds causing me to grow concerned.

The man reaches up and tears her shirt apart on her back before I can protest making me growl protectively. "What? It's nothing I haven't seen before," he says aggressively with a suggestive smirk and a raised eyebrow leaving me gritting my teeth and understanding his innuendo.

The smirk drops from his face quickly into concern when I look over her back. "Oh no. Sunshine … sweetheart. I'm so sorry!" he chokes out the last part with a strangled sob. Clearly, he cares for her behind that arrogant attitude.

"Let me help," I say grabbing the bandage he used to clean the other wounds and then holding together a deeper laceration for him to suture. He hesitates for a second before nodding his head and getting to work. I hear someone curse behind me and look over my shoulder seeing the man she called Cadoc flush with anger staring at her back.

"How the fuck did she get whipped? And why is she unconscious! I swear the girl needs tied and kept under lock and key to prevent herself from being harmed!" he yells frustratingly while running a hand through his hair.

I whip my head around so fast and growl angrily at him saying, "Don't you *dare* threaten to imprison my mate. You sick son of a bitch." I would punch him straight in his perfect nose if I wasn't holding my mate's wounds together.

"Easy man. He wasn't serious," the man suturing says. "*Prince* Cadoc, you dick, you really shouldn't be insinuating anything about locking people up right now." He looks over his shoulder then back at this prince.

Cadoc actually seems to look slightly embarrassed for a moment looking around at the slave camp in realization and then looks down. "Sorry. You're right but I was just angry and not serious. Solveig tends to find trouble more than anyone I know. I hate seeing her in danger." Then pausing he says, "Also, what the fuck do you mean by mate?"

Elder Aren takes that moment to clear his throat and say, "We need to grab supplies then get out of here. There are wagons near the mountain entrance we can load with the injured and supplies. Let's save any further discussion until my granddaughter wakes up."

CHAPTER
Thirty-One

SOLVEIG

I wake up to the sound of arguing voices and ruffling of feathers. *Feathers?* I think.

You were injured young one. I couldn't reach you in the mountain. You should have brought me! Tyr, my friendly goshawk, projects to me clearly upset with a picture of him clawing at the mountain door.

Sorry, my friend. I will heal in time. You couldn't have done much in there, most of it was narrowed tunnels and halls. I send back to him and open my eyes.

I'm lying on my back on a blanket in the back of a wagon with Tyr perched on my shoulder (the good one without injury). His wings are extended out fully and he's snapping his beak aggressively at someone while making a *ki-ki-ki* high pitched scream. Next to him perched on the side of the wagon is another bigger goshawk that's speckled all over with white and grey. She's beautiful although appears just as angry as him with her wings extended and her head down. They're clearly in full on protector mode which makes me smile. I reach up and pet Tyr's underbelly of feathers then project, *Is this your beautiful mate, Tyr?*

Tyr projects smugly back, *She is beautiful, isn't she? My mate is fierce when angered. She already considers you one of her eyas.* I know from him that he means a baby hawk.

You are reckless, my child! Must I constantly watch out for everyone? First Tyr likes to fly off wildly hunting enemies with metal sharp things and now I must keep an eye on you who is injured so bad she sleeps, Tyr's mate projects to me with a huff of frustration. *I am Allira. You are now under my protection child. Tell these men to back up unless they want their eyes poked out of their skulls.*

"Oh, thank Valirr! She's awake!" I hear a male voice shout out when I started to pet Tyr.

"Solveig, can you calm your hawks? Tyr won't listen to me," Elder Aren asks.

"Sunshine! Get the birds off you. I need to check your wounds, please! They won't let any of us near you," Vidarr says lastly making me jerk and attempt to sit up.

He's okay! I think to myself and smile. I was so worried I had lost him.

Suddenly, I'm filled with the urgent need to hold Vi and feel his arms around me making me feel safe. I don't know what kind of world this would be without Vidarr there watching my back. Hopeless. That's what. He's ... starting to become way more to me than I care to acknowledge. Nearly losing him, made me realize I'm definitely falling for him. *Damn.*

The goshawks flutter and with a questioning look at me like- are you sure you don't want me to peck their eyes out? I let them know I'll be ok then they nod and fly off into the trees with a *cak-cak.*

I jump up and crawl to the end of the wagon stumbling in my haste and weakness. I'm feeling better but still low on energy. The lacerations on my back feel tight and tender while the wound on my abdomen is still painful. I make it to the end of the wagon just as Vidarr comes racing up with several other people. Throwing myself into his arms, I wrap my legs around his waist and hold onto his neck. Then before I can be too conscientious about people watching, I kiss him.

I kiss him like I almost lost him. Like he almost died, which he almost did. He squeezes me back just as tightly and moves his hands to my ass. Once he gets over his shock at me throwing myself at him and kissing him publicly, he starts to kiss me back hungrily and without restraint. It's a claiming in and of itself.

He pulls back between us kissing and whispers, "I'm okay, sunshine. I'm all better. Damn, you scared me. Why did you heal me like that? You could have killed yourself." He kisses me some more nipping my bottom lip then kissing down my neck as we get lost in each other. "Thank you, Sol. You—you're amazing. But don't ever do that again. Also, we need to stop since you probably pulled your stitches," he reprimands me with a smile and squeezes with one of his hands on my ass before setting me on the end of the wagon.

Everyone is silent around us staring with disapproval. Elder Aren steps forward and gives me a hug saying, "I'm glad you're okay, Granddaughter. You had us all worried. I told you to be careful with your gift. You can't do so much at once especially while carrying your own injury. We will have a talk regarding your power once you are fully healed. And about your newly public relationships … you need to remember you are a princess and future queen of Elaria." He steps back with look of reprimand on his face before a smile turns up one corner of his mouth and he reaches forward. He tucks a piece of my, I'm sure totally disgusting and messy, hair behind my ear asking, "When did you get this rune, dear? You didn't have it going into the mountain. How many does that make? Four?" He shakes his head in disbelief.

"I've never heard of an Elarian with four runes," says Yaeril standing to my right in an awe filled voice. He places a hand over his heart and bows his head. "Glad you are awake, Solveig, my queen."

"Thanks, Yaeril. Glad to be awake," I say while Vidarr lifts my shirt some and he inspects my wounds grunting when he sees blood leaking from the abdomen wound.

"You tore a few stitches here on your abdomen but as long as you're careful we shouldn't have to redo it. I'll put a pressure bandage over it and wrap it until you heal it yourself with time. No more jumping my bones until you're healed, sunshine," he says in a serious voice but lessens it with a smile. I can't help but smile back at him, seeing him alive and healthy makes me feel so fortunate after all we've been through.

Looking back over at my grandfather, I try to answer his questions. "I felt my fourth rune develop when I was in the mountain with Kaeden. I heard his voice in my head and then I felt the burning pain that I've come to associate with a rune developing shortly afterwards. What does it look like?" I ask.

Elder Aren nods his head and stares at my neck. "You are very powerful and very special, Granddaughter. The rune is beautiful and very detailed compared to your others. Yaeril is right, we have never had an Elarian with four runes in our history as a people. This rune," he says while tracing it with a finger and a teary-eyed look, "it stands for mind-speak. I knew one other person with this. It's rare, very rare." Then he looks me in the eye, swallowing with difficulty, trying to get the words out. "Your grandmother, my mate, had a similar rune. She was able to mind-speak with me. It was an amazing blessing to have, being able to speak with my mate so intimately."

I reach over and hold his hand. "I'm sorry you lost her. She died?"

"Yes. She died many, many years ago from a mortal wound. We had no healers at the time in Elaria. Lochlann was young. My mate—she was amazing. I miss her every day and will continue through the rest of my time. You have a part of her within you and I'm sure you will use this gift well."

Vidarr finished with his inspection and tending my wounds. He sits up on the wagon next to me listening to my grandfather and I feel him grab my hand and hold it while he listens. It feels … good to have someone touch me in a caring way. Or at least it did until I turn my head and see the scowling angry faces of Kaeden and Cadoc.

Kaeden looks like he's about to go full barbarian, storm over and throw Vidarr to the ground before wrapping me up in his arms. I don't quite understand it since we only just met. I mean he's extremely attractive in a rough lean barbarian way but it makes me anxious feeling an intense pulling towards a man I hardly know. *Ugh. Damn indigestion.* I think rubbing my chest and feeling the burning in the center of my chest again.

Cadoc looks pissed off with his arms crossed standing like he's braced for a fight. His fists are clenched and nearly white. He makes an impressive sight with his powerful stance, large broadsword hanging at his hip and intense gaze towards me. I'm still not quite sure why he followed me and assisted us. Especially now that I know he's a prince! *Fucking deceiver.*

"What exactly, Grandfather, do you mean when you say mate?" I ask softly while shiftily peeking at Kaeden from the corner of my eye. I feel Vidarr's grip on my hand tighten and his gaze narrow at my grandfather.

Clearing his throat, I notice my grandfather seems uncomfortable with a subject for the first time. "Well … we hadn't gotten to discussing Elarian customs and much of our culture yet, Solveig." He runs a hand over his face then continues, "Let me see if I can clearly explain."

"Yes, please explain. We are all very curious about the whole mate thing," Cadoc grits out angrily between his teeth looking over at Kaeden who looks … proud?

"As I was about to say … mates are something Elarians can either choose or find through fate. They are a life partner, similar to when you marry someone through your customs, yet so much more. They are your everything, your world, your love. Although you can be mated without love through fate it is rare since most mated couples develop strong affection rather quickly for one another through their connection. Once bonded, you can share emotions and feelings if the bond is strong enough. And if you are lucky, like I was, then your mate has the rune for mind-speak you get to share not just emotions and feelings but also their thoughts. Think of it as a soul connection with the one you are meant to be with. Elarians strive for finding their mate and in some cases—mates. It's every Elarian's purpose in life other than protecting our home and forest. The more powerful the Elarian or as such, more runes, the likelihood that person has more than one mate. I only had one mate myself, the love of my life, however you had a great aunt that had two mates herself. Your father also had two mates, though he lost his first mate to a raid before he met your mother."

Shocked and trying to process his words, I look over at Kaeden with anxiety. Then I look back at Elder Aren and curiously ask, "You mentioned you can choose a mate as well? Do Elarians ever refuse a mate bond?" I see a stricken look cross Kaeden's face when I ask my question but I focus on my grandfather needing to know the answers. I can't feel trapped anymore. I need to control my own fate. Too long, too long I've been under the control of Counselor Malphas and my father.

"Yes, child. You can choose. Fallia, our Goddess of family and fertility, has blessed us with the choice although few rarely reject a mate bond when fated. You would be rejecting someone that was specifically made for you, your perfect match." My grandfather says seriously to me with an intense look. "It would feel like breaking your own heart and could potentially lead to an immortal life of loneliness. I've only known one Elarian to reject a fated mate bond. You can also choose a mate without waiting for fate. We live long lives, which can sometimes be lonely, and we develop feelings for others. It is a much more common mate bond but still cherished just as a fated mate bond would be."

I'm looking at my hand in my lap with my head down contemplating his words when I hear a soft sob in front of me causing me to look up. Kaeden dropped to his knees in the grass before me with a look of devastation on his handsome face while gazing up at me.

"What's—" I start to ask him concerned he's injured or something worse. I mean, the man looks like his world is ending.

He reaches his hands forward to hold mine and interrupts me before I can finish asking him what's wrong. "Please, please Solveig, my mate. Give me a chance to prove myself," he starts asking with his head down holding my hands and I realize with a start he's begging! The warrior I just witnessed fight his way to freedom after being beaten. He never once begged those men for mercy when he was tied to that post and being whipped nearly to death. But now … he's on his knees in front of me! Begging for a chance with me!

I don't even know what to say. He must have thought I was going to reject him after asking my questions. *Shit!* I mean, I'm freaked out and not exactly excited to have a stranger be connected to me but I don't want him to feel alone and rejected. *I've been there too many times to count.*

"You really think we are mates? How do you know? Also, please stand up. I—I wasn't rejecting you. I simply know nothing about Elaria or our culture. I'm trying to understand," I say to him. He looks up at me with relief and breathes out a shaky breath. Then he stands and sits on my other side at the end of the wagon giving Vidarr a look that I can't decipher.

"I know we are mates. There is no question," he says with a determined voice and patting a hand in the center of his chest. "I feel it here. You make my heart burn for you." Then he taps his head saying, "And I hear you here. I cannot think of anyone or anything else. I'm constantly pulled toward you, my mate. You feel like everything that should matter in the world. I want you and will prove to you that I am a worthy mate." He looks down at himself in disgust. "I may not look like much now but at one time, I was a strong warrior and would be able to protect you. I will love you fiercely and no other. Just give me a chance." I'm flabbergasted that such a strong rugged handsome man would want me so surely.

Everyone is silent while they wait for my response.

You don't know me yet. You'll be disgusted with me once you see the mess I am *inside. I'm unclean, dirty … used.* I think to myself sadly. *Whore. A disappointment. Disfigured.* Those are the words that Malphas always called me. I don't know anyone that would want someone so bad if they knew my history. Well, other than Vidarr. He doesn't seem to think differently of me.

Kaeden suddenly sits up so straight his back should have snapped with the sudden force. Then he gets a murderous angry look on his face. Reaching out with both hands he cups my cheeks and looks intently into my startled blue eyes while I stare at his golden amber ones.

Ugh oh! Did he somehow hear what I said? I need to figure out this mind-speak thing ASAP, I think nervously and a bit embarrassed.

Kaeden starts to speak, confirming my fears. "Now listen here, mate, I never want to hear that again. Who is the man or woman that put those thoughts in your head? I will fucking destroy them. I will rip their heart from their body and dissect it with your dagger before giving it to you for your hawk to eat," he grits out angrily before taking a deep breath to calm himself. He's eerily attractive when he gets all murderous and defensive of me and—quite inventive. Definitely a turn on.

Then he says softly, "You could never disappoint me. It makes me sick and angry to think you consider yourself that way." He slowly leans forward and kisses my forehead causing that damn burning in my chest which I now know is connected to the mate bond. However, the fluttering in my stomach with the beginnings of attraction feels almost more dangerous to me since this man could easily get under my guard and make me feel things for him.

Vidarr breaks the moment by leaning forward and saying, "What did she say? I want in on the murder part and feeding their body parts to the hawk …" He's smiling in a teasing manner, but I can see he's tense looking at me with Kaeden. *Uh oh. What about Vidarr and me? Or my evolving "friendship" with Jorah for that matter? Will… Vidarr still want to be with me now that he knows I have a potential mate? Is my relationship with Jorah something to consider in this scenario? Oh shit—what will Kaeden think when he finds out I'm sleeping with Vi? Solveig, you've really gotten yourself into a tangled mess of men.* My thoughts keep tumbling around in my head.

Luckily, Darritt chooses that moment to walk up, totally oblivious to the intense conversation, and says, "We need to get moving again. We still have halfway to go and need to get these people back to rest. You ready to move out, again Sol?"

"Wait, we are halfway back? What happened? Where are all the prisoners from the camp?" I ask rubbing my head. I must have been out longer than I thought from my injuries.

"We are almost back to the capital, Falal, halfway there like Darritt said. Most of the people in that abhorrent camp decided to scatter once set free so they can travel back to their hometowns." My grandfather states while thinking over his words. "About twelve people from Falal are traveling back with us that were abducted from the city streets. There were around twenty Elarians in the camp that we rescued, and they are traveling further back in a wagon sleeping. We've taken plenty of supplies for them to use for a time. Out of the twenty Elarians freed, there are five Elarians that are prior warriors in your father's army and have volunteered to be part of your protection duty once they've recovered." At his words, I flick my gaze over his shoulder and see four rough looking men with one tall woman who all nod their heads respectfully.

"Wait—where will the Elarians all go? To live? They can't return to the city or my fath—King Batair will capture and kill them! Can they return to this Elaria that you spoke of before?" I ask Elder Aren.

He looks into the forest for a bit then responds, "The forest will provide for us, Granddaughter. Don't worry. We have supplies now. They will stay with us for a time hiding in the Elarian Forest. It was once ours and it will be again, I've seen it." He gets an unfocused far off look in his eyes. "We cannot return to Elaria yet even though it is the seat of our power."

"Why not? Why not go back?" I ask confused.

"Because we are cursed," he says turning his gaze back to look directly at me. "And you, granddaughter, are going to save us."

"Cursed? What do you mean?" I ask frustrated and honestly just exhausted. I mean—why does everything have to be so complicated.

"Back during the rule of King Gaargon in Laevaris, we lived in peace hidden deeply in the Elarian Forest with our capital and seat of power as Elaria. It was a central area for us all to come together and was deeply rooted in our power. Many of our people preferred to live in the forest but Elaria was special for us where many of our gatherings and festivals were held. We were once a powerful well-respected kingdom. It is said that a majority of our power and connection to the forest was given to us not only by the Gods but also from our connection to the Drakoni."

He pauses and I go to interrupt, but he holds up a hand.

"Let me finish, child, or we will never get out of here. The Drakoni are an extinct nation now similar to ours and were known to be able to shift from human to dragon with simply a thought. They were deeply connected to the land and magic. We lived entwined with them and shared Elaria gratefully. They used to inhabit a distant part of land farther up near the coast of the Aruvian Sea. Then, King Gaargon started a war against anyone with magic and more power than himself. He destroyed the Drakoni, hunted them down like animals during their weakest time, and as you know waged war on the Elarians. Elaria became abandoned since many Elarians were killed or thrown into slavery afterwards. Many don't know this but the king at the time paid a witch, they are very rare, to cast a curse over our people. Supposedly, she cursed Elaria preventing anyone from stepping foot there."

He looks sad and frustrated when he looks up at me.

"So how do we break this curse? And why do you think I can help?" I ask him in shock. I mean dragon shifters? Witches? Curses? I had never even known about magic and power until recently when I developed runes. How did our kingdom wipe out all traces of this from our history! It's insane!

"The curse—we don't fully know how to break it. It's not like the witch would tell an Elarian being thrown into slavery however there were rumors that it involves the Drakoni, may even require one." He says somberly. "So, it's almost not even worth discussing since the Drakoni are extinct now. I haven't seen one for nearly two hundred years. And the only person that would know how to break the curse is potentially a witch."

We both become silent afterwards lost in our thoughts.

Maybe Jorah and I can find something about this. There has to be rumors or something about witches in history.

"You, Granddaughter, need to rest and gain back your strength. We will handle the rest of the journey. Prince Cadoc can watch your back once you leave the forest since he has access to the castle. And I will take care of our people for now."

Suddenly exhausted as I think about everything that's happened in the past day, I don't even argue instead just nodding my head and laying back into the wagon as it starts to rumble through the forest. Vidarr jumps out of the wagon and grabs a nearby horse mounting up and riding alongside the wagon. Kaeden though stays in the wagon sitting by my side and leaning up against a bag of supplies. He pulls a blanket up over me and runs a hand along my hair all the way to the bottom of my long braid before he quickly falls asleep sitting up. He must be just as exhausted.

Cadoc jumps up on his horse alongside Eirik who is already mounted.

Just before I pass out into sleep from utter exhaustion, I hear him say to me, "Rest up, Solveig. Once we are back, you're in my hands. And I don't intend to let you go."

EPILOGUE

I feel as though time is slipping through my talons.

I'm used to sleeping for long periods of time during specific seasons however this is more than usual. I'm trapped. Unable to open my eyes and view the world around me. My memory is foggy, and I only have snippets of awareness on why I'm here.

Subconsciously, I know I'm still in my lair. There's the sound of water and the sensation of hot steam in the air. I feel tired and almost as if I'm chained to my dreams.

I dream a lot and usually they involve my family, my lost people, and flying. Sometimes hunting. Sinking my teeth into not just prey animals for hunger but also into my enemies. I have a lot of them. Enemies—that is. That I remember. A molten anger is resting inside me ready to explode when I encounter them but for now all I can do is dream.

However lately, my dreams have changed. I keep dreaming of her … the beautiful, brown-haired female with sad, sapphire eyes.

She's always staring at me with darkness and sadness in her eyes. Sometimes longing.

I feel this intense need to go to her... but I can't. I'm chained to my dreams and subconsciousness, unable to wake up.

I'm not sure who she is but I know I must have her. She's mine! My treasure! The most rare and special gem that I could possess in my entire horde. All I need to figure out is how to wake up ...

AUTHOR'S NOTE

Hi there! Thank you so much for reading my first book! I truly feel connected to Solveig's story and I hope you did too! Her story is one filled with darkness, but I'm totally in love with her strength and perseverance. Just wait until you meet more of her love interests in book two! Can I say the word…dragons? Things start to get even more spicy in the next book, so you best get on with reading it. If you're wanting to strangle Malphas or perhaps slice his throat for Sol, hang in there since it's a journey to get justice.

I want to shout out a special thanks to my best friend Kate and her husband (also my friend) Kyle who were the first to read my unedited, rough draft of a novel. It's a very sensitive thing to be a new author and have people read your inner thoughts written out into a book, but they never made me feel that it wasn't something worth pursuing. Also thanks to my husband and kids for putting up with me and my craziness while I changed careers from the medical world into writing. Lastly, thanks to my new readers for giving me a chance!

Coming soon by J.L. Cres

Kiss of the Sun

Book 2 in the Blade of the Sun series

War of the Sun

Book 3 in the Blade of the Sun series

Printed in the USA
CPSIA information can be obtained
at www.ICGtesting.com
LVHW060355150524
780269LV00017B/393

9 798990 553514